SHINJI TAKAHASHI
INTO THE HEART OF THE STORM

JULIE KAGAWA

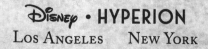

DISNEY • HYPERION

LOS ANGELES   NEW YORK

First Edition, April 2023
10 9 8 7 6 5 4 3 2 1
FAC-004510-22322
Printed in the United States of America

This book is set in Adobe Caslon Pro/Monotype.
Designed by Marci Senders

Library of Congress Cataloging-in-Publication Data
Names: Kagawa, Julie, author.
Title: Shinji Takahashi : into the heart of the storm / Julie Kagawa.
Other titles: Into the heart of the storm
Description: First edition. • Los Angeles ; New York : Disney-Hyperion,
   2023. • Series: Society of Explorers and Adventurers ; book 2 • Audience:
   Ages 8–12. • Audience: Grades 3–7. • Summary: Thirteen-year-old Shinji
   and his S.E.A. cohorts travel to a forgotten island in Polynesia in search of
   a lost culture.
Identifiers: LCCN 2022014963 • ISBN 9781368074148 (hardcover) •
   ISBN 9781368075046 (paperback) • ISBN 9781368075176 (ebook)
Subjects: CYAC: Adventure and adventurers—Fiction. • Magic—Fiction. •
   Animals, Mythical—Fiction. • Secret societies—Fiction. • Japanese
   Americans—Fiction. • LCGFT: Novels. • Action and adventure fiction.
Classification: LCC PZ7.K117443 Shm 2023 • DDC [Fic]—dc23
LC record available at https://lccn.loc.gov/2022014963

Reinforced binding
Visit www.DisneyBooks.com

SUSTAINABLE FORESTRY INITIATIVE
Certified Sourcing
www.sfiprogram.org
SFI-01681

Logo Applies to Text Stock Only

TO NICK

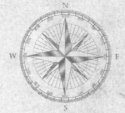

CHAPTER ONE

The thugs were closing in.

Panting, Shinji gazed around the crowded marketplace. It was hard to see through the press of bodies meandering aimlessly among the dozens of stalls and booths, but he caught glimpses of the pursuers through the crowd. And they were coming right for him.

"This way!" he hissed at Lucy, and darted between a goat and a stall selling chickens. Lucy followed as Shinji pushed deeper into the square. The throngs of the marketplace surrounded them, getting in his way and blocking their path. Shinji ducked and wove between bodies, darting under limbs and slipping through tight spaces, but he could still see the dark sunglasses of their pursuers bobbing through the crowds, getting ever closer.

Heart pounding, Shinji ducked behind a fish vendor's booth, pulling Lucy with him, watching the group of men comb the marketplace. Lucy was breathing hard. Her blond hair had come free of its ponytail and was sticking out around her face. Her cheeks were red, her blue eyes wide as one of the large men stalked past their hiding spot. Shinji and Lucy hunkered down and held their breath until he had passed.

"I think the exit is that way," Lucy whispered, pointing across the marketplace square. "If we can just get past those booths, we can hide in the city and escape."

Shinji peered in the direction she was pointing. He saw the opening, but he also saw a pair of large men standing menacingly under an overhang nearby. "There are two agents blocking the exit," he said, ducking back. "If we run that way, they'll catch us for sure."

"Well, we can't stay here," Lucy whispered back. "We have to do something. Come on, Shinji." She gave him an encouraging look. "You have guardian powers now. You should be able to pull something off."

"Yeah." Shinji took a deep breath. She was right. He did have guardian powers. Or he was *supposed* to, anyway. It had been a few months since a legendary winged serpent that guarded a mystical font had gifted him with magical powers.

The tattoo of a serpent with huge golden wings still graced his forearm, marking him as special.

There was just one slight problem.

Ever since they left the jungle, Shinji had been having a really hard time accessing any type of magic at all. It wasn't as if he hadn't tried. Back at SEA headquarters, he would routinely try to call on the wind, or to communicate with different animals, or to summon a giant snake with magnificent gilded wings. All things that he had done in the Mexican jungle, when the Coatl had first granted him its power. Back then, when he and his friends had been in danger, he had been able to use the magic without thinking about it. Now he couldn't even summon up a slight breeze.

"Shinji!" Lucy's voice pulled him out of his memories. One of the agents had noticed their hiding place and was stalking toward them with a murderous gleam in his sunglasses.

"Run," Shinji said, and they bolted from behind the stall, trying to lose their attackers in the crowded marketplace once more. But this time the agents seemed to converge around them. Everywhere Shinji looked, there was an enemy closing in on them.

Desperate, he darted around a booth and plunged down an alley with Lucy behind him, only to be met with a high brick wall.

"There's no way out," he panted. "Turn around. Go back."

They spun, only to find two of the men standing at the mouth of the alley. Another pair joined them, guarding the exit while the first two began stalking into the alley. Shinji's gaze darted from side to side, as he searched for a way out, but there was nothing. They were trapped.

"Up there!" Lucy grabbed his sleeve as the men came forward, pointing to something above them on the roof. Shinji looked up and saw several potted plants sitting precariously on the corner of a balcony railing. If he could make them fall somehow, the heavy pots might hit the men and give him and Lucy a chance to escape.

Taking a deep breath, Shinji searched for the magic inside him. *I'll only get one shot at this.* As the men stepped forward, closing the distance, he exhaled and flung out a hand toward the plants overhead.

There was a pathetic puff of wind, barely more than a fart, from his open palm. That was it.

The two men closed in, trapping Shinji and Lucy against the wall. One of the men raised an iron club overhead, sneering with contempt. Shinji felt Lucy tense beside him and braced himself for the club to come smashing down.

The lights suddenly flickered, and the two men froze, as did the world around them. A voice, flat and robotic, echoed in Shinji's ears.

Pause. Simulation ended. Please remove your headsets and wait for further instruction.

Beside him, Lucy slumped in relief. Bowing her head,

she pulled off the thick VR goggles she had been wearing, shaking out her hair as the headset came free. Shinji reached back and did the same, stripping off the goggles and the headset attached to it.

Reality came into focus as the goggles were removed. They were no longer in a crowded market square in some far-off, exotic country. They were in a very large room with no windows and smooth walls that stretched up more than twenty feet. Stalls and booths were scattered about to resemble a marketplace labyrinth even though they were indoors. The "agent" in front of Shinji was now a highly mobile robot holding a plastic stick in one metal clamp. But if Shinji peered at everything through the goggles, the men, the crowds, and the sunny marketplace overlaid reality, making him really feel like he was somewhere else. It was just a skin, though. An augmented reality designed to make everything feel real. And it had felt real, up to the point where Shinji had failed to call on his powers. If this had been the real world, he and Lucy would have been captured. Or dead.

A familiar voice echoed over the speakers, the same speakers that had been playing marketplace and crowd noises in the background. "All right, kids," said Oliver Ocean. "You're done. Come on back."

Oliver didn't sound angry or disappointed, but Shinji clenched his fists. Lucy gave him a look that was both worried and sympathetic, which only made him angrier. Glancing at the now-immobile robot, he resisted the urge to kick it in its tanklike treads. A sudden breeze rattled a vase sitting on a nearby stall, which made him grit his teeth. He hoped Lucy didn't notice.

Oh, now *you show up, huh? Where were you two seconds ago when I needed you, stupid magic?*

"It's all right, Shinji," Lucy said, trying to be encouraging. "Like Oliver said last night, you're still learning how to use your magic. You're not supposed to know how everything works all at once."

Shinji's jaw tightened. Lucy meant well, but she wasn't the one with the power of a guardian inside her. He had accepted the mantle of the Coatl; he was supposed to be able to do something with this magic. So far, he hadn't been able to do anything. At least not willingly.

I'm a guardian now. Why doesn't the magic work? What is wrong with me?

When Shinji didn't answer, Lucy's brow furrowed. "You okay?"

"Yeah, I'm fine," he said flippantly, and rolled his eyes. "It's not really a big deal."

Only, it was. He had been trying to master these stupid powers for three months now, and nothing was working. The Society had even gotten involved. Maybe because they felt responsible for him, or maybe because they were worried that a thirteen-year-old running around with the uncontrolled power of an ancient mythological creature was a bad combination. But for all their knowledge, research, and access to old books and artifacts, the Society didn't seem to know any more about how his magic worked than Shinji did.

This latest exercise in augmented reality had been their—or rather, Oliver's—attempt to trigger Shinji's powers, at least enough to study them a little. And though it had been super cool to run around SEA's version of the "Danger Room," it didn't negate the fact that he had failed miserably.

Shinji appreciated that Oliver and the Society were trying to help him, but at the same time, he wished they would stop. The Coatl had given its magic to him; it was his responsibility to learn how to use it.

"Come on," Lucy said, and turned away. Thankfully, she didn't seem to notice the mysterious breeze from nowhere. "Oliver and the others will be waiting for us."

Still annoyed, Shinji followed her, walking back through the maze of makeshift stalls and booths. Without the VR goggles, the room seemed dim and cluttered. It still felt like they were walking through some kind of market square, only this time an indoor one. Even though the marketplace had been an illusion, the booths had been put together to look like the real thing. There were even a couple of chickens clucking away in cages and a goat tethered to one of the carts. The Society of Explorers and Adventurers had been to *a lot* of places; when they decided to re-create a marketplace of a distant foreign country, they did it right.

Lucy was quiet as they wove their way through the cluttered room. Normally she would be talking excitedly about the robots or the VR goggles or other tech-related stuff, but today she kept it to herself. Clearly, she knew Shinji wasn't in the mood.

A green exit sign glowed brightly on the far wall of the room, showing the way out. They pushed through the door, climbed a long flight of metal stairs, and entered a room that overlooked the simulation chamber.

There were two people in the room, standing in front of the glass wall that showed the marketplace on the lower floor. The slight, blue-haired woman in a wheelchair gave Shinji a bright grin when he and Lucy walked through the door. Even though he was feeling morose and irritable, Shinji smiled back. It was hard to keep a sour face when Zoe Kim turned her beaming grin on you.

The person next to her, a lean, rugged-looking man in a long coat, did not smile when they came in. Young and handsome, he carried a walking cane in one hand, and its golden parrot head glittered under the fluorescent lights as he pointed it in their direction. "I am supposed to inform you that you did not, in fact, escape the Hightower agents," Oliver Ocean remarked in his wry tone of voice. "You have been captured and are on your way to Hightower headquarters to be dissected for your magic."

"Oh good," Shinji said flatly. "That was what I was hoping for."

Lucy wrinkled her nose. "Hightower wouldn't dissect Shinji," she stated confidently. "Not if they know he has magic powers. They would first try to buy the magic from him, and if that didn't work, they would move on to threats and blackmail."

"Regardless," Oliver went on, "Shinji would now be in Hightower's clutches. And we would probably have to rescue you. Again." He gave Shinji a knowing look. "So, what happened down there, kid? I saw you tried to do something. You were either attempting to use magic or you were shooing away a fly. Were the 'agents' not convincing enough? I know you felt you were in a giant video game, but still. This is real-world survival training. You're going to need to control your magic if Hightower really is after you."

"I did try," Shinji protested. "I just . . ." *I can't do it. I don't know how to use the magic yet.* "Maybe if the 'agents' looked more like humans and less like coatracks with wheels, I'd do better," he finished with a smirk.

"Hmm, maybe you're right," Oliver mused, twirling his cane in one hand. "Maybe next time we'll run the jungle simulation with the angry velociraptors."

"Oh, give the kid a break, Oliver," Zoe broke in. "I'm sure he tried his best." She gave Shinji an understanding nod, which made him feel a little better. "Anyway, you can't stay here; Priya wanted to see you all in the meeting room after you were done with the training simulation."

Oliver winced, and Shinji nearly did as well. Priya Banerjee was the chairwoman of this branch of the Society and essentially the person in charge. She had been nothing but nice to Shinji ever since he arrived at SEA, but she was also a strict, no-nonsense woman who everyone, even Oliver, was a little bit afraid of.

"Go on, then," Zoe continued as she wheeled her chair gracefully toward the exit. "I have things to do in my lab, but I told Priya I'd send you guys on. You don't want to be late."

They left the training room, walking down the long tiled hallway toward the elevators at the end. On the way, they passed Zoe's lab, where dozens of electronic and mechanical doodads were scattered over every possible surface. Other doors along the hallway led to storage rooms or small offices, though only Zoe had a permanent workshop down here. Shinji hadn't even known about this part of SEA headquarters until recently. Lucy had, of course. She would disappear for hours, sometimes skipping meals, and when Shinji asked where she'd been, she would shrug and say she had been working with Zoe. Shinji knew Zoe had a workshop somewhere; he just never thought about where it could be. And since the elevators to the undercity, as Oliver called it, had been cleverly hidden behind an ordinary-looking bookshelf, Shinji hadn't suspected anything was there.

The Society of Explorers and Adventurers did love to hide things behind bookshelves.

As they followed Oliver down the hall, Lucy suddenly tapped his arm. "Hey," she began. "I don't have guardian powers, but I do know a little about how magic works. I mean, just look at Tinker."

She held out her arm, palm facing up. The pocket of her overalls moved, and a tiny creature crawled out of it. It was a mouse made completely of metal, but it moved and acted like a real mouse. The tiny robot creature was one of Lucy's own creations, a marvel of tech and magic fused together in a way only Lucy knew how to do. Tinker wasn't just a cool pet, though; he was super intelligent and could do some very handy things, like open locked doors and turn off security cameras. And even though Tinker wasn't really alive, he and Lucy were inseparable. Tinker's copper ears and tiny copper feet glittered in the light as he scampered into Lucy's palm and sat up, nose and whiskers twitching.

"Tinker is a mechanical construct," Lucy said, though Shinji had heard this all before, "but I still needed a little magic to bring him to life. I know more about working with magic than Zoe or Oliver, or anyone here at Society headquarters. Maybe I could help you."

"Thanks," Shinji said, and he meant it. "But you can't. I have to figure this out myself."

"Why?"

"Because I'm the guardian," he replied. "No one else has these powers; the Coatl gave them to me. I have to learn how to use them."

"You don't have to do it by yourself," Lucy began, but at that moment they had stepped into the elevator with Oliver, who immediately pressed the button for the top floor. The doors slid shut, and they started to ascend.

Priya Banerjee was standing alongside the large, sturdy wooden table in the meeting hall. The room itself was enormous, with a high ceiling painted with depictions of numerous animals, both real and mystical. The walls were covered with letters, paintings, and postcards, and the numerous shelves held artifacts from around the world.

Kali, Priya's large, aggressively friendly black bear, lounged on the nearby couch, all four paws in the air. She huffed a greeting when Shinji entered the room and started to rise, as if to give him one of her infamous bear tackles. But Priya cleared her throat in a firm manner, and Kali lay down again with a groan.

Priya's dark eyes met Shinji's for a moment and narrowed before they shifted to Oliver. "Oliver," she greeted, "Zoe has already informed me of what happened, but I wanted to hear it from you. I take it the simulation did not produce the desired results?"

Oliver looked uncomfortable for just a moment but managed to shrug. "It was the kid's first time in augmented reality," he said. "I wouldn't write it off as a failure just yet. I think once he gets used to the goggles and the weirdness of the training simulations, he'll have a much easier time."

"Hmm." Priya did not seem convinced. She turned to Shinji then, her gaze intense. "And what do you think, Shinji? Are you able to better control your powers now? Is any of this working?"

"Um." Shinji didn't really want to lie. "I don't know," he said evasively. "Maybe a little? It's hard to tell. It's not like I've ever done something like this before."

"In Mexico, you showed extreme power when you called on the Coatl's magic," Priya went on. "It was reported that you could summon wind, speak to animals, and even call upon the Coatl itself when you were in danger. Have you been able to do any of that since you returned from the jungle?"

"No," Shinji admitted. That day, when he had used the full extent of the Coatl's magic, felt like a dream now. "But I haven't really been in any danger," he joked. "Maybe I need a bunch of Hightower agents, real Hightower agents, not coatracks on wheels, chasing me down to be able to use it again."

Priya's frown deepened. "That is what we are trying to prevent," she told him firmly. "You have an untested magic that, left uncontrolled, can be very dangerous to you and the people around you. Learning how to harness it is vital." She sighed, tapping her fingers on the table beside her. "Clearly, the methods we've been trying are not working. Which is why I've called for a specialist to help."

A specialist? Like he had some sort of mysterious disease no one had ever seen before? "No," Shinji said. "I'm fine. I don't need a specialist; I can figure this out on my own."

"We've got this, Priya," Oliver broke in at the same time.

"I said I would help him get a handle on this magic, and I will. We just need a little time."

"Unfortunately, Oliver, time is what we do not have." Priya walked around the table to pick up a folder, holding it up somberly. Shinji could see the word *Classified* written in large red letters along the top. Priya paused a moment, gazing at the folder, before turning back to Oliver.

"Have you ever heard of the Natia people?" she asked.

The ex-pirate frowned. "Vaguely," he replied. "They were a lost civilization that supposedly lived somewhere in the Polynesian Triangle of the South Pacific. But no one has ever found evidence that the Natia actually existed, other than a few vague references here and there. There are even a couple seafaring legends that their island moves or is hidden by a constant fog that never goes away."

Priya nodded. "Yes. The location of the Natia's island, and the Natia people themselves, has never been discovered. But . . ." She raised the folder. "Recently, I received word that a shipwreck has been discovered in a remote section of the Polynesian Triangle. According to my contacts, that ship might be carrying several artifacts belonging to a lost civilization, possibly the Natia."

Oliver straightened, a flash of excitement crossing his features. "Well, that is something," he said. "The Natia have been nothing but rumor and legend until now. Nothing but ghosts."

"Yes," Priya agreed. "If we could discover something about them, something real and concrete, we could share their existence with the rest of the world. They wouldn't be ghosts any longer. However, there is one small problem."

For just a moment, her gaze flicked to Lucy. It was only a split-second glance, but Shinji caught it. And he knew what she was going to say next.

"Hightower has also gotten wind of the shipwreck," Priya said, making Lucy's lips tighten. "And we can be sure that they will be looking to claim it and whatever treasures they find. We cannot allow that to happen. Hightower would simply sell or collect the artifacts, and whatever we could learn about the Natia would be lost forever."

"Yeah," Lucy chimed in. She sounded disgusted, but it was directed at Hightower, not at the people in the room. "That sounds like them."

Priya gave her an approving nod. "Given this information, we have no time to waste. Hightower could already have a head start on us. I know you are determined to help Shinji, Oliver, but you are our most experienced member when it comes to shipwrecks and underwater extractions. Captain Mano of the *Seas the Day* has specifically requested your presence for this mission. You leave for the South Pacific tonight."

"Mano?" Oliver snorted, and a wide grin crossed his face. "That scurvy walrus is still at it, huh? Why am I not surprised?" Glancing at Shinji, he sobered. "What about the kid?"

"Oh, don't worry about that," said a new voice behind them. Shinji saw Oliver tense, fingers tightening around his cane. "I'll be taking extra good care of our young guardian."

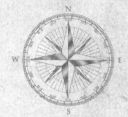

CHAPTER TWO

A woman stood in the doorway, beaming a bright smile as she peered into the room. Shinji had never seen her before, but by the way Zoe gasped and Oliver's eyes widened, the Society members recognized her. She was almost painfully thin, with jet-black hair pulled into a messy bun, and wore a bright sea-green coat. A large red umbrella, thankfully closed, was clutched in one hand, though there hadn't been any rain for weeks.

"Hello there!" she called, raising the umbrella in greeting. "Sorry I'm late. There were a few complications with the plane before we took off. Nothing serious—I'm here now!"

On the couch, Kali jerked up with a grunt. Seeing the

newcomer, she gave a happy bellow and rolled onto the floor. With a huff, she started loping across the room. Shinji knew from experience that a bear tackle was imminent, and hoped Kali's overenthusiastic greeting wouldn't break the thin woman in half.

To his surprise, the woman laughed, waving cheerfully at the three hundred pounds of bear lumbering toward her. "Hello, Kali!" she called, sticking her free hand into the pocket of her long coat. "Yes, I have something for you! I wouldn't forget my favorite *Ursus americanus*." She pulled out a peppermint stick that was nearly a foot long, holding it high above her head. "Sit!"

Kali skidded to a halt a mere two feet away. With a grunt, she plopped into a sit, nose twitching as she gazed up at the candy. "That's my adorable elite predator," the woman crooned, handing her the stick. Kali snatched the peppermint in her jaws and turned, snuffling happily, to waddle back to the couch.

Impressed, Shinji leaned in toward Lucy and whispered, "I gotta try that."

"Phoebe?" Oliver sounded surprised, and not entirely happy about the sudden arrival. "What are you doing here?"

"I called her," Priya said, stepping around the table. "Shinji, Lucy, this is Phoebe Mystic. She and her family have been part of the Society of Explorers and Adventurers for a very long time. She has advanced degrees in philosophy, anthropology, kinesiology, world mythology, and juggling."

"You can have an advanced degree in juggling?" Lucy whispered.

"She has also studied ancient magic, yoga, and meditation with some of the world's finest practitioners," Priya continued. "Phoebe was kind enough to travel all the way from Tokyo to help Shinji better understand his magic."

"*Phoebe* is your specialist?" Oliver asked incredulously, but Phoebe was already bounding into the room, coat flapping behind her, that beaming smile directed fully at Shinji.

"And this must be Mr. Takahashi!" Coming right up to him, she stuck the umbrella in the crook of her elbow and thrust a dainty hand out before her. "Shinji Takahashi, it's a pleasure to finally meet you. We of the Eastern chapter house have heard all about your exciting adventures with Hightower and the font. Imagine seeing the legendary Coatl with your own eyes . . . Oh!" She gave a dreamy, dramatic sigh. "I can only hope to be so fortunate one day."

"Yeah. Fortunate." Uncertain, Shinji glanced at Oliver, who rolled his eyes. Not wanting to seem rude or awkward, Shinji grasped the offered hand, and the woman's fingers immediately clamped over his like a vise. He jumped as the smiling woman pulled his arm forward and turned it over, revealing the tattoo of the Coatl right above his wrist.

"There it is," Phoebe whispered, staring at the winged serpent with wide eyes. "The mark of the Coatl. Oh, it's even more beautiful than I imagined. Interesting that the wings are gold instead of rainbow colored like in the common renditions of the myth. Very interesting." She traced the sweeping golden wings with a painted teal nail, causing goose bumps to creep up his arm. Gritting his teeth, Shinji tried pulling back, but her grip was like steel. "So, given that the Coatl was referred to as a god of wind, among other things," Phoebe muttered, completely absorbed in her study of his tattoo, "I'm thinking we'll have to take a more . . . creative approach in unlocking this magic. Something whimsical and free-flowing. Perhaps we'll start with some simple meditation to control one's breath. . . ."

Meditation? Nope, not happening. Shinji finally managed to pull his arm free. "Thanks," he began, taking a rather large step back, "but I don't need a specialist. I'm doing fine." He nodded at Oliver, who watched them with a dark expression. "Oliver has been helping me, and everything is going great. I really don't need anything else."

Lucy gave him a slight frown, knowing he wasn't really telling the truth. He wasn't "fine," and things—at least concerning his magic—were not "great." But Shinji trusted Oliver a lot more than this so-called specialist. And he really did not want to spend the next few days in boring meditation while learning how to breathe properly. The magic was his, and the Coatl had chosen him; he had to figure it out on his own.

"Oh?" Unperturbed by this news, Phoebe glanced up at Oliver. "Well, that is wonderful to hear," she said, "but now

I'm confused. I thought Mr. Ocean had been called away on a very important mission for the Society this week."

"He has," Priya said with a stern look at Oliver. "A *very* important mission. He departs tonight, in fact."

Oliver met Priya's glower for only a moment, then sighed. "Yeah," he said, giving Shinji an apologetic look. "Sorry, kid. I gotta go. As much as I want to help you conquer your magic, this mission is important. The Natia people have been nothing but myth for decades. Finding concrete evidence of their culture and ways of life would be a massive discovery. Besides"—he smirked, returning to his swaggering, ex-pirate self—"I'd rather be tied to an anchor and tossed in with a school of starving barracuda than let Hightower beat us to this ship. Mano is a great captain but a terrible strategist. He's going to need a retired scoundrel to outmaneuver a corporation like Hightower."

"Take me with you, then," Shinji offered. "I'm part of SEA now, right? And I've lived most of my life on a ship. I can help."

Oliver scratched the back of his neck with the golden parrot beak. "Look, kid," he began, "you know me. Personally, I'd have no problems taking you along, but I don't think that's an option." He shot a glance at Phoebe. "We all have a mission, and yours is to get a handle on your guardian powers. Your new teacher isn't going to let you go traipsing off to the South Pacific in search of sunken treasure."

"Why not?" Phoebe asked, surprising them all. "In fact, I think that sounds like a fabulous idea!"

Priya blinked. Clearly, she had not been expecting this, either. "Phoebe," she said, "are you sure? Shinji might be a member of the Society, but he is still just a boy. It would be safer to keep him here while he is under your tutelage. Oliver is an accomplished adventurer, but this mission might bring him into contact with Hightower. It could be dangerous for Shinji to be on that ship."

"Exactly!" Phoebe jabbed a finger at the ceiling. "When dealing with magic and mystical powers, I've found that they are often triggered when there is something exciting going on. Danger and adventure seem to draw them to the surface much faster than, well, silence and boredom. So, it would actually benefit Shinji to be a part of this mission, rather than sitting in an ordinary classroom trying to tap into his powers. If this trip is not extremely hazardous, I see no problems with letting Shinji accompany Mr. Ocean. A fun adventure might be just the thing he needs for his magic to show itself."

Shinji felt a swell of hope and glanced expectantly at Priya. "See?" he said. "That's perfect, then. Oliver will still be there to help, and I can concentrate on learning magic."

To his surprise, it wasn't Priya who gave a long, extended breath at the suggestion, but Oliver. "A Mystic aboard a ship," he muttered. "I'm not sure Mano is going to go for that. He still doesn't allow bananas on board because he thinks they're bad luck. The kid might be better off here."

Betrayed, Shinji gave Oliver an incredulous look, but Priya held up her hand.

"Leave that to me," she said. "I'll talk to Mano and work something out, if . . ." She glanced at Phoebe again. "You really think bringing Shinji along will help him learn to control his magic?"

"I do!" Phoebe said enthusiastically. "Trust me, nothing awakens mysterious powers better than going on an adventure. Like walking into a dragon's lair in North Wales smelling of fish. Be sure to have fire-resistant pants on if you do—little life advice there."

"What about me?"

This was from Lucy. Shinji had nearly forgotten about her and felt a tiny prick of guilt when she stepped forward. She had been with them for so long, he'd just assumed she was coming, too.

"Oh, of course Miss Frost should come as well," Phoebe stated loudly. "She's the other half of the daring duo, after all. Having a familiar element around will also help Shinji when he is trying to tap into his powers. Besides," Phoebe went on, still smiling at Lucy, "I heard all about your exploits in Mexico, Miss Frost. Bravo, standing up to Hightower like that. Shinji is very lucky to have you as a friend. Of course, you will accompany us on our important mission, right, Mr. Ocean? Another hand on deck never hurt."

"No arguments here," the ex-pirate said, tipping his cane at Lucy. "She's always welcome on my ship."

Lucy's smile made Shinji weirdly proud. The Hightower Corporation was the bitter enemy of the Society, believing in completely opposite ideals. While SEA tried to preserve the land, cultures, and wonders of the world, Hightower only wanted to exploit and use them for their own gain. Lucy's full name was Lucy Frost, and she was a direct descendant of Harrison Hightower the Third, the founder of the Hightower Corporation. Her father, Gideon Frost, currently ran the entire company.

When Oliver first met Lucy, he didn't trust her at all. He thought she might be a Hightower spy. Lucy had to prove herself to him and everyone in the Society that she wasn't working for Hightower, that she hated them and everything they stood for. She had earned Oliver's trust, and even more, she had earned his respect. That was saying something.

Priya looked like she might be regretting calling on Phoebe, but she sighed. "Very well," she said after a moment, "if you really think it will help Shinji, then I suppose I will allow it. On one condition," she added quickly, and darted a fierce glare at Oliver. "I am trusting you with the well-being of our two youngest members, Oliver. Their safety is going to be *your* number one priority. I do not want to hear about having to drag them out of a smuggler's den, or off a kidnapper's boat, or from the bottom of the ocean. If things become too dangerous, you will send these two back to the Society immediately, is that clear?"

As Oliver assured her that they would be fine, Lucy looked at Shinji and gave him a triumphant smile. He grinned back, but mixed feelings swirled inside him. He was happy that he'd be going on this important mission with Lucy and Oliver. He was happy to be doing something about his magic. He just wished Phoebe wasn't coming along to peer over his shoulder the entire way.

And, deep inside, he was worried. The Coatl had chosen him to carry the power of the font, but . . . what if it had chosen wrong? What if Shinji was just no good at being a guardian and screwed everything up?

"Wonderful!" Phoebe clapped her hands together. "It's all decided, then. This is so exciting! Oh, I should get my bags, shouldn't I? Be right back!"

She started to bound off, but then a rumble went through the floor, like a mini earthquake. On the couch, Kali sat up with a growl of alarm as spiderweb cracks appeared in the ceiling above Priya's desk. There was a sudden, deafening crunch as part of the ceiling came loose, and the miniature chandelier attached to it abruptly plunged toward them. Oliver yanked Lucy and Shinji out of the way as the glass fixture smashed to the carpet, where Phoebe had been standing moments before. Tiny crystals flew everywhere, peppering the carpet and walls, and Shinji's heart nearly lodged itself in his throat.

In the stunned silence, Oliver shook his head. "And there it is," he said dryly. "The Mystic curse is still alive and well, I see. Mano is going to be *so* thrilled to have you aboard."

Mystic curse? Shinji blinked. Had Phoebe been cursed? Before all this happened, before Shinji had even known about the Society, he thought he had been cursed by the Coatl statue. It was this supposed curse that caused him and the others to venture deep into the Mexican jungle, searching for the Coatl's temple, to return what had been stolen. Shinji's curse turned out to be fake, but he knew that real curses existed. Had Phoebe angered something or touched an artifact she wasn't supposed to?

"Oh dear." Phoebe gazed up at the ceiling. Bits of plaster floated to the ground from the hole left behind, ruining the mural's image of a Pegasus. Plaster dust had settled in her hair, turning it gray. "Don't worry," she announced, pivoting back to the table. "I can pay for that. At least it wasn't a one-of-a-kind eighteenth-century Ming vase like last time. Um . . ." She gazed down at the shattered crystals inches from her toes. "Do you have a broom anywhere?"

Priya was pressing two fingers to her forehead. "It's fine, Phoebe," she said, forcing a smile as she lowered her hand. "I'll take care of it. You just . . . go to your quarters and relax." *Without breaking anything else* was the unspoken request.

"Of course," Phoebe said genially. "I need to do a bit of study on ancient Mesoamerican practices, anyway. No need to show me the guest room; I remember where it is." She bounced to the door, shedding plaster dust as she did, but paused and smiled broadly at Shinji from the frame. "Our first adventure together, Shinji," she announced, raising her umbrella like a conductor's baton. "This is going to be great!"

Shinji was pretty sure she was the only one who thought that.

CHAPTER
THREE

Back in his dorm room, Shinji dragged the suitcase the Society had given him out from under his bed and plopped it open on the mattress. His mind was spinning so much that he could hardly concentrate on what he needed to pack.

Another adventure. Another mission with SEA. Only this time, instead of trying to find the Coatl's temple to return a statue to the font, they had to find a sunken ship that held the ancient artifacts of a lost culture. And they had to reach it before Hightower got there first.

Also, Phoebe Mystic would be there, to "help" him learn to control his guardian powers.

Shinji clenched his jaw. He wished he could make them all understand. The Coatl had chosen him, but more important, Shinji had accepted the mantle of the guardian. Which meant it was up to him to figure his magic out. If he couldn't learn how to control his own magic himself, he would be a failure as a guardian. He didn't need help, especially from someone who seemed to be cursed herself.

As he was tossing clothes and other necessities into his suitcase, his phone vibrated. Pulling it from his pocket, he stared at the screen, seeing a new text had come through.

Hey Shinji. Having fun here in New Zealand but it is C.O.L.D. Hope you're enjoying your classes and not giving SEA any trouble. Wish you were here.

The text also came with a picture of a slender Asian woman in an enormous puffy coat, waving to him against a backdrop of snowdrifts taller than her head.

Aunt Yui. Shinji grimaced. His legal guardian had been worried about leaving him with the Society while she went on a business trip to see an old friend. Shinji had urged her to go, insisting he would be fine. Aunt Yui was very understanding, but if she knew he was going on a mission for the Society, and that the nefarious Hightower corporation could be involved, she might be worried enough to come home. She might even forbid him from going in the first place. Shinji didn't want that to happen, so after some quick thinking, he texted back:

Hey Aunt Yui. No troubles here. Me and Lucy are going on a field trip to the SOUTH PACIFIC with Oliver tomorrow. I'll order a fruity drink with a tiny umbrella for you. Enjoy your snow.

He added a sun emoji, a palm tree, and an ocean wave before sending the text off with a grin. A few minutes later, his phone buzzed a second time.

Not jealous was all it said, next to the sobbing emoji. With a smile, Shinji stuck the phone in his pocket and continued packing.

As he was tossing in the last of his socks, there was a knock on his door, and Lucy poked her head in.

"Hey," Lucy greeted, coming into the room. "Are you done?"

"Almost," Shinji grunted, forcing the lid of the suitcase closed and zipping it shut. The clothes he'd stuffed in would have fit better if he'd folded them beforehand, but who had time for that? Grabbing the handle, he heaved the suitcase off the bed and set it on the floor before turning to Lucy. "There. I'm finished. You?"

She snorted. "Not even close. I'm still choosing what shirts I'm going to wear for the next week. Plus, I need to figure out what's going in my emergency kit. So far, I have bandages, mosquito repellent, disinfectant, and hand sanitizer. Can you think of anything else?"

"The kitchen sink?" Shinji smirked. "You know, there's this thing called 'traveling light' that's really popular these days."

"I like to be prepared." As she glanced at Shinji's suitcase, her nose scrunched up. "And at least none of my clothes are going to be a wrinkled lump of nasty when I take them out again."

He shrugged. Wrinkled clothes never bothered him, though Aunt Yui would sigh in exasperation if he wore a shirt for more than three days. "Did you need something?" he asked Lucy.

"Yes," Lucy said. "I lent you a book a couple weeks ago. On the different mythologies around the world. Remember? Did you ever read it?"

"Not really," Shinji admitted. It was a massive tome that could break his toes if he dropped it on them. "I *meant* to. But I kept getting distracted by, you know, not-boring things."

Lucy sighed. "Predictable. You're only the guardian of one of the last magic fonts on earth, with the spirit of the Coatl inside you. Why would you need to read up on other myths and possible guardians around the world?"

Shinji rolled his eyes. "Don't you have packing to do?" he asked Lucy. "Or did you just come in here to be sarcastic?"

"Says the king of sarcasm himself," Lucy retorted, but her faint smile said she wasn't being mean about it. "But no, I want to take that book with me. In case we spend a lot of time on the water, I can do some light reading."

Light reading she called it. Shinji shook his head and went to his desk. The large book lay beneath a stack of comics, where it had sat, untouched, since Lucy had lent it to him. "You know, the Society probably has a bunch of ancient encyclopedias gathering dust somewhere," he said, holding the giant book out to her. "You could just borrow one of those if you get bored."

"Some of us *like* studying." Lucy took the tome, holding it to her chest, but she didn't leave. "Hey, Shinji, you know who Phoebe is, right?" she said. "And why her family is so important?"

"Not really," Shinji said, making her sigh.

"Henry Mystic?" she went on, as if he should know the name. He stared at her blankly, and she rolled her eyes. "Really, Shinji, there is a huge portrait of him hanging on the wall in the meeting room. How have you never noticed it before?"

He shrugged. "You mean the old guy with the monkey and the funny hat? Yeah, I've seen it. So what?"

"It's called a fez." Lucy sighed again. "Henry Mystic was an extremely important and influential member of the Society, and part of SEA history," she went on. "He lived at the same time as Harrison Hightower, and there were rumors that they were acquaintances, maybe even friends, before Hightower's falling-out with the Society. The Mystics have been part of SEA for decades; plus, they're also very rich. If the Society does anything big, you can be sure the Mystics know about it and are probably involved in some way themselves.

"So, just be careful with what you tell Phoebe about the tattoo and the Coatl," Lucy finished. "She is a member of SEA, but there are stories about her family and what they've done in the past, and some of it is kind of shady. The Mystics are just as powerful as the Hightower Corporation, maybe even more so. We don't want you getting caught up in another power struggle over the tattoo."

"Is that why she's cursed?" Shinji asked, making her frown. "Oliver said something about a 'Mystic curse.' Do you know anything about that?"

"Sort of." Lucy shifted the tome to a more comfortable position in her arms. "Just stories, really. There were rumors about the Mystics in the Hightower Corporation. Things just . . . happen around them, things that can't be explained. My father used to be terrified that he would run into a member of the Mystic family and that their strange curse would latch on to him. Apparently, it dates all the way back to Henry Mystic and an old music box he found."

"Great," Shinji muttered. "And this is the person who's going to try to teach me magic. I'll probably start meditating and a lamp will fall on my head."

"*I* can teach you magic," Lucy said, a bit indignantly. "I probably know more about how magic works than Phoebe Mystic does. I'm sure she's *read* all about it, but I've actually used magic in my creations. *Without* making things explode. I could help you if you would just let me."

"I can't." Shinji shook his head. "I mean, I appreciate it,

but . . . I can't explain it. It's something I gotta figure out myself."

Figure it out. That was how it had always been. Aunt Yui was great, and Shinji knew she did everything she could for their well-being, but it had always been just the two of them. Sailing around the world, managing the shop, taking care of everyday life; sometimes his aunt simply *couldn't* be there when he needed someone. So Shinji had learned to take care of himself. He didn't like asking for help, especially with something he felt responsible for. That was just how he was wired.

"Don't you trust me?"

The question caught Shinji off guard. He gave Lucy a surprised look. "What? Of course I do. What kind of dumb question is that?"

She glared at him over the book. "You're keeping secrets," she accused. "About your powers. I know something else is going on, Shinji." She paused a moment, as if recalling something painful, then said, "Remember when I didn't tell you that my father was part of Hightower? I kept that a secret because I was scared of what the Society would do if they found out who I was. But it just backfired on me: Oliver thought I was a spy, and you thought I'd been sending secret messages to my dad."

He did remember. And he still felt guilty for accusing her of being a spy when all she had done was help him. "Yeah," he muttered. "Secrets bad. I get it."

"Let's trade," Lucy suggested. "You tell me what's been going on with your magic, and I'll tell you a secret of mine. A small one." She held out her hand, palm facing him. "Nothing serious. Just something that's been bothering me, and I can't say it out loud. But I'll tell you. Because we're friends and I trust you," she added emphatically.

Shinji sighed. "Fine." Sitting on his bed, he studied his hands for a few seconds, feeling Lucy's eyes on him. The Coatl tattoo on his forearm seemed to mock him, and he made a frustrated gesture. "So, you know I've been having trouble getting the magic to work," he said at last, and Lucy nodded. "But that's not the only problem. I . . . can't control *when* the magic happens, either. Sometimes it wakes me up in the middle of the night, or sometimes it makes things blow off shelves or across the room. Last night, it happened again. I wasn't even trying to call on it, and there was this gust of wind out of nowhere. I'm just glad no one was around to notice."

"I noticed," Lucy said.

Surprised, Shinji glanced up, and she raised both palms in a shrug. "It's kind of hard *not* to see a soda can rolling across the table on its own," she said. "But I thought you were practicing your magic at weird times. I didn't know you were having this much trouble."

"Yeah." Shinji raked his fingers through his hair, shoving it back. "And it's been getting worse," he admitted. "I've been trying to keep this a secret from Priya and Oliver. I don't want them to think I'm dangerous because I can't control the magic. It's not like I'm starting fires or flipping cars. It's just been small things: papers blown off my desk or random bursts of wind when I leave a room."

"Ah," said Lucy, as if just realizing something. "So that's why I keep hearing slamming doors."

Shinji clenched a fist on his leg. "I have to figure this out," he said. "The Coatl chose me to be the guardian of the font, not that I even know what that means." He threw up one hand in frustration. "So, I'm supposed to protect people. Is that *all* people, or only the ones I know? And what am I supposed to protect them from? Small things, like spider bites? Or big things like . . . wars? I don't know. I don't know what I'm supposed to do, but I can't screw this up."

"I think you're being too hard on yourself," Lucy said gently. "And I don't think you should take all this on alone. It took me years to learn to work my magic, and I had tutors helping me. Even then, sometimes I'd miscalculate the magic-to-tech ratio, and it would malfunction. It was a pretty delicate process. You can't rush magic. I don't think you can rush learning to be a guardian, either."

Lucy possessed a rare and special talent for blending magic and technology together. It was how she created Tinker, and to Shinji, she was a genius when it came to gadgets and gizmos. But she hadn't promised a mystical Coatl that she would become a guardian to protect people. She didn't have the magic from one of the last fonts in the world inside her. This was different. Shinji had taken on a huge responsibility, and he was determined to get it right. Even if he had no clue about what he was supposed to be doing.

But he didn't want to argue with Lucy, either, so instead he asked, "So, what's your big secret?"

She paused. "It's nothing, really." She shrugged, though her hesitancy said otherwise. "But sometimes . . . I miss Hightower."

Shinji stared at her. "You *miss* Hightower?"

"A little." She shrugged again and looked away. "I shouldn't miss it," she went on, as if disgusted with herself. "It was a terrible place. I'm much better off here. But . . . I do miss my room. And my workshop. Sometimes I wonder if anyone thinks of me." Tinker crawled to her shoulder, curling up in the collar of her shirt, and a bitter smile crossed her face. "I doubt my dad even cares that I'm gone."

Unease bloomed inside Shinji, and a breath of wind fluttered the comics on his desk. Lucy was homesick. Was she unhappy at the Society? Did she want to leave and go back to the Hightower Corporation? His stomach clenched at the thought. Lucy was his friend; he didn't want her to leave, but more than that: She knew a ton of SEA secrets that she could take back to the enemy. She had been on the inside; she had seen the hidden places of the Society. If her father commanded her to come home, would she go?

Lucy shook herself, giving Shinji a normal smile again.

"Anyway"—she shrugged—"that's my silly little secret. It's stupid, right?"

Shinji shrugged, too. "I mean, I guess I get missing your room and your super-fancy workshop. As long as you don't have the urge to make zombie rats or killer robots, I think it's fine."

She laughed. "What about killer-zombie-rat robots?"

"*Those* might actually be cool."

She laughed again. "I need to finish packing. Thanks for not losing my book." She hefted the enormous tome in both hands. "I figure *one* of us needs to research the different world mythologies so we'll know what to do if you're ever attacked by a dragon."

"That would be awesome," Shinji replied. "And I hope the answer is throw a saddle on it and ride it around."

Lucy rolled her eyes. Holding the book to her chest, she turned and walked out of the room, Tinker's beady red gaze peering at Shinji as she left.

Alone again, Shinji sat down on his bed, thinking of what Lucy had revealed. For a second, he wondered if he should tell Oliver. They were in a race to beat Hightower to a sunken treasure. Which meant that they would probably run into the greedy corporation somewhere along the journey. But he didn't want to rat Lucy out, especially if Priya decided she couldn't come. That would suck for both of them.

Besides, he trusted Lucy. With everything that happened,

she wouldn't just leave the Society to go back to Hightower. She despised their greed and their ruthlessness.

But then, if she hated them so much, why was she feeling homesick?

Shinji held up his arm, gazing down at the tattoo standing out against his skin. A brilliantly colored serpent with a feathered hood and golden wings framing its body stared back at him, though there was no spark of life or sentience behind its emerald gaze. Just flat, lifeless ink. Since the last adventure, Shinji had snuck furtive glances at the tattoo more times than he could count, hoping to catch it moving or peering back at him, like it used to do. He had always been disappointed.

"I still have no idea what you want me to do," he told the Coatl, ignoring the strange feeling he got from talking to a picture on his arm. "You haven't given me any instructions. I'm trying to figure everything out by myself, but a little hint would be nice."

No response from the winged snake on his forearm. Not that he was really expecting one. It seemed he was on his own after all.

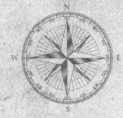

CHAPTER FOUR

Standing on the tarmac of a tiny private airport somewhere in the city, Shinji watched the small red plane approach with a mix of excitement and utter dread.

"Oooh, is that Scarlett I see?" Phoebe called, shading her eyes as the whine of the propellers got closer. "How exciting. I haven't seen her in a minute. Last I heard, she was forced to land somewhere in the Himalayas because one of *Rhett*'s engines supposedly burst into flame."

Oliver visibly blanched. "Thanks, Phoebe. I could've gone the rest of my life without knowing that."

Shinji stifled a groan. Scarlett J. Blaurhimmel and her infamous plane were well known and respected throughout the Society. Supposedly, she flew all around the world in the ancient red airplane she lovingly called *Rhett*, but the two flights Shinji had been on with Scarlett were not what he would call comfortable. Terrifying would be a better description. And Oliver hated flying even more than Shinji did. He wondered if the plane still only had the one parachute.

The plane bounced once on the runway, landed, and came to a rather screeching halt that left wisps of white smoke curling into the air. After a few moments, the pilot door opened, and a woman with flaming-red hair emerged, a pair of flight goggles perched atop her head. She smiled at Shinji, Lucy, and Oliver, but her blue eyes widened when they landed on Phoebe.

"Phoebe? Phoebe Mystic, is that you?" Scarlett shook her head, crimson hair whipping about in the breeze. "What are you doing here? I thought you were in Scotland trying to track down the Loch Ness Monster."

"Sadly, that didn't pan out." Phoebe gave a dramatic sigh. "Nessie was being very camera shy and didn't make an appearance. It's fine, though. I know she's there. I'll get a clear picture of her one day." She sniffed, then glanced down at Shinji. "Today, I'm here for Mr. Takahashi. We're off to the South Pacific, and Priya was kind enough to let me tag along."

"Oh? That *was* very kind of her." An amused smile tugged at Scarlett's mouth, and she looked over at Oliver. "And are you in on this, too, Ocean?"

Oliver snorted. "Unfortunately, I've been outvoted."

"Oh well, cheer up. Nothing but blue sky and sun where you're heading. And don't you worry"—she reached back and patted the side of the plane—"*Rhett* and I will get you across the Pacific in record time. There's even a cooler full of drinks and sandwiches, so we're all set to fly." She turned away, but Shinji thought he heard her murmur, "Let's just hope those repairs on the second engine hold. . . ."

It was definitely not a luxury trip.

Flying with Scarlett was just as loud, unpleasant, and jarring as last time, only much, much longer. Shinji felt every dip, jolt, drop, and tremor of the plane through the metal seat he was sitting on, and the vibration of the engines made his teeth itch. Scarlett had attempted to make things a bit more comfortable by putting down cushions, but it was still a long, shaky trip. The engines were so loud Shinji couldn't even talk to Lucy or Oliver without nearly shouting, so nobody spoke much. And sleeping was out of the question. Except for Phoebe Mystic, who propped her cushion up on the wall, leaned against it, and started to snore. Shinji occupied himself with games and movies on his phone, munched the peanut-butter-and-jelly sandwiches that came out of Scarlett's cooler, and fantasized about being on the ground.

A couple of hours into the flight, *Rhett* gave a violent

shudder. Glancing out the window, Shinji saw one of the propellers sputter and stop moving. The plane gave a loud cough and then dropped out of the air.

Lucy shrieked, and Shinji's stomach jumped all the way up to his throat. Oliver's face turned green, and he braced one arm against the side of the plane, looking like he might throw up. Before Shinji could take a breath to let out a yell himself, *Rhett* gave another cough and the propellers started spinning again. The plane stopped its free fall and started climbing once more, but from then on, every little jolt made Shinji's stomach clench.

Phoebe didn't even wake up.

Shinji was never as happy to feel a plane's wheels touch the runway, though it was a very bouncy, jarring landing that would've clacked his teeth together had he not been braced and ready for it. Glancing over, he saw Lucy pressed into the seat as well, and Oliver's clenched jaw. In the corner, Phoebe Mystic continued to snore.

The plane didn't stop immediately upon landing but continued across a tiny strip of pavement toward what looked like a hangar bay at the end. Through the plane's small windows, Shinji caught glimpses of blue sky and palm trees, and a rush of excitement went through him. They were finally here.

Oliver was out of his seat before the plane even stopped moving. He grabbed his backpack off the floor and swung it over one shoulder as the engines shuddered and came to a stop. Lucy let out a sigh of relief as the noise level in the cabin dropped, though Shinji could still hear the echo of the engine drone in his ears.

"And that's three." Oliver sighed, shaking his head. "Three times I've been on this flying deathtrap this year. Which is three times more than I wanted. How are you two doing?" he asked Shinji and Lucy. "Everyone okay?"

"When do your teeth stop vibrating?" Shinji muttered. Oliver snorted.

"Give it a couple of minutes; it'll go away soon. The real annoyance will be the ringing in your ears. You'll hear that for at least an hour."

"Mm?" Phoebe grunted, and raised her head. "Goodness, are we there already? I was having a nice nap. Time flies." She yawned, stretched, and stood up. "So, that was easier than I thought. Where to next?"

Oliver glared at Phoebe, as if he blamed her for the plane dropping out of the sky. Shinji remembered the "Mystic curse" and wondered if it really had been Phoebe who'd caused the plane's malfunction, or if it was just *Rhett* being *Rhett*.

The door behind Oliver opened with a grinding screech, revealing Scarlett's smiling face on the other side.

"Welcome to Pula!" she announced, crimson hair whipping around her in the hot breeze sweeping through the hangar. "A little-known place halfway between Tahiti and Easter Island. I do apologize for the rough ride. *Rhett* got a little cranky there in the middle of the flight and decided to act up. I don't think he likes you much, Ocean."

"Trust me, the feeling's mutual."

A taxi pulled into the hangar, rolling to a stop a few yards away. Scarlett stepped back a pace and motioned them out. "All right, everyone, off you go! Have fun out there, and don't let Oliver sail into a reef again. I'd hate to have to come and rescue you in the middle of the ocean."

"You sailed into a reef?" Phoebe asked.

"I did not sail into a reef," Oliver said indignantly. "My boat was pushed into the rocks by a hurricane; there's a difference."

"Yes, but the question you have to ask yourself," Scarlett broke in, smiling as she leaned casually against the side of her plane, "is *why* he was out on his ship in the middle of a hurricane in the first place. Have him tell you that little story one day; it's sure to be entertaining."

With a wink, Scarlett pushed herself off the side of the plane and walked around the front, vanishing from sight. Shinji stared after her a moment, then looked questioningly at Oliver.

He grimaced. "Yeah, not a story you're gonna hear anytime soon, kid. Sorry." He jerked his head at the taxi. "Let's go. My butt cheeks have been clenched for the past nine hours. I need to be on a boat."

Now this is what I'm talking about, Shinji thought. Sitting in the backseat of the taxi, windows rolled down and a cool wind blowing in his face, he stared out at the sparkling waters, gleaming sand, and tropical paradise beyond the road. Palm trees grew everywhere, seabirds wheeled through a cloudless sky, and the distant ocean was the turquoise green of a precious jewel. Pula itself was an interesting mix of rural and modern, with gravel side roads and tiny huts giving way to looming resorts and hotels. The breeze blowing into the taxi smelled like seawater, which made Shinji all the more eager to get down to the ocean.

Lucy sat beside him, also staring out the window with wide, eager eyes. Tinker's nose poked out of her hair and twitched, like he was a real mouse.

"So, Oliver." Abruptly, Phoebe twisted around in her seat to peer at them over the headrest. "I know we're in a frantic race to beat Hightower to this ship at the bottom of the ocean and recover evidence of a culture that has been lost for decades, but what's the likelihood of running into a kraken in this part of the world? Any hope of a long, sucking tentacle reaching up from the abyss and dragging us into the void?"

"A kraken?" Lucy shuddered.

For a second, Shinji thought Phoebe was joking, before he remembered who he was in the car with.

"As fun as that sounds, probably not," Oliver answered with a dismissive shrug. "Not at the depths we'll be diving. The kraken and all their squiddy cousins like deeper, darker waters. Plus, for such a giant, scary sea monster, they're kind of wimps. The noise of the ship engines will likely scare one off long before we'd ever get to see it."

"Aw." Phoebe pouted. "Darn it. Why are all the underwater monsters so painfully camera shy? Someday I'll see one. Someday. So, Shinji!" She turned to him, making him jump. "Speaking of monsters, I heard you came face-to-face with the Weaver while you were in the temple of the Coatl. Tell me *all* about that. Was she really half-human, half-spider, or was it more of a sixty-forty split?"

Shinji blinked. "I don't—"

"And when the Coatl made an appearance," Phoebe went on without letting him finish, "what did it look like? Were you scared? Was it a terrible winged snake creature of vengeance, or more of a benevolent demigod? Did it speak to you, or did you just *know* what it wanted?"

"Well . . ."

"Oh, and don't forget about the fight between the Weaver and the Coatl!" Phoebe waved both hands, hitting the top of the taxi roof. The driver, Shinji noticed, was giving her a side-eyed look of concern. "I want to hear all about that battle, every tiny detail, even the ones you might've missed. What an epic sight that must've been, two legendary creatures trying to tear each other apart." She sighed dreamily. "I would've happily given up my collection of dragon scales to see that.

"So, go ahead, Shinji," Phoebe finished, staring at him

intently now. "I'm all ears. Tell me exactly how everything happened. Leave nothing out."

Shinji was trying to think of a way to point out that the backseat of a taxi wasn't exactly a good place to recite what would likely sound to the driver like the plot of a monster B-movie. Thankfully, before he could speak, the taxi slowed and came to a rather jolting halt next to the sidewalk.

"Kiani Harbor," grunted the driver, pointing with a weathered hand. Glancing out the window, Shinji saw a distant line of sails bobbing against the sky. Seabirds wheeled above the masts, and sunlight glinted off the water. "You'll have to walk from here."

As Oliver scooted forward to pay the driver, Shinji took the opportunity to escape and quickly opened the car door, sliding out onto the sidewalk. Instantly, the breeze coming off the water and smelling of salt and fish tossed his hair. A bicyclist rolled past him, ringing a bell, and a small dog yapped at him from the end of a leash.

The hair on the back of Shinji's neck prickled, making him pause. It was the same feeling he got whenever he and Aunt Yui found themselves in a strange city or on the questionable side of town. That uncomfortable sensation of being watched.

Carefully, Shinji looked around. They were on a sunny, fairly busy corner, with traffic from both cars and pedestrians passing them on the street. Around them, large hotels rose into the cloudless sky, windows catching the sun. People ambled down the sidewalks, seemingly in no hurry. It was, as far as he could tell, a fairly lazy, normal day around the harbor.

And then Shinji spotted a boy. A kid around his own age, leaning casually against a palm tree with his arms crossed. He wore shorts and a sleeveless shirt and looked like he spent all of his time outdoors in the sun. His long, dark brown hair hung in his eyes, and those eyes were definitely watching him. When their gazes met, the boy gave a smirk that was clearly not friendly, and the challenge there made Shinji bristle.

"Shinji? You okay?" Lucy stepped out beside him, nudging his arm. "What are you staring at?"

"Nothing." Shinji glanced back at the other kid, but the boy was now gazing down the street and not looking at them at all. Behind them, Oliver and Phoebe were still in the cab with the driver, and he could hear Phoebe's voice drifting through the glass. "It's beautiful here, huh?"

"Yeah," Lucy said, distracted. She gazed warily around the street, as if searching for attackers hidden in the bushes and alleyways. Tinker emerged from a pocket, crawled up her arm, and perched on her shoulders, delicate copper ears rotating around like miniature satellite dishes.

"What are *you* looking for?" Shinji asked.

"Hightower," Lucy replied without hesitation, and Shinji's nerves prickled. Why was she looking for Hightower? Did she want to talk to them? If she saw any members of the

Hightower Corporation walking around, would she decide to go back and work for them?

Shinji shook himself. He'd had these suspicions about Lucy before, and nothing good had come of it. Lucy was his friend. She was part of SEA now, just like him. She wouldn't betray them just because she was homesick.

As if sensing his unease, Lucy glanced over with a faint frown. "Everyone at Hightower knows who I am," she explained. "Or at least, they know who my dad is. If Hightower is already here and recognizes me, it might put the mission in danger."

Shinji relaxed. That made sense, though it made him feel even more guilty for doubting her loyalty. "Kinda feels like we're in another training simulation," he joked, making her smile. "At least if there are any Hightower goons wandering around, they're not going to jump us in the middle of the city—"

Something slammed into Lucy from behind, pushing her into Shinji. He stumbled back, just managing to stay on his feet while holding Lucy upright. Before he could even get his balance again, someone rushed by, and Shinji caught a split-second glimpse of the boy who had smirked at him. The kid didn't stop to apologize, but kept right on running.

"Did he do that on purpose?" Shinji said. He took a breath to shout something after the rude boy, but Lucy suddenly clutched at her shoulder and let out a horrified gasp.

"Tinker!" Lucy shrieked. "He stole Tinker! Catch him!"

"What?" Shinji said, but Lucy took off across the road in the direction the boy had fled. With a curse under his breath, Shinji sprinted after her. He heard Oliver shout his name over the sounds of cars and traffic, but he couldn't stop. If the strange boy had stolen Tinker, Lucy would be inconsolable. They had to get him back.

The boy ducked between buildings, crossed another road, and vaulted over a fence to escape. He was very fast. Probably did this kind of thing all the time. But Shinji also had experience fleeing pursuers in crowded markets, and there was no way Lucy was going to lose Tinker. She scrambled over the fence with a determination that impressed him, and kept going. They followed the boy past shops and buildings, weaving around cars and sidewalks lined with palms, and finally chased him through an indoor market filled with stalls and vendors selling everything from purses to bananas.

As they drew closer, catching fleeting glimpses of the boy through the crowd, Lucy suddenly shouted something. Shinji couldn't tell if it was directed at the thief or at Tinker, but a few seconds later, he heard the boy ahead of them yelp in surprise. And then what sounded like a muffled curse.

Ducking between stalls, Shinji and Lucy finally caught up to him near the bathrooms. He was crouched behind a potted plant in the hall between the women's and men's rooms, and Shinji could hear him groaning in pain. As they rounded the corner, trapping him in the hallway, he glanced up at them, panting, and held out a hand.

"Okay, okay. Take it easy. You got me, okay? Just back off."

"Where's Tinker?" Lucy demanded, stepping forward with her fists clenched. "What did you do with him? Tell me."

"You mean your robot rat? It's here." He gestured to a potted fern in the corner. "I stuffed it in there after the stupid thing nearly burned my fingers off."

"Good. You got what you deserved," Lucy said icily, brushing past him and heading toward the potted fern. Reaching under the fronds, she emerged with Tinker, who made happy squeaking noises as she pulled him free. Lucy put the mouse to her face, making sure he was all right, then glared daggers back at the thief. "Thanks for letting me test out my antitheft protocols," she said. "I hope it hurt. A lot."

The boy raised one hand, where a line of burned red skin streaked his palm. "There. Happy now?"

Her eyes narrowed, but she didn't answer, stalking back to Shinji with Tinker held close. The boy's gaze shifted, meeting Shinji's glare with a raised eyebrow. "What?" he challenged. "Gonna beat me up now for stealing your girlfriend's rat?"

Shinji snorted. The kid was baiting him, trying to make him mad, but little did he know, Shinji was a professional smart aleck himself. "I wouldn't have to," he drawled. "She could kick your butt on her own if she wanted."

The kid laughed. It wasn't a mocking laugh now, though it did make Lucy's lips tighten. "Yeah, I'm not gonna call that bluff," he said, and raised both arms in a placating gesture.

"You got your rat back. How 'bout we walk away and forget we ever saw each other—deal?"

"Already done," Lucy said in a voice of cold disdain. "Let's go, Shinji."

Shinji started to turn away but hesitated. He could feel something stir inside him, a faint curiosity that wasn't his own. It made his stomach jump and his heart beat faster at the realization. Was it . . . the Coatl, reacting to this stranger?

"What's your name?" he asked the boy.

One brow arched in wary surprise. "Why?" the kid asked. "The cops around here already know me. You're not going to surprise them by turning me in."

"I wasn't going to." So the kid had had dealings with the police before. Shinji wasn't surprised. "I'm Shinji, by the way," he went on. "This is Lucy, and her *mouse* is called Tinker."

Lucy gave him a look of confused disgust. "What are you doing?" she whispered.

Shinji shrugged. He didn't really know. He just hoped the exchange of names would get the kid to talk.

The boy gave him a weird, puzzled look, then shrugged. "It's Roux," he said, pronouncing the name with a long *oo* sound.

"Why'd you steal Tinker?"

"What? I don't know." Roux shrugged again. "It looked cool? I wanted to see what it did? I thought I could outrun a pair of tourists? Take your pick."

"You could've just asked," Lucy said, still in a stony voice. "I would have let you hold him."

That made Roux laugh again, but it was a bitter sound now. "Yeah, asking doesn't get you crap around here."

"Shinji? Lucy?"

Oliver appeared at the end of the hallway, Phoebe behind him. When Roux saw the two adults, his jaw tightened, and his eyes darted toward the exit behind them. Oliver's gaze swept over the situation, lingering on Roux, and he raised a knowing eyebrow.

"Everything okay here?" he asked, keeping his eye on Roux. He moved himself to further block the exit from the hallway, in case the new kid decided to bolt. "Shinji, Lucy, you all right? What happened?"

"Ahhh-haaaaaaa!" Phoebe lunged past Oliver, both arms held in front of her in a karate stance. "Are you in danger? Where are the bad guys? Don't mess with me!" she warned an invisible attacker. "I am trained in Shaolin Kempo, Brazilian jujitsu, and Wing Tzun kung fu!"

"We're fine," Shinji blurted before Lucy could say anything. She frowned at him, but he ignored her. "There was just . . . a misunderstanding. It's been taken care of."

"A misunderstanding," Oliver repeated. He sounded dubious and cast an appraising glance at Roux. Shinji could tell Oliver knew what was going on, but he shook his head and moved aside so he wasn't blocking the hall anymore. "Well, misunderstanding or no, let's not take off without warning in the middle of a strange city, okay? You nearly gave me a heart attack, and we haven't even left land yet." He sighed and ran his fingers through his hair. "If I managed to lose you two before we even got on the boat, Priya would never let me hear the end of it."

"Aw." Phoebe lowered her arms. "I was hoping we would get a chance to put our fighting skills to the test, Oliver. You and me, battling hordes of bad guys?" She gave the air a dramatic chop. "That would have been amazing!"

"Ah, no, it would not," Oliver countered with a shudder. "I don't know what fighting skills you're talking about, but mine are limited to me flailing about with a cane and hoping I hit something."

Shinji knew this wasn't true. Oliver could fight *very* well. Their self-defense classes with the ex-pirate proved that. But Oliver also liked to downplay his fighting skills, either to maintain the element of surprise or because he truly despised fighting even though he made it look easy. Shinji didn't get it, but there was still a lot about Oliver Ocean that was an enigma.

"I would like this trip to not involve any encounters with large scary bad guys, if at all possible," Oliver continued. "Kids, let's go." He turned away and motioned them all out of the corridor. "The ship is waiting for us in the harbor, and Mano has already called to see if we're on our way."

Shinji started to follow Oliver but caught Roux's gaze before he did. The other boy was watching them leave, his expression unreadable. Once again, Shinji felt that weird sensation inside that wasn't his; it was as if the Coatl was intrigued by the stranger who had stolen Tinker. He wanted to know more about the kid, but Oliver and the others were already walking away. With a final glance and an apologetic shrug, Shinji hurried after them.

On the long walk back to the harbor, Lucy abruptly and rather aggressively punched him in the arm. "Ow!" Shinji exclaimed, frowning at her while rubbing his bruised shoulder. "What was that for?"

"What do you mean, what was that for?" Lucy scowled back at him, and her angry voice startled him even more than the punch. Lucy rarely became embroiled in an argument. Probably due to her Hightower upbringing, but the angrier she got, the colder and icier her demeanor became. Usually. "That boy stole Tinker!" she went on indignantly. "He would've gotten away with it, too, if we didn't chase him down. Why were you even talking to him?"

"What did you want me to do, punch him in the face?"

"I wouldn't have complained."

"It turned out fine," Shinji pointed out. "We got Tinker back. Besides . . ."

He trailed off. He was going to say that the magic seemed interested in Roux or maybe it was trying to warn him of danger, but then he noticed Phoebe Mystic watching them over her shoulder. If she heard him mention anything about the tattoo or the Coatl, she would definitely want to know about it, and Shinji didn't want to spend the next hour detailing what had happened.

"Besides, what?" Lucy prodded.

"Um, besides . . . he didn't seem so bad at the end," Shinji finished. "I mean, he gave Tinker back without a fight. And he said he was sorry." And, in some strange way, Shinji could sympathize with him. He recognized that wary, suspicious look on Roux's face when Oliver and Phoebe joined them, that instant distrust of grown-ups. Shinji didn't condone what Roux had done, but he did sense that the boy, much like himself, had seen the rougher side of people.

"Hmmph." Lucy sniffed, unappeased. "Well, whether he's sorry or not, that doesn't make it right to steal from people. At least we won't see him ever again." Scooping Tinker from her shoulder, she placed him carefully in her pocket. "You stay hidden until we get on the boat. I don't want you grabbed by another lowlife."

They finally reached the harbor, following Oliver down a long cement embankment that ran alongside the ocean. Dozens of ships floated in the bay, sails and masts pointed at the sky. Shinji, having spent a large part of his life on a boat, recognized most of the vessels. From the smaller, sleeker sailboats to bulkier, twin-hulled catamarans to enormous private yachts, he had glimpsed them all before, in harbors around the world—though he had never been on a ship with the Society before, exploring the unknown. He was excited to get started, and wondered which of the dozens of ships in the harbor was the one they would be sailing on.

As they neared the end of the piers, a shout suddenly rang out, echoing over the breeze.

"You got some nerve showing up here, Ocean!"

Shinji looked up. A man was striding toward them over the docks. A very large man, with dark hair and eyes, muscles bulging through his shirt as he plowed forward. Lucy gasped, and Phoebe immediately raised her arms in the same karate pose she had assumed before, though the large man ignored her, his gaze riveted on Oliver.

Frowning, the man stomped up to them, towering over Oliver. Shinji couldn't see Oliver's expression, but the ex-pirate didn't appear wary or tense, though that could have just been his nonchalant attitude toward everything. Arms crossed, Oliver stared up at the large man, seemingly unconcerned that one swing from those ham-size fists could send him flying into the water. Phoebe was rigid, arms raised and muscles coiled, ready to launch an attack. Though Shinji doubted she would be able to do much harm to the stranger. He looked like someone could smash a vase over his head and he wouldn't even feel it.

For a moment, the large man stood there, scowling, fists clenched and nostrils flaring like an angry bull. Squaring his shoulders, he leaned forward, getting right in Oliver's face, glaring at him like he was about to knock him out. Beside him, Lucy looked on with wide, fearful eyes, and Shinji held his breath.

The man's jaw clenched, lips twitching, and then he suddenly broke into a loud guffaw that made Shinji jump. "Darn it, Ocean," he exclaimed, straightening and stepping back. He was grinning now, and it transformed his face entirely. "Absolutely nothing? Come on."

"I keep telling you, Mano," Oliver replied, and from his tone, Shinji could tell he was grinning, too. "You're not scary. Your face and hands and mouth all say *I'm gonna punch your lights out*, but your eyes are laughing. Every time."

"Nuts," the large man said, and without warning threw both of his enormous, muscular arms around Oliver with a laugh. "Ah, it's good to see you, Ocean," he exclaimed, lifting the smaller man off his feet with no effort at all. "I was wondering when we would go on another adventure together. You, me, the open sea. Just like old times again."

He squeezed once, then set Oliver back on his feet. "Well, don't just stand there, my friend," the big man said, slapping Oliver in the shoulder. "It's rude to keep everyone waiting. Introduce me."

"Right." Oliver took a quick breath, probably to reinflate his lungs, and gave the rest of them a wry smile. "Everyone, this is Mano, an old sailing buddy of mine, the captain of the *Seas the Day*, and the worst poker player in the world. Mano, this is Shinji and Lucy, the protégés you've heard about."

"Nice to meet you," Lucy said politely while Shinji raised one arm in a wave.

"Mano means 'shark,'" the big man announced. He seemed proud of that fact. "But don't worry, I don't bite." He winked at Lucy, then turned to Shinji with a smile. "I heard all about your expedition to Mexico, Shinji, and your run-in with a rather mystical feathered snake. That is fantastic; I would've loved to have seen it myself." He shook his head in disbelief. "You know, in some cultures, snakes are considered signs of good fortune, which is very nice to have before you go on any kind of sailing adventure. Our last lucky totem washed overboard in a storm, so you can be our good luck for the trip."

"It washed overboard?" Shinji grinned. "That wasn't very lucky of it."

"No," Mano agreed. "No, it was not." Leaning over, he rapped three times on one of the wooden posts lining the pier. "Knock on wood, hopefully luck will be with us on this trip."

"Hello, Mr. Mano!" Phoebe interrupted, stepping in front of Oliver with a smile and extending a hand. "It's a pleasure to meet you. I'm Phoebe Mystic, as I'm sure Oliver just forgot to mention."

"Yes, Priya told us you were coming." Mano didn't take her hand, as if Phoebe had some terrible disease that he might catch. Taking a long step back, he reached into his pocket and pulled out something small and bright. Shinji saw it was a penny as he rubbed it between thumb and forefinger. "Unfortunately, I still have concerns. I tried contacting you about this, Ocean," Mano went on, glancing to Oliver. "You didn't reply to any of my messages."

"I would have," Oliver said, "but I was with Scarlett, and it's really hard to text when you're about two seconds away from puking at any given time. Besides, there's nothing to be concerned about." He jerked a thumb at the still-smiling Phoebe. "We flew together on *Rhett*. If there was any sort of bad luck, we would be at the bottom of the ocean right now."

"Scarlett makes her own luck," Mano replied with a wave of his large hand. "It's the only reason that she can keep flying that rust-covered contraption." He stuck the penny back in his pocket and crossed his arms. "I'm sorry, but a Mystic on board a ship is a recipe for disaster. I can't condone bringing her along."

Neither Mano nor Oliver seemed concerned that Phoebe was standing right there, listening to them talk about her, but Phoebe didn't seem to care, either. Or, at least, she was doing a really good job of hiding it. Shinji wondered if this sort of thing happened to her often.

Lucy suddenly stepped forward. "Not that I believe any of this," she said, frowning at Mano and Oliver. "But what about Shinji? You said his Coatl tattoo was good luck. Having a guardian with us has to count for something, right?"

"Hey." Shinji raised both hands and took a step back. "Don't bring me into this," he told Lucy. "Do I look like a lucky rabbit's foot? It's not like I can wave a hand and make it stop raining or anything like that."

"But you are a guardian," Lucy insisted. "At the very least, you have a little magic. A little magic is better than none, even if you can't control it yet."

Lucy! Shinji glared at her, making her eyes widen. *That was a secret! You weren't supposed to tell anyone!*

Lucy winced, looking immediately guilty. *Sorry,* she mouthed, but Shinji turned away, still fuming. That was the last time he would tell Lucy a secret.

"Hmm." Mano folded his arms, looking thoughtful. "I suppose that is something," he mused. "Having a guardian around should act as a counter to any bad fortune the Mystic name might bring aboard." He gave a gusty sigh. "I still don't like it, but I guess it'll do. She's welcome to come along." He scratched the back of his neck, giving Phoebe a guilty look. "Sorry, Miss Mystic. No offense taken, I hope?"

Shinji glanced at Phoebe. For just a moment, her eyes were hooded, a shadow of some dark emotion crossing her face. But then she brightened, and the shadow was gone so quickly he thought he had imagined it.

"Oh, not at all." Phoebe waved off the tense moment with a cheerful smile. "Don't worry, Mr. Mano. I am well aware that my family name might carry a bit of baggage for some. Especially after the whole music-box incident." She snorted a laugh and made a dramatic gesture with one arm. "Really, you'd be surprised how often this sort of thing comes up. Shall we go? I'm eager to see this boat you all keep talking about."

"This way, then." Mano gestured down the pier. "The *Seas the Day* is waiting for us at the end of the harbor."

CHAPTER FIVE

"There it is," Oliver announced a few minutes later, nodding across the pier. "The *Seas the Day*. That's our ship."

Shinji followed his gaze, and his brows rose. An enormous blue-and-white ship sat in the glittering waters at the end of the dock. It was, Shinji estimated, over two hundred feet in length, with a yellow crane at the back and a radio tower stabbing into the air up front. No tiny sailboat or clunky barge, it would've towered over the *Good Tern*, and it dwarfed most of the other boats in the harbor.

It was probably one of the bigger ships he'd seen, certainly the biggest he would ever be a passenger on.

"Pretty impressive," Oliver said, arms crossed as he gazed

up at the vessel. "Not as fast as the *Salty Siren,* of course," he added, referring to his own ship. "But as a research vessel, it's better set up for these types of missions. Plus, there's a full team of Society scientists and researchers aboard, so things are going to be interesting. What do you think, kid?" he asked, glancing at Shinji. "Not a bad place to be spending the week, right?"

"Oh, I can't wait," Phoebe exclaimed. "A ship like this will surely have all sorts of underwater cameras and motion sensors. I still hope we can see a kraken. Or a siren, though the boys might have to stuff wax in their ears to keep from being lured overboard."

Oliver snorted. "Wax. What are we, in the fourteenth century?" Reaching into his coat pocket, he pulled out a small plastic bag, which he tossed at Shinji and Lucy. "Here, kids. Not that I think we'll need it, but just in case."

Shinji caught the bag and gazed down at the contents. "Earplugs?" He frowned.

"Never leave home without them." Oliver nodded. "Especially if you're a sailor. Siren songs are no joke."

As Shinji stuck the earplug bag into his pocket, his nerves prickled a warning. It was that same sensation of being watched that he'd had right before Roux slammed into Lucy. Turning, he scanned the dock and the surrounding harbor, staring at the boats, searching for anyone who might be watching them. For a figure with long, sun-bleached hair and dark eyes. This time, though, he didn't see anything weird or out of place. If someone was spying on them, they were doing it out of sight.

Following Oliver and Mano up the ramp, Shinji, Lucy, and Phoebe were met by a dark-skinned, dark-haired woman in a long white coat. "Welcome to the *Seas the Day*," she said, holding out a hand to Oliver. "I'm the chief archaeologist, Dr. Tamara Grant. It's an honor to have such an esteemed Society member on board, Mr. Ocean."

"Just call me Oliver." Oliver grinned at her. "Also, who is going around calling me 'esteemed'? I'm going to have to work on my reputation around here."

The archaeologist chuckled. "Your reputation already precedes you, Oliver Ocean, trust me on that." She glanced at Lucy and Shinji with a smile. "And these must be the new members of SEA," she went on. "Welcome aboard."

"Thanks," Shinji replied. "This is a big ship."

"It is." She nodded. "And I know you're probably tired, having flown all the way from the US, but would you like a little tour before we cast off? I'll show you what we do here and where everything is. If nothing else, it'll be a good way to combat that jet lag I'm sure you're feeling."

"Sure! If that's okay?" Shinji added, glancing at Oliver. He really wanted to check out the ship, but the operation he was on wasn't exactly a vacation. They had a mission to complete. But Oliver waved them off.

"You kids go ahead," he told them. "Get the grand tour.

I'll be catching up with Mano and seeing what we'll need to do for this little excursion."

"We cast off in an hour," Mano announced, turning away with Oliver. "Sorry for the shortened time line, but I want to be well under way in case Hightower is already here. Be ready by then, Doctor."

"Yes, Captain."

As Mano and Oliver walked off, the doctor turned to Shinji and Lucy with a wink. "You two don't have to be so formal," she told them. "Call me Tamara."

"I'll come, too," Phoebe announced. "I would love to see more of the ship, if that is allowed?"

"Of course, Miss Mystic. We're happy to have you," Tamara said. "All right, everyone." The scientist gave a brisk nod and started walking up the ramp toward the ship. "Follow me."

For the next hour, Shinji and Lucy received the grand tour of the *Seas the Day*, with Phoebe trailing along behind them. It was a huge ship. There was a specimen lab and a metal shop, a chart room and a chemistry station. They walked through the galley and said hello to the crew cooks, then visited the doctor in the medical bay. Dr. Grant then showed them the bridge, where they could look out over the glittering ocean and see where it touched the sky.

"And this is the cargo hold," she explained a few minutes later, pushing back a large metal door. "This is where we keep the *Seabeetle*, which is the submarine we'll be using to explore the shipwreck when we get there."

Standing next to Shinji, Lucy gave a gasp of delight and rushed into the room. In the center of the hold, sitting on a wooden platform, a bright yellow submarine gleamed under the fluorescent lights. It wasn't long or torpedo-shaped like the subs Shinji had seen in the movies. This one was sleek and modern-looking, with twin propellers at the back and a glass bubble up front to permit passsengers to see everything around the sub. It did remind Shinji vaguely of a beetle or some kind of bug, but it was also one of the coolest things he had ever seen.

"I've heard about these," Lucy exclaimed, stepping back from the submarine with her hands clasped beneath her chin, as if she really wanted to get close but was afraid to touch it. "They're super high-tech and really amazing. They can dive to depths most personal submarines can't even touch, and have retractable legs to better move along the ocean floor."

Tamara Grant smiled at her excitement. "You know your stuff," she told Lucy, who beamed. "That is correct, although this is SEA's own creation. Safer than any underwater exploration vehicle ever assembled, thanks to its patented design. The *Seabeetle* also comes with two remote-controlled drones for underwater surveillance. They can get to places even the *Seabeetle* can't reach, so we will be well prepared once we arrive at the shipwreck site."

"That's so cool," Lucy breathed. "Can I . . . ?" She

hesitated. "I mean, I don't want to get in the way, but is it possible to see the schematics?"

Dr. Grant chuckled. "They told me you were somewhat of a tech wiz, Miss Frost. One moment." Raising an arm, she beckoned to someone on the other side of the *Seabeetle*. "Hayley," she called. "Would you come here a moment, please?"

A young woman walked around the *Seabeetle*, wiping her hands on a rag. "This is Hayley Frye," Dr. Grant said. "She's the one who keeps the *Beetle* up and running, who knows it inside and out. Hayley, this is Lucy Frost."

"Hi there," the young woman greeted Lucy. "Nice to meet you."

"Would you be amenable to showing her the *Seabeetle*? I think she has some questions for you. That is"—Dr. Grant turned to Lucy—"if you don't mind staying here and missing the end of the tour. All that is left is to show you your quarters and join the captain on deck when we cast off. But I can have Ms. Frye take you there later if you really want to stay."

"Could I?" Lucy's eyes widened. "That would be great! Um, if that's okay with Shinji."

"Fine with me." Shinji knew if Lucy didn't get to stay, she would either be so distracted she wouldn't hear anything else, or she would talk about the *Seabeetle* the rest of the night. Or both.

"Thanks." Lucy turned back to the mechanic. "I'd love

to hear more about the *Seabeetle*," she said eagerly. "Is it anything like the Nemo or Pisces subs? What depths can it dive to? How does the hull withstand the pressure of the ocean past two thousand meters?"

Shinji rolled his eyes as the two walked off, already talking about submarine engines and mechanics and things that made no sense to him. If he knew Lucy, she would likely be here until dinnertime. He probably wouldn't see her for the rest of the night.

Shinji crossed his arms. *Good,* he thought. He was still a little mad at her for spilling his secret earlier. He'd told her that he couldn't control his powers, and she let that slip in front of everyone. Worse, she'd let it slip in front of Phoebe Mystic, who was standing next to Shinji now, smiling down in a way that made him slightly nervous.

"All right," said the chief scientist as Lucy and Hayley disappeared around the *Seabeetle*, "let's get you to your quarters, and then we'll nearly be ready for castoff."

Shinji's quarters were tiny and cramped, with a narrow bed set into the wall, a desk, and a set of drawers, with barely enough space to walk between them. It was strangely comforting, as his room aboard the *Good Tern* was much the same. He was used to small ship quarters and easily maneuvered his way around the room. Dropping his duffel bag on the floor, he sat on his cot, leaned back, and listened to the faint sound of the waves lapping against the sides of the ship.

A sharp knock on his door jerked him out of his doze.

Thinking it was probably Lucy, Shinji slid off the cot, making sure to duck his head to avoid the low ceiling, and walked across the room to open the door.

It was not Lucy.

"Hello, Shinji!" Phoebe beamed at him through the frame. He stifled a groan. "I was thinking," she went on, "since Lucy is busy and Oliver is with the captain, this would be the perfect time to talk about your magic problems."

"I don't have problems," Shinji said. "I'm doing fine. I can handle it on my own."

"Of course you can," Phoebe said matter-of-factly. "And I want to hear all about it! That's the first step in figuring out the solution to a problem after all. Let's make use of the ship's library we saw earlier, shall we? It will be the perfect quiet spot to talk about your magic. With any luck, we'll have this figured out by dinner."

She wasn't giving him any opportunity to back out. Shinji could've claimed he was tired and not feeling well, but that would only delay this meeting to a later time. Phoebe wasn't going away, and unless he wanted to dodge her the entire trip, he was going to have to talk to her sometime.

"Sure," he muttered with a shrug. "Let's get this over with."

"Wonderful!" Phoebe beamed. "Just give me a few minutes to retrieve some things from my room. I will meet you in the library in ten minutes."

"Can't wait." Shinji sighed.

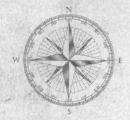

CHAPTER
SIX

The library, much like many of the other rooms on the ship, was small. Metal bookshelves lined the walls, filled with different tomes and texts. Shinji, gazing at the shelves, noted that most of the books were nautical or ocean-centered textbooks, and there were no comics, novels, or storybooks of any kind.

Reading the spine of the closest book, he wrinkled his nose. *Hydrostatics and Stability of Marine Vehicles*, it said. Definitely not something he would be picking up. *It's like Professor Carrero's library, only even more boring*, he thought, gazing around to see more of the same. *I bet Lucy could spend all day in here.*

"Ah, Shinji, there you are. Over here."

Shinji turned to see Phoebe waving to him from the center of the room. She sat cross-legged on a cushion on the floor, with another pillow directly across from her. A stack of books sat on her left side, a small box on her right.

"Have a seat, Shinji," she told him, motioning to the pillow in front of her. Shinji bit down a groan.

Ugh, meditation. I knew it.

"Now, before we begin," Phoebe continued as he knelt on the cushion, "I want to ask: What is the extent of your magic so far? What have you been able to do or feel?"

Shinji shrugged. "Summon the wind, call on the jungle animals to help me, shoot beams of light from my hands. Oh, and there was that time the Coatl burst out and ate someone—"

"Yes, but all that was right after you received the magic from the Coatl, yes?" Phoebe did not seem shocked or put out by any of what had happened, even the part where the Coatl devoured a Hightower agent right in front of Shinji. "What was the extent of your powers after you got home from the jungle? What have you been able to do since then?"

Shinji gritted his teeth. He didn't want to tell Phoebe the truth, but he couldn't keep lying to her, himself, and everyone. With a sigh, he slumped his shoulders.

"Nothing," he finally admitted. And with that, the anger, shame, and guilt for not being the guardian he had promised to be burst inside him like a popped balloon, and he raked his hands through his hair. "I don't know what I'm doing wrong," he snapped in frustration. "I can *feel* the magic, but I can't *use* it. I can't control it."

Phoebe watched him in silence, and Shinji's anger grew.

"I'm supposed to be the guardian," he said. "The Coatl gave me the magic of the font. Why can't I use it? I didn't have any trouble before when I was in the jungle fighting Hightower."

"Ah, well, there was much at stake then," Phoebe said calmly. "As I said before, adventure and danger tend to draw magic to the surface. Besides, it wasn't you summoning the magic as much as it was the Coatl itself using the last of its power to protect you and the font. You were the conduit for its power. It sacrificed itself to move the font inside you, and it had just enough magic left to defend you, one last time."

"Oh." Shinji sobered. "Wait, so you're saying the Coatl died to give me the magic?"

"Essentially, yes," Phoebe said. "Though I suspect it knew the font was not safe in the temple any longer. No matter what happened, Hightower would eventually return and try to claim the magic for themselves. Transferring the font inside you would keep that power out of Hightower's hands. Though it cost the Coatl its physical existence to do so."

"Great," Shinji muttered. "I can't use the magic, and the Coatl is gone. Now I feel even worse."

"Maybe not," Phoebe said. "Mythological creatures like guardians are extraordinarily hard to kill for good. It could be that the Coatl bonded with you, and that part of its spirit still resides somewhere within."

"If it has, it hasn't responded to anything I've tried," Shinji said.

"Well, that is what we are going to try to fix." Phoebe smiled and settled herself onto the cushion, putting the backs of her hands on her knees. "When dealing with magic, I've observed that it often comes out in one of two ways. One: in moments of high stress, danger, or emotion—"

"Like trying to outrun fake Hightower agents in a simulated environment?" Shinji asked.

"Mm, yes. However, this type of magic use is unpredictable and hard to control. The magic spikes with your adrenaline and it's difficult to calculate when it will appear." Phoebe raised her chin and closed her eyes. "To truly master your power, you must first master your emotions. Frustration, anger, and fear will cause the magic to lash out in ways you cannot control."

Shinji bit down a smirk. "Give in to anger, you must not," he rasped in his best Yoda voice. "Anger, fear, regret . . . the Dark Side are these."

"Exactly!" Phoebe did not seem to get the reference. "So first, you must clear your mind of any negative emotions and thoughts. Close your eyes, just like this. Now, breathe in . . . breathe out. In and out. Imagine your breath inflating your lungs, filling your whole body." She demonstrated with a lifting of her thin shoulders. "Just like that." She opened one eye and squinted at him. "Are you doing it?"

Shinji rolled his eyes, then shut them with a sigh. "How is breathing going to help me?"

"You are clearing your mind," Phoebe said. "You're trying to awaken the power inside you. To tap into the deep well of magic that exists somewhere within. Now, breathe with me. In and out. In and out. Let the magic flow through you. We are calm. We are . . . empty. There is no barrier between us and the magic. In and out."

This is so boring, Shinji thought, but he did as Phoebe said. In and out. Inhale and exhale. Trying to think of nothing as he did. *Is this really going to do anything?*

"Feel the breath within your body," Phoebe went on, a droning chant in his head. "Feel the light, the power, the magic. It is yours to take, to wield, if you only reach out and possess it. Do you feel it? Do you feel the magic?"

Shinji didn't feel any magic. He didn't feel any power or light or warmth. He tried doing as Phoebe instructed, but all he felt . . . was sleepy.

Shinji blinked, opening his eyes. He was flying over the ocean, barely skimming the tops of the waves as he glided through the air. Wind and spray hit him in the face, and he could smell the salt in the air as he soared like a pelican over the water. Looking down, he noticed that the water was almost crystal clear, and he could see something on the seafloor, far below. It looked like the hull of an ancient shipwreck, but so covered in algae and barnacles it seemed part of the ocean itself. Clouds of fish and other ocean life swarmed around it, darting into cracks and crevices as his shadow rippled over them.

A much larger shadow emerged from beneath the shipwreck, long and sleek and torpedo shaped, causing a chill to skitter up Shinji's back. He thought it could sense his presence as well, but he only caught a moment's glimpse before whatever force was moving him along swept him away, rising over a swell, and he continued on toward the horizon.

Looking up, he shivered. A dark shape suddenly appeared against the sky, rising up out of the ocean. An island, Shinji realized, with a tall, narrow mountain pointing up from the center like a finger.

No, not a mountain, he thought after a moment. *A volcano.*

The wind picked up, and dark clouds began forming in the sky above the volcano. They swirled overhead like a whirlpool, flickering with lightning, casting an ominous shadow over the whole island. As Shinji flew closer, he thought he could see a shape in the clouds, something huge and terrifying moving through the storm. There was a flash, and for just a second, Shinji saw a pair of eyes, blue-white and glowing, peering at him from the mist. Those eyes grew bigger, and Shinji could feel the anger behind them, in that white-hot glare getting closer and closer.

FREE ME, roared a voice in his head.

Crash!

Shinji jerked up, and the vision faded instantly. He was

back in the library with Phoebe Mystic, who was sitting ramrod straight on the cushion with her eyes open. One of the shelves behind her had mysteriously toppled over, spilling books and texts all over the floor.

"Shinji, are you all right?"

Lucy stood in the doorway, eyes wide as she stared at Shinji, Phoebe, and the fallen shelf. On her shoulder, Tinker twitched his ears back and forth in alarm. "What happened?" Lucy demanded, glaring at Phoebe as she came into the room. "What's going on?"

"Hmm, oh dear." Phoebe casually glanced over her shoulder at the mess. "I'm not entirely sure which one of us did that," she mused, "or if it just fell down on its own. Oh well. So, Shinji!" She turned back to him with a beaming smile. "Did you feel anything? Were you able to get in touch with the magic?"

"You're learning magic? With her?" Lucy glanced at Shinji, a shadow of hurt crossing her face for just a moment. "You didn't tell me."

"You were busy with the *Seabeetle*," Shinji protested, his heart still pounding from whatever it was that had just happened. "I didn't think I could drag you away from your precious machines."

Lucy's eyes narrowed. "I was looking for you to see if you wanted to watch the boat cast off," she said in a chilly tone that told him she was angry. "I guess next time I won't bother." She glanced at Phoebe. "Or care if you get yourself magically blown up."

"Oh, that won't happen," Phoebe interjected, cheerfully oblivious to Lucy's mood. "Based on the Coatl, Shinji's magic is mostly wind-centered. There's no possible way he could blow himself up. The worst thing he might do is summon a tornado that destroys everything around it, though I would not recommend producing funnel clouds in the middle of the ocean. The captain would not be happy."

Lucy didn't answer. With a last look at Shinji, she turned and left the room, Tinker's glowing red eyes peering back at him as she left.

Phoebe blinked. "I hope Miss Frost is all right," she said, finally catching on that Lucy was upset. "Anyway, Shinji, did you feel anything while you were meditating? Were you able to connect with the magic?"

Shinji hesitated. The image of the volcano and the angry voice now felt more like a dream than anything else. Maybe it had been. Maybe he had fallen asleep while meditating and dreamed the whole thing.

Or . . . maybe it had been real, and there was something out there that needed his help. Maybe it was something that only a guardian could do, a task that only he, Shinji, could accomplish. The Coatl had sacrificed itself to grant Shinji its power, and now Phoebe had given him some really good tips on how to use the magic. Now it was up to Shinji to actually master his powers. He could do this, and he could do it on his own. He had to prove, to the Coatl and himself, that he was a real guardian after all.

"No," he told Phoebe. "I didn't feel anything."

"Ah well." Phoebe stood up with a smile and brushed off her knees. If she was disappointed with his lack of progress, she didn't show it. "You know what they say, then: Practice makes perfect! Keep trying to master those emotions and connect to that magic. One day it's just going to click."

She took one step to the right, just as a large book fell from the shelf beside her and hit the cushion with a thump. Shinji started, but Phoebe barely gave it a second glance. "Come along, then," she told him. "I should probably get you back to Oliver before he worries that we've been tossed overboard. This time of year, it is not something I'd recommend."

That night, Shinji woke up and couldn't go back to sleep. For a few minutes, he lay on his narrow cot in the darkness, wide-awake and staring at the ceiling. Maybe it was the weird time difference, his body thinking they were back home in the US, or maybe it was everything that had happened that day, but once Shinji opened his eyes, he wasn't remotely sleepy anymore. He thought about the magic lesson with Phoebe earlier in the day, and the strange dream/ vision he'd had. The angry voice calling to him, demanding to be freed. He thought about the race to the shipwreck and wondered if he would even see Hightower on this mission. So far, the nefarious corporation didn't feel like much of a threat. But just because Shinji hadn't seen them didn't mean they weren't out there. Plotting against the Society right now.

Thinking of Hightower also made him think of Lucy, of her confession that she missed Hightower and what she used to do as a part of their operations. She was always so excited when it came to gadgets and new inventions, always spending time in Zoe's workshop, tinkering away. Back at Hightower, Lucy had her own workshop—the place where she had created Tinker, the marvel mouse of technology and magic. Because the Hightower Corporation had been built on a font, Lucy could use its magic to create her inventions, blending tech and magic together in a way only she could. Without the font, she was still a genius inventor, but she couldn't create anything magical like Tinker.

No wonder she missed Hightower.

Fumbling for his phone, Shinji tapped the screen to see it was 2:43 a.m., way too early for anyone to be up and about. Nonetheless he swung his legs off the bed and stood, reaching for his shirt. He couldn't stay in bed with his brain spinning in circles; he had to get up and move.

Grasping the handle, he pulled his door open, wincing as it gave a rusty squeak that sounded very loud to his ears. The ship wasn't exactly silent; Shinji could hear the muted drone of different machines, and a faint conversation down the hall between a pair of crew members who happened to be walking by.

Stepping into the hall, Shinji softly closed the door behind him, then went exploring for himself. As he crept through the narrow halls and tight ship corridors, the *Seas the Day* felt even more mazelike and labyrinthine than before. But Shinji was used to ship life, and even though the *Good Tern* was many times smaller than the research vessel, he could still navigate the larger ship fairly easily. And without any grown-ups ushering him along, peering over his shoulder, he could wander around the ship at his own pace.

In a dusty storage room, he found nearly a dozen old steamer trunks stacked in a corner, covered in stickers from around the world. Africa, Cancún, Taiwan, the Bahamas, and more. Another room held a collection of fossils and marine skeletons in glass cases. Shinji paused at the display of a long white tooth the size of his hand. For a second, he thought it might be a tooth of a megalodon, the giant shark that lived around the time of the dinosaurs. But then he read the sign below the case. *Sea serpent fang. Gakkel Ridge, 2001.*

Phoebe would probably love this place.

As he stepped back into the hallway, a cold breeze blew down the corridor, ruffling his hair and making his skin prickle. Shinji paused, rubbing his arm and gazing warily down the hall. Mysterious breezes belowdecks were definitely not normal. There were no windows down here; everything was airtight. Maybe—and Shinji's heart beat faster at the thought—was it the Coatl, trying to tell him something?

The wind was coming down the corridor that led to the

cargo hold. Curious and wary, Shinji headed in that direction. Surprisingly, the metal door to the cargo hold was unlocked, and he pushed it open with a faint creak.

The space beyond the frame was cloaked in darkness. The *Seabeetle* still sat in the center of the room, yellow hull glittering faintly in the light coming through the door. Shinji's nerves prickled a warning. For a second, he was almost sure he had seen a shadow dart behind the submarine, but that might've been a trick of the light.

Cautious now, Shinji stepped into the room and gazed around, all senses alert for anything out of place. He heard the hum of the engine and felt the ship gently rocking beneath him, but other than that, everything was still.

"Hello?" Shinji took another step into the room. His voice echoed weirdly in the empty space overhead. "Anyone here?" No answer, though Shinji didn't actually expect one. "I know you're there," he went on, even though he really didn't. "You might as well come out. I saw you try to hide."

"Not very smart, are you? What if I was an ax murderer, and you're down here all alone?"

Shinji's heart jumped. A figure stepped away from the *Seabeetle*, arms crossed, a faint smirk on its face. He recognized the longish, unkempt hair, the dark eyes, the challenging look on the face. Glancing around, he realized he was alone in a dark room with the thief they'd met the other day, and Shinji was blocking the only way out.

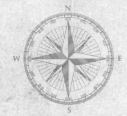

CHAPTER SEVEN

"Roux," Shinji exclaimed, and the other boy raised an amused eyebrow. "What are you doing here? How did you even get on the ship?"

Roux made an offhand gesture. "Easy." He grinned. "I snuck on board while you guys were having your fun little tour. Everyone was so busy with you and the tourist girl, no one even noticed me. That's how I get into most places." He gave Shinji a mocking salute. "Thanks for being a good distraction."

"Yeah, sure," Shinji said. "It's what I'm good at. But *why* are you here?"

"Why not?" Roux said casually, running his palm over

the side of the *Seabeetle*. "I was curious. I've never seen a boat like this before. Seemed like a good time to take a vacation. Besides, I'd jump at any chance to get off that island." He held both hands up and edged toward the door, as if Shinji would just move out of the way and let him pass. "Don't mind me; you won't even know I'm here."

"Hold on," Shinji said. "Have you done this before? Stowed away on a stranger's boat and hoped they didn't see you?"

The other boy shook his head. "Nah, this is my first time off the island," he admitted. "Don't turn around on my account, though. It's not like I have anything to go back to."

"What about your home?" Shinji asked. "And your parents? They won't miss you?"

"They might." Roux shrugged. "If I had any."

"Oh." Shinji sobered. "You're an orphan, then."

"That's usually what having no parents means." Roux gave a twisted little smirk. "Don't look at me like I'm some baby deer whose mama just got shot. My parents have been gone for years; I don't even miss them."

Shinji knew what it was like to be an orphan. He'd lost his parents in a fire when he was just a toddler. He also knew Roux was lying. He was acting like he didn't care, trying not to appear weak, but Shinji knew that it was just a mask. Because he had done the same thing himself.

"I don't need anyone's help," Roux insisted. "But there's nothing on that island, and I'm sick of staring at the same things every day. Look . . ." He held up a pair of long-fingered, grime-stained hands in a placating gesture. "You don't have to say anything, okay? I'll stay down here, keep out of everyone's way, and when this ship stops at any port, I'll leave. I'll disappear, like a ghost. No one will have to know I existed at all. *If*"—and he narrowed his eyes at Shinji—"you don't squeal on me. Deal?"

"I . . ." Shinji hesitated. On the one hand, he didn't want to get Roux in trouble. He wasn't a snitch, and he could sympathize with a fellow orphan. On the other, Roux had stolen from Lucy, run off with Tinker, and stowed away on their ship. If he agreed to hide Roux and not say anything, he would be siding against the Society, which he was now a part of. He would be turning against the ones who had saved his life on numerous occasions. And if Roux stole from his friends or did anything to the ship, Shinji would be the one responsible.

He remembered the panic in Lucy's voice when Tinker had been taken, and set his jaw.

"No." Shinji shook his head. "Sorry, Roux, but I can't agree to that. I'm going to have to tell the others that you're here."

Roux's dark eyes narrowed, and a dangerous smile crept over his face. "So, that's how it is, huh?" he said. "I should've known you were just like everyone else." He shifted his weight, glancing at the door behind Shinji, as if preparing to make a break for it. Shinji took a step forward, and Roux's expression turned threatening. "Get outta my way, tourist. I'd hate to break your nose."

"You can't run," Shinji said quickly. "I know you're here, and we're in the middle of the ocean. Even if you hide, there's nowhere to go. You're just going to be found again." Roux's expression didn't change, and Shinji tried keeping his voice reasonable. "Look, just come with me. We'll go and see Oliver; he'll know what to do. He can talk to the captain, and we'll figure this out. It's not like we're going to throw you overboard to the sharks or anything like that."

For a few seconds, the other boy didn't move, glaring at Shinji with dark eyes. But then he slumped and made a disgusted motion. "Fine," he muttered. "If you're going to be a rat anyway, I guess that's how it's gonna be." He gave Shinji a resigned look and rolled his eyes. "Come on, then. Let's get this over with."

"It won't be that bad," Shinji promised, turning toward the door. "The Society is okay. They helped me out when I was in trouble—"

Movement from the corner of his eye was all the warning Shinji had. He spun back just as Roux lunged, his shoulders hunched like a linebacker with a football, in order to knock him aside and bolt past him into the ship.

Shinji only had a second to act, and in that moment, the self-defense lessons he had received from Oliver over the past few months suddenly kicked in. Instead of letting Roux slam into him, he spun aside, letting the other boy barrel past, and gave him a hard shove as he did. Roux lost his balance, tripped, and went tumbling into the opposite wall with a clatter of mops and metal buckets. Grimacing, he looked up as Shinji loomed over him, fists clenched, ready to act if the other boy leaped up and threw a punch. Roux blinked, staring up at him, then gave a weak laugh.

"Okay, wow. So, the tourist actually has some moves. I wasn't expecting that. Good to know."

Shinji didn't smile. "Are you done now?"

"Yeah." Roux struggled to get himself upright, shoving mops and broom handles aside. "I'm done. This is stupid. Let's go talk to your Oliver friend or whatever he is and get this over with."

Shinji took a step back, gesturing to the door that led to the hall. He wasn't about to allow Roux to get behind him again. "You first."

The other boy smirked, as if he knew what Shinji was thinking. But he got to his feet and started walking out of the room. Shinji followed, ready to lunge if Roux suddenly took off. But the other boy didn't try to escape, and together they walked through the lower ship halls, climbed the ladder to the upper decks, and started down the hall to the guest quarters.

As they turned a corner, a body in a bright teal coat suddenly blocked their path. Roux jumped, flinching back and nearly running into Shinji. Phoebe blinked in the relative dark and then broke into a wide smile.

"Oh, Shinji. Hello!" Her voice echoed through the corridor, making Roux wince. "You're up early. You know, if you're not doing anything, I would love to ask you a few more questions about . . ." Suddenly she noticed Roux. "Oh, I didn't see you there. Wait. Isn't this the boy from yesterday? How did he get here?"

"I swam," Roux told her. Phoebe's brows arched, like she really believed him. Shinji spoke up before she could ask any more questions.

"I'm looking for Oliver," he told Phoebe. "Have you seen him? Is he still asleep?"

"Oliver?" Phoebe shook her head. "No, he's up on the deck right now, staring at the moon or something. Why?"

"I need to talk to him."

"Oh well, come on, then," Phoebe said, and gestured down the hallway. "We can all go see Oliver. I have to ask him something as well."

Shinji saw Roux set his jaw before he marched down the hall after the SEA agent. Phoebe moved quickly, striding along with her head high, humming to herself. Roux wouldn't be getting around her so easily, and with Shinji guarding his back, there was nowhere for him to go. He was probably feeling very trapped as they escorted him through the ship halls and onto the upper deck. As a cool ocean breeze hit Shinji's face, he briefly hoped Roux wouldn't do something completely stupid like jump overboard into the dark water.

Shinji spotted Oliver near the railings, long coat flapping behind him, seemingly staring at the moon or out over the ocean as Phoebe had said. He seemed fascinated or deep in thought but turned his head as Shinji approached and gave a puzzled smile.

"Hey, kiddo. You're up early. Couldn't . . ." His gaze strayed to Roux, and both brows arched. "That's funny. I don't remember inviting anyone else aboard. Isn't this the kid you ran into yesterday? The one with whom you had your 'misunderstanding'?"

"Oliver." Shinji took a step forward as Roux's gaze narrowed. "This is Roux. He's—"

"A stowaway?" Oliver interrupted. "Yeah, I can see that."

"A stowaway?" Phoebe echoed, staring at Roux. "Well, I suppose that makes sense now that I think about it. How else could he have gotten aboard?" She shot a questioning glance at Oliver. "What is the protocol in dealing with stowaways? Should we toss him in the brig?"

"We don't have a brig," Oliver said, making Roux slump a bit in relief. "Though Mano is not going to be happy with this little development. Captains do not look kindly on stowaways, just a friendly warning." He glanced at Roux and raised an eyebrow. "Sneaking on board a vessel; you got guts, kid. I've done that a time or two in my life. Though I don't know why you picked the *Seas the Day*. There's nothing on this boat but sciencey things and no valuables. As far as targets go, you would've done better with a yacht."

"If I wanted to steal stuff, I would have," Roux said. "I just needed a ride off the island, that's all." He shot an annoyed glance at Shinji. "If this snitch didn't find me, you wouldn't even know I was here."

"Yep, that's Shinji," Oliver said in a cheerful voice. "Always ruining someone's slightly nefarious plans. But the question is, now what do we do with you?" A contemplative look crossed his face. "You know, on a couple ships I've been on, they make stowaways walk the plank."

"Oh dear," Phoebe said as Roux went rather pale. "That seems a little extreme. Are we really pirates? Do we even have a plank? Oh," she added, smiling and waving a hand at Oliver, "that was a joke. You were joking, right?"

Oliver just gave a weird little smile, then sighed. "Well, come on, both of you. I think we're going to have to go talk to the captain."

Mano was not happy. He stood behind his desk with his arms crossed, glowering down at Roux. His jaw was tight, his expression like a thundercloud. His office, Shinji noticed, was full of things like rabbit's feet, magic 8 balls, and four-leaf clovers. A rusty horseshoe had been tacked over the door, and a shaker full of salt sat on a corner of the desk.

"Well, this is annoying," Mano said at last. "A stowaway. On my ship. Do you know how unlucky it is to have a stowaway on board? Not to mention all the legal headaches I'm going to have to go through because of this." He snatched a rabbit's foot off his desk and squeezed, while shooting a rueful look at Oliver. "Too bad the old method of throwing them overboard in a barrel has fallen out of favor."

"I know." Oliver shrugged. "But we can't do anything about it now," he told the captain. "We certainly can't turn around and go back. Hightower is still out there, trying to get to the wreck before us. If we slow down, for any reason, they're going to beat us. The kid is just going to have to stay aboard the ship until we reach land again."

"That's fine, but what do I do with him until then?" Mano asked. "I'd feel bad locking up a kid, and there's really nowhere on this ship I can put him even if I wanted to."

"Shinji can keep an eye on him!" Phoebe volunteered, making both Shinji and Roux start. "He's got a good head on his shoulders and a good moral compass. Plus, they're about the same age, so they should get along fine, right, Shinji?"

"Sure," Shinji said flatly. "Because I get along so well with everyone my age."

"Hang on," Oliver said, raising a hand. "I don't know if I like that idea. No offense, kid," he went on, glancing at Roux, "but I was raised by pirates and cutthroats. I know what they're capable of."

Roux shrugged, as if he was used to this kind of treatment, and raised both arms away from his sides. "You can search me if you want," he told Oliver. "I left my shiv in my other bag."

"Oh, Oliver, he's not going to do anything," Phoebe

interjected. "He's just a boy. Besides, Shinji has the magic of the guardian looking out for him. He'll be fine."

Roux blinked, as if he wasn't entirely sure he'd heard that right. Shinji saw Oliver stiffen, as if he, too, realized Phoebe had blurted something about Shinji's magic to a complete stranger. But Roux didn't say anything, and after a tense moment, everyone acted like they hadn't heard Phoebe's strange statement.

Mano observed them both for a few seconds, then sighed. "I suppose that will have to do," he muttered, and knocked the surface of his desk three times. "We don't have an extra cabin, so that means you two will be bunking together. I'll have someone scrounge up a sleeping bag. Look, kid . . ." He glanced at Roux and raised a large finger. "*Don't* get into trouble. I don't want to see you wandering around my ship by yourself. There are still a few large barrels belowdecks; if anything goes missing, you might find yourself floating back to Pula. Understand?"

Roux's lip curled up in a smirk, and he glanced at Shinji. "Guess you're coming with me to the bathroom, then."

"Can't wait," Shinji replied, just as sarcastically.

"All right, kids." Oliver shook his head and took a step back. "You can hash it out in your room. Let's go, before the captain makes us all walk the plank."

"There you are," Lucy greeted when Shinji walked out of his room a couple hours later. "Oversleeping again, I see. Did you hear? The captain has some kind of special announcement to make this morning. There are rumors going around that we had a stowaway on board last night."

"Yeah, about that . . ."

Roux stepped through the door into the hall behind him. Lucy's eyes got huge.

"You!" she snarled, making Shinji flinch. "What are you doing here? Why . . . ?" She paused a moment, then drew in a breath as she figured it out. "*You're* the stowaway," she said accusingly. Reaching up, she quickly snatched Tinker off her shoulder, ignoring his startled squeak, and stuck him in her pocket. "Why are you in Shinji's room? What were you trying to steal?"

"Calm down, Snowflake," Roux said. "Your robot rat is safe; I'm not going to steal anything." He shot her a wide grin, making a great show of looking around. "I just wanted to see your ship, that's all. And your captain decided to let me stay aboard. So, I'll be hanging out with Shinji until we reach land. Hope that's okay with you."

Lucy's face darkened, and she glared at Shinji, who raised his hands.

"Hey, don't look at me," he protested. "I had nothing to do with this. I just found him hiding out in the lower decks last night. We went to see Oliver, talked to the captain, and somehow, I got stuck with him."

"And we're best pals already, right, Shinji?" Reaching out, Roux looped an arm around Shinji's shoulders before Shinji could stop him. "So, you might as well get used to me,

Snowflake," he told Lucy as Shinji pushed him away. "You'll be seeing my face a lot."

Lucy glowered, then took a breath and drew herself up, that chilly air of Hightower settling over her like a cloak. "I see," she commented, in a voice as cold as ice. "Well, if the captain made the decision, then it's already done. But that doesn't mean I trust you. Stay out of my room, and don't touch Tinker. If he ever goes missing, I'll know exactly who to blame when I inform the captain."

Turning, Lucy strode off down the hallway without a second glance at either Shinji or Roux. Shinji groaned. He had a feeling that he was going to be stuck between Lucy and Roux, and that as a result, the race to the shipwreck had gotten even more interesting.

"Brr." Roux mock-shivered and rubbed his arms. "I don't think she likes me very much."

CHAPTER
EIGHT

The next few days were busy but uneventful. Shinji barely saw Lucy; she was either in the metal shop or down in the cargo hold with her new favorite thing: the *Seabeetle*. The only times Shinji talked to her were when she emerged for meals. Roux, however, followed him everywhere, seeming to take Mano's warning to heart. Shinji suspected that part of the reason he never saw Lucy was because she was deliberately avoiding the other boy. When they were together, she barely said two words to him, radiating a stony, distrustful silence and speaking mostly to Shinji. For his part, Roux didn't seem to care. He didn't talk much, especially when the adults were around. He was, Shinji noticed, very good at fading into the background, making himself scarce and unimportant. Sometimes he forgot Roux was there at all.

Surprisingly, Phoebe did not track Shinji down to talk to him about his magic, either. Maybe because Roux was always there now, and she didn't want to discuss things like Coatls and guardian powers around a non-Society person. Shinji was glad for the distraction, but that also meant he couldn't focus on figuring out how to use guardian powers.

One night, Shinji was plagued by a recurrent dream. An island. An angry, swirling storm. Those same electric-blue eyes, glaring out of the clouds. Only now the clouds parted, and a massive form emerged, silhouetted against the storm. Shinji's heart dropped as he stared into the face of an enormous boar. Lightning snapped along its bristling hide, and huge tusks curved up from its jaw as it swung its head toward Shinji. Those powerful jaws opened, and a booming voice made the clouds swirl madly and threatened to split his skull.

FREE ME!

Shinji jerked awake, breathing hard, his heart pounding in his chest. On the floor, Roux was sprawled out on the sleeping bag, snoring loudly. He didn't even twitch as Shinji sat up, raking his hands through his hair as he waited for his heartbeat to go back to normal.

What was going on? Why did a giant scary lightning boar keep invading his dreams, shouting at him to be freed? What was that island? Shinji thought about going to Lucy;

she could usually make sense of this type of stuff. But things had been kinda weird with her lately, especially with Roux around, and he didn't want to deal with that now. Very briefly, he thought about talking to Phoebe and quickly discarded that idea. If she knew he was having dreams of a magical boar and a mysterious island, she would never leave him alone.

I'm a guardian, he thought at last. *Whatever this thing is, it's calling me because I have the magic. I have to figure out what it wants and help it myself. That's what a guardian would do.*

Bolstered by his thoughts, Shinji put the pillow over his head to drown out Roux's snores and tried going back to sleep. Maybe if he had the dream again, he could get a hint of what he was supposed to do. But his thoughts swirled madly around his brain, and sleep did not find him again that night.

"You have raccoon rings under your eyes," Lucy remarked the next morning at breakfast. "Are you having trouble sleeping? I thought you were used to being on a boat."

"I am," Shinji muttered. The dream with the boar flickered through his head again, and he shoved it down to deal with later. "It's just hard to sleep when your roommate snores like a motorcycle."

"What are you talking about?" Roux grinned at him around a mouthful of scrambled eggs. His plate was always piled with breakfast food, but he never wasted any of it. In fact, he ate more than any kid Shinji had ever seen. "Motorcycles don't snore."

Roux stuck a piece of bacon into his mouth, chewing noisily. Lucy wrinkled her nose. "You know, forks were invented for a reason."

"Oh, sorry, Snowflake." Roux scrubbed the back of his hand across his face and gave her a greasy smile. "I think I lost my silver spoon. Can I borrow yours?"

Lucy's gaze hardened, and she turned back to Shinji. Leaning in, she lowered her voice. "I heard some of the scientists talking last night," she told him. "They said a Hightower ship might've been spotted close by."

Shinji straightened, suddenly wide-awake. "Where?"

She shrugged. "I don't know," she whispered. "But if they are close, you can be sure they know *we're* out here, too."

"You think they'll try something?"

"Almost certainly."

"You know I can hear you guys, right?" Roux commented.

"Shinji, Lucy." Oliver strode up to their table before Shinji could answer. "Hurry up and finish," he said, rapping his knuckles against the tabletop. "You're needed on the bridge."

Shinji and Lucy shared a glance, then immediately got up to follow. Roux watched as they started to leave, then quickly stuffed another slice of bacon in his mouth before trailing after them.

Mano was waiting for them, looking grave, as they followed Oliver onto the bridge. Phoebe was there as well, though she was staring at a large portrait on the wall across from them. The picture showed a woman in a white captain's hat holding a golden cutlass, a colorful green parrot perched on her shoulder. The parrot, Shinji saw, had an eye patch over its left eye.

Oliver saw what Phoebe was looking at and winced. "I keep telling you to take that down, Mano." He sighed as his fingers subconsciously rubbed the golden head of the parrot cane in the crook of his arm. Shinji had never noticed it before, but Oliver's parrot head also wore an eye patch.

"And I keep telling *you*, Oliver, you should be proud of your ancestry." Mano shook his head with a frown. "Captain Oceaneer was a highly respected member of the Society and one of our most prominent explorers. She accomplished things we can only dream of."

"So everyone keeps telling me," Oliver said. "Every time I see that picture."

"Oh, Captain Oceaneer," Phoebe said in a dreamy voice as she turned back. "What a legend. Discovering sea serpents, finding pirate gold, sailing through the Bermuda Triangle with only a pocket watch and her parrot. I can only hope to accomplish what she has."

Oliver rolled his eyes. "Every single time."

Mano cleared his throat. "Regardless, we have larger problems," he went on, glancing at Lucy and Shinji, who had come in behind Oliver, followed by Roux. For a moment, his gaze lingered on Roux, and he hesitated, as if debating whether or not to continue. But then he went on. "I've gotten word from some friends in the coast guard," he said as everyone crowded around the console in the center of the room. "There's good news, bad news, and worse news. So, brace yourselves."

"Well, that's ominous," Oliver said. "Let's hear the bad news, then."

"The bad news. The Hightower ship the *Sea Plunderer* has been spotted moving thirty knots in a southeasterly direction from Pula. As of now, they are heading straight for the wreckage site. The good news? They're about a day and a half behind us. At their current speed, we should reach the shipwreck first."

"That's the good and bad news," Oliver said. "What's the worst news?"

"The worst news . . ." Mano sighed and pressed a button on the console. "Is that we just picked up this message."

A grainy, staticky signal sputtered to life. A few seconds later, Shinji heard a voice, garbled and indistinct, through the white noise. ". . . *day, Mayday! If anyone . . . ear this, our vessel . . . broke down near . . . stranded with no . . . Sharks are starting to circle . . . send help . . . please!*"

The message started to repeat, and Mano turned off the radio. "That signal is about a day away from us," he said. "There are no other ships or vessels in the area. The coast guard is too far away to help. Therefore . . . Ocean?"

Oliver let out a loud groan and rubbed at his eyes. "Therefore, good marine protocol says we need to go help them."

"What?" Lucy glanced at him in concern. "But Hightower is closing in! If we veer off course, they could get to the shipwreck before us. At the very least, they'll get a lot closer."

"They might," Mano said solemnly. "But I checked, and we're the only ones in the area. If Hightower receives that distress signal, do you think they'll change direction to help?"

Lucy fell silent. The answer was pretty obvious, and Shinji clenched a fist on his knee. Time was precious, and they were just barely ahead of Hightower. But they couldn't ignore a call for help out in the open ocean. As much as Shinji hated the thought of losing to the corporation, he agreed that the decision to rescue the stranded vessel was the right one.

Mano sighed. "I know this is frustrating," he said. "Believe me, I don't want Hightower to snatch those artifacts out from under us any more than you do. Dr. Grant has already chewed my ear off. But I think, under the circumstances, we have to do the right thing. Artifacts and lost treasures are not as important as human lives. We have to remember that. It's what makes the Society different from Hightower—"

"Oh, come on," Roux broke in.

Everyone stared at him. He gestured at the console screen. "You don't see what's going on here? You guys are trying to beat these Hightower guys to a shipwreck, and a distress signal comes in out of nowhere?" He snorted. "Where did it come from? There's nothing around here for miles. This is obviously a trap. You're blind if you can't see that."

Lucy bristled. "And what would *you* do?" she challenged. "Ignore a call for help? Pretend it doesn't exist so you can get to the treasure first?"

"I am aware that it could be a trap," Mano said, frowning at Roux before rapping three times on his wooden desk. "It certainly is convenient timing. However, what if it's not? We can't take that chance. If it is someone in trouble, it is our obligation to help. That's my decision. Again, I apologize to all of you, but this is not negotiable."

"Don't apologize, Captain," Phoebe exclaimed. Even through the palpable disappointment in the room, her cheeriness never waned. "You are right, of course. Helping people should always take precedence over discovering treasure."

Roux snorted. "Speak for yourself," he muttered.

It took nearly five hours to reach the stranded vessel.

"There it is," Oliver murmured, standing on the deck with a copper spyglass in hand, pressed to his eye. "Well, you guys certainly have gotten yourself into a pickle, haven't you? That is not a boat for deep-sea exploration."

"Can I see?" Shinji asked, and Oliver handed him the spyglass. Peering through the glass, Shinji saw a medium-size catamaran, a ship with two parallel hulls instead of one.

The twin hulls, plus the wider stance of the ship, made a catamaran hard to capsize. This one, however, seemed to be dead in the water. A trio of figures, two men and a woman, milled around the upper deck, looking lost.

"Tourists." Oliver sighed. "They probably came down here for the weekend, rented a boat without knowing what they were doing, and headed merrily out to sea." He took the spyglass from Shinji, folded it, and stuck it in his coat pocket. "This is why you should always know how to use your sails. In case your engines malfunction or you run out of fuel."

"Looks like they see us," Roux observed. "They're all waving their arms now."

"Yep," agreed Oliver, and shot a quick glance at the three of them. "You kids leave the talking to me," he said. "Keep your eyes peeled, and if something seems strange, go tell Mano on the bridge. With any luck, this will be a normal rescue operation."

"And if it's not?" Lucy wondered.

"Then we gun the engines and get the heck out of here."

The *Seas the Day* drew alongside the vessel, the waves from its wake making it rock heavily from side to side. "Hey there," Oliver called down to the three strangers on deck. "Looks like you're in a bit of trouble."

"Oh, thank goodness," one of the men replied. Removing his sunglasses, he squinted up at Oliver and the others. "Yes, we could certainly use the help; we've been stuck out here for nearly a day. Our engine stopped working for some reason."

"Both of them?" Oliver sounded surprised. "This is a twin-engine cat; it's unusual for both to go out at the same time."

"We really don't know anything about boats," called the woman, stepping up beside the first man. "Are you the captain? Would you be able to come aboard and take a look at it?"

Oliver didn't move. "Captain is on the bridge at the moment, in case he needs to radio for help. How did you guys get yourselves way out here?" he asked conversationally. "The nearest port is back in Pula. Where were you heading, if you don't mind my asking?"

The two men exchanged a glance. "Nowhere," said the first. "We . . . uh . . . we were just out here doing some fishing."

"Marlin," added the other man, a little too quickly, Shinji thought. "We wanted to try our luck fishing for marlin."

"Marlin, huh," Oliver mused. He leaned his elbows on the railing in a nonchalant manner. "Generally, fishing for marlin requires some pretty heavy-duty gear," he continued. "You don't have any fishing rigs from what I can see. Unless you're leaping overboard and wrestling them with your bare hands."

A ripple of movement from the corner of Shinji's eye caught his attention. He turned his head, and all he saw was glittering ocean and waves lapping against the side of the ship. But he was almost certain he'd seen a shadow moving beneath the water.

"We . . . um . . . lost our fishing gear." The men on the boat were sounding more and more nervous. And more and more suspicious. Shinji's heart rate ticked up. "But our engines are the real problem. You wouldn't mind coming aboard and just checking them out, would you?"

"You seem awfully eager to get me down there," Oliver said, still smiling in a genial manner. "Why don't we just stop bluffing one another and playing dumb? How much did Hightower pay you to send that distress signal?"

The men's faces hardened, losing the hapless-tourist look in an instant. "Self-righteous SEA scum," the first one snapped. "Wouldn't you like to know?"

Shinji's stomach clenched, and he narrowed his eyes. "You *are* from Hightower," he said accusingly. "Your ship isn't in trouble. That signal was completely bogus."

The trio gave him cold smiles.

"And you followed the bait just like they said you would," the woman said. "Still too idealistic for your own good. You should've ignored the distress signal and kept going."

"That shipwreck is ours," the second man announced, pointing at Oliver. "Everything in it belongs to Hightower. You Society meddlers can back off."

Lucy leaned over the railing, her voice furious as she glared down at the Hightower agents. "That wreck contains artifacts from a lost culture!" she shouted. "Hightower would just sell them off to get more money. Or they would sit in someone's private collection doing nothing. At least the Society is trying to do something good."

"Lucy Frost." The woman's voice didn't sound surprised. "They said you might be aboard this ship. Your father sends his regards. He would still like you to return home . . . *if* you have come to see reason."

Lucy's eyes narrowed. "See reason. You mean become ruthless and power-hungry like the rest of Hightower," she said in disgust.

"Your workshop is still there." The woman ignored Lucy's comment. "Your father hasn't shut it down or moved anyone else in. If you return to the corporation, you can have access to whatever you like. Magic, gizmos, new blueprints, the latest tech. Anything you need, as long as you agree to work for the company again."

For just a moment, Lucy hesitated. Shinji saw the flash of longing in her eyes, and it made his heart pound. "Everything is still there?" she asked in a shaky voice.

"It is. And you can come back with us right now," the Hightower agent went on. "The Society can't stop you. Step down from that boat, come with us, and we'll take you to your father. You can go home and be part of Hightower again. That's what you want, isn't it?"

Lucy glanced at Oliver, who was still leaning casually against the railings, though his expression was grim now.

Say something, Shinji thought at him. *Tell her she's with the Society now. Tell her she can't go back.*

Oliver sighed. "It's your decision," he told her in a low voice. "Your life. If you really want to go, we won't try to stop you."

"Are you freaking kidding me?" Shinji shouted. He glanced at Lucy again, seeing her hands clench on the railings. Would she leave them right now? Climb down the ladder to the Hightower boat and go belowdecks? His stomach twisted at the idea, and his thoughts swirled frantically. *Don't leave. You're my friend. We've been through all this crazy stuff together, and you're with the Society of Explorers and Adventurers now. You don't belong at Hightower. You never did.*

But, if she decided to return with the Hightower agents, maybe she did belong with them after all.

"Lucy," he began. Not really knowing what to say, feeling he had to say *something.*

But Lucy straightened, cutting him off before he could speak. Raising her chin, she glared down at the Hightower agents all waiting for her decision. "Tell my dad," she said in a clear, frosty voice, "that I can't be bought like the rest of his acquisitions. He can wave all the money, magic, and expensive toys he wants in my face; I'm still not going back. Unless he or Hightower itself changes, I'm staying right here, with the Society. At least they know what's right."

"You are making a serious mistake, Miss Frost," the Hightower agent said, and shrugged. "But very well. If that is your choice. You SEA scum will never reach the wreck in time. You've lost this race; you just don't know it."

"And how do you figure that?" Oliver asked, still candidly. "By my calculations, it took us five hours to get here; it'll take less than that to get back on track. This little side jaunt will cost us less than ten hours total. Hightower is speedy when it comes to snatching valuables, but they're not going to be able to plunder an entire ship before we get there."

The woman smiled. She held out her hand, palm up, and one of the other men immediately placed something in it: a rectangular device with an antenna poking up from the top. Putting the walkie-talkie to her mouth, she spoke loud enough for Shinji and the others to hear.

"James? Are the charges set?"

A staticky voice answered almost instantly, "Set and ready to blow, ma'am."

"Do it."

A pulse went through the air. Shinji felt a jolt through his whole body, like he had grabbed an electric fence or stuck his finger in a socket. A startled yelp caught in his throat. The world around him sputtered like a bad television signal, and for a split second, everything went white.

He blinked and gazed around. He was standing in the same spot with Lucy and Oliver, and they looked just as confused as he felt. Everything seemed normal, though. The ship bobbed on the waves, but it didn't feel like it was sinking. There had been no explosion. No fire or smoke. Carefully, Shinji waggled his fingers and toes; they appeared fine—nothing seemed hurt or broken.

"Weird." He glanced at Lucy. "What *was* that? Some kind of bomb or electromagnetic pulse?"

"I don't know." She looked up at the sky, her brow furrowed in confusion. "I couldn't tell what it was."

"Well, they did *something* strange." Oliver took a step back from the railing with a grave look. "Hightower is gone."

"What? How?"

Shinji peeked over the railing and saw that Oliver was right. The three Hightower agents, as well as their boat, were gone. In fact, there was no sign of a boat on the water, no hint of a vessel anywhere in the distance or on the horizon. The ocean was blue, clear, and completely empty. As if the boat and the people on it had just blipped out of reality.

"Weird," Shinji muttered again, making Lucy frown at him.

"It's not weird," she said, "it's impossible. Even Hightower can't instantly poof out of sight." Her eyes widened. "Unless . . ."

A booming shout came from somewhere in the pilothouse. "Ocean!" Mano bellowed, poking his head out the doorframe. "Get in here, now!"

They all hurried onto the bridge. Mano was standing before a console of blinking lights and switches, his face pale in the eerie glow.

"Impossible," he muttered, shaking his head. "This is impossible. How did Hightower do this?"

"What's going on?" Oliver said.

Before Mano could answer, pounding footsteps could be heard, and a moment later, Phoebe burst into the room. "Captain!" she exclaimed. "This is incredible! Did you feel that pulse? Do you know what has happened? Oh, hello, Shinji, Lucy, Roux. You're here, too. Did you feel the energy field across the ship a few moments ago?"

"I would have to be dead not to," Shinji replied impatiently. "What was it? What does it mean?"

"Look at your phones," Phoebe replied. "Do you notice anything strange about them? The date and time, perhaps?"

Frowning, Shinji dug out his phone, wishing Phoebe would just tell him what was going on already. He noticed that Lucy had already pulled her phone out and was staring at it in alarm and disbelief. Flipping up the screen, Shinji first saw that a text had come in from Aunt Yui, and that it had arrived . . . two days ago?

Behind Shinji, Oliver let out an explosive breath. "Tell me this is wrong," he said, looking at Phoebe. "According to my phone—and everyone else's, I assume—it is *forty-eight hours* later! How in Poseidon's beard did we lose two days?"

"Hightower," Lucy whispered. "I thought it was impossible, but . . ."

"But what?" asked Shinji.

Lucy's face was pale as she glanced up. "A couple of

years ago, one of our alchemical physicists was working on something called a time bomb. It was another device that blended tech and magic; you really can't develop anything time-oriented without using magic. Unfortunately, the person working on it just . . . vanished one day, in his own workshop. No one knows what happened to him, and the project was declared too unstable to continue. Which is really bad. If even Hightower decides to abandon something, then, well, it's gotta be super dangerous."

"A time bomb?" said Mano, looking ill. He fumbled across his desk for the saltshaker, poured a liberal amount of salt into his palm, and tossed a large pinch over his left shoulder. Then his right one. Then the left one again. "How is that even possible?"

"I'm not sure how it works exactly," Lucy continued, "but I think the device is supposed to cause a blip in time, like a hiccup, that sort of freezes everything it touches in a stasis bubble. Outside the bubble, the world continues and time goes on. But inside, it's like no time has passed at all. Eventually, it bursts, and everything goes back to normal."

"Thank goodness that it did," Phoebe added. "Time is not something one can play around with safely. We're lucky we're here and not hurtling through a rift into the unknown. Although . . ." She paused, a somewhat dreamy look crossing her face. "I would love to see fourteenth-century Japan. . . ."

"Except we're now two days behind," Mano said, slapping his hand onto a table with a resounding whack. "Curse that Hightower! There's no way we're getting to that wreck before them now."

Shinji clenched his jaw. As cool and unbelievable as the time bomb was, it still meant Hightower was ahead of them. "They cheated," he declared furiously. "They couldn't beat us in a fair race, so they rigged the contest. Isn't there some kind of rule against playing dirty?"

"Not for Hightower." Oliver sighed and stuck his phone into his coat pocket. "And there's nothing we can do about it now," he said practically. "We'll just have to get to the wreck and see if they left anything behind. Two days is still not a lot of time for underwater extractions. Maybe there will still be something that can tell us more about the Natia people. The least we can do is go down and look. We didn't come all this way to leave empty-handed."

"Yeah," Mano agreed, and gave a gusty sigh as well. "I'll inform the team of what happened. If you hear yelling, that's probably the doc chewing me out and cursing Hightower."

"Um, sorry." Roux, who had been silent until now, raised his hand. "Can I just ask something quickly?" he said. "Is this real, or did I somehow hit my head really hard and I ended up in Wonderland?"

"Hey, you wanted to sneak aboard the ship." Shinji clapped Roux on the shoulder. On the one hand, he got it.

When he'd first met the members of the Society, he had felt the same way: overwhelmed and incredulous. On the other hand, Roux had brought this on himself. "Welcome to the Society of Explorers and Adventurers. It's not exactly normal around here."

CHAPTER NINE

Shinji's heart pounded. Staring out a round window of—he hoped—extremely thick glass, he listened to the groan of a metal crane as it swung the *Seabeetle* out over the water.

After the incident with Hightower and the time bomb, they had raced to the shipwreck as quickly as they could. But when they reached the site, it was as they feared; Hightower was gone, and from the stuff bobbing on the ocean waves—wooden planks, plastic chunks, and other debris—the corporation had already plundered the wreck and snatched what they could. Still, after some discussion with Mano and Dr. Grant, they decided to take the *Seabeetle* down anyway, to see if Hightower had missed anything. The *Seabeetle* only had room for four passengers and the pilot, and after much begging by Lucy, and much assurance from Hayley Frye about how perfectly safe the *Seabeetle* was, Oliver had consented to take Lucy along for the ride. Then Phoebe had chimed in, arguing that this might be the perfect opportunity to awaken Shinji's inner magic, and suddenly Shinji and his new sidekick, Roux, had been signed on for the journey.

Now, gazing out the window at the roiling waves below him, Shinji felt his stomach starting to creep up to his throat, the same feeling he got when he was on a roller coaster, slowly climbing up the highest drop on the ride.

"All systems normal, Mr. Ocean," said Dr. Grant's tinny voice from the speaker overhead. "Once the *Beetle* is clear, we'll detach the sub, and you can take over the controls from there."

"Roger that," Oliver replied. "Waiting on your signal."

Shinji took a deep breath. The interior of the *Seabeetle* was small and cramped, with himself, Oliver, Lucy, Roux, and Phoebe sitting in a tiny space surrounded by curved metal walls and numerous blinking lights. Beyond the glass was the vast, sunless ocean, and whatever lurked in its depths.

Phoebe suddenly gave a high-pitched squeak that made him jump. "Oh, this is so exciting!" she exclaimed, her voice bouncing off the walls of the tiny chamber. "Aren't you excited, Shinji?"

"Excited, terrified; it's the same thing, right?"

With a mechanical hum, the crane began lowering them into the water. Waves sloshed against the sides of the *Seabeetle*, splashing over the glass. Shinji watched as they sank below the surface, blue sky being replaced with the blue-green haze of the ocean.

"This is amazing," Lucy whispered, eyes bright as she watched the *Seabeetle* sink lower into the water. "I'm so glad I actually get to see the *Beetle* in action. Even though Hightower probably took everything that wasn't nailed down, I'm happy we decided to go see the wreck anyway."

"Yeah," Shinji agreed. "I just wish we had gotten there first. There's not going to be much left now that Hightower has come through."

But Oliver chuckled. "Don't get too gloom and doom yet, kids," he said, glancing back at them. "It's only been two days, and this isn't a tiny fishing boat we're talking about. Trust me, Hightower didn't have the time they'd need to grab everything from a ship this size. My guess is they snagged the most valuable pieces first—artifacts worth the most cold, hard cash—and got the heck out before we arrived. Statues, coins, weapons, things like that. But that's not what we're looking for."

"True," Phoebe chimed in. "We're looking for items of cultural importance. Things that would tell us more about the Natia and their lost civilization. I doubt Hightower would consider an old bowl or a cracked plate important.

I'm sure they left some pieces behind in their rush to loot the ship."

Lucy nodded, and Shinji felt a ripple of both relief and hope. Maybe this mission hadn't been for nothing after all. But Roux, sitting across from Lucy, looked disappointed. Shinji was sure he was hoping they would find treasure like gold and jewels, and didn't consider a cracked plate very valuable.

"We're about to detach the sub," said Dr. Grant over the speaker. "Is everyone ready?"

"Ready," Oliver confirmed.

"Detaching *Seabeetle*. In three . . . two . . ."

There was a jolt as whatever was holding the sub aloft was released. Immediately the *Seabeetle* began to drift downward. Oliver took the controls, and Shinji heard the whir of engines as the pod began a controlled descent into the ocean depths.

For several minutes, Shinji could only stare out the window in amazement. Colorful schools of fish swarmed around the sub, from tiny creatures no bigger than his finger, to fish as long as his arm. The deeper they went, the dimmer the light became, until Oliver hit a button and a spotlight flickered to life. More fish swam around the sub, perhaps attracted to the light, or maybe just curious about the strange metal creature drifting through their world.

"This is ironic," Roux muttered beside Shinji. "It's like we're in a fish tank, and the fish are the ones staring at us.

This must be what everything at the aquarium feels like from the perspective of the fish."

The *Seabeetle* continued downward. After what seemed like an eternity, the seafloor finally came into view in the hazy beam of light.

"Lucy," Oliver said as they continued to descend. The ocean floor was just a few yards away now. "See that red switch over there? Push it."

Lucy blinked, her face lighting up with excitement. "Now?"

"Yes."

Lucy flipped the switch, and Shinji felt a mechanical vibration below them as the *Seabeetle* responded. From the sides of the sub, panels opened, and four jointed metal legs curled out, reminding him of enormous insect appendages. The *Seabeetle*, now truly looking like some kind of huge water bug, touched down on the ocean floor, and Lucy literally clapped her hands with excitement.

Oliver pressed the controls, and the *Seabeetle*'s metal legs moved, crawling over sand, rock, and dirt as it scuttled along the seafloor. Leaning against the window, Shinji watched the bottom of the ocean scroll by, shadowy and surreal in the hazy spotlight. Fish swarmed around them, small creatures darted away over the sand, and stingrays fluttered past like ghostly pancakes. At one point, a cloud of jellyfish appeared, their pale bodies ethereal and transparent as they floated in the water. The sleek form of a shark passed overhead once, its silvery-gray fins barely moving as it glided like a torpedo through the darkness.

They crested the rise, and suddenly the hulk of something large and boat-shaped appeared at the bottom, sprawled in the sand and rock of the ocean floor.

Lucy gave a little gasp. "There it is! We found it."

It was lying on its side, covered in algae and seagrass, and looked like it had been there for decades. But it was definitely a ship. It was, from Shinji's perspective, enormous. Far bigger than the *Good Tern*, it even dwarfed the *Seas the Day*. The details of the vessel were impossible to make out, having been lying on the ocean floor for decades, but Shinji thought it might have been an old military ship, sunk and left to rot miles from the ocean surface.

But then, that raised the question, why was there a warship here?

"Still intact, too," Oliver muttered. "At least Hightower didn't blow it to smithereens when they were done with it."

Roux, Shinji noticed, had been staring out the window in awe, eyes bright with amazement as he gazed at the sunken ship. Quickly, he shook himself and wrenched his gaze from the boat, his normal bored expression falling into place.

"Too bad we're down here to find cups and plates," he muttered. "And not real treasure."

Lucy narrowed her eyes. "And what would you consider real treasure?" she asked in a cold voice.

"I don't know. Gold? Jewels?" He shrugged. "Old statues

that are worth lots of money? Don't rich people pay a fortune for that kind of stuff?"

"They do." Phoebe nodded. "But you see, there is more to it than money. We believe history should be preserved. Whatever was on this ship could've taught us a lot about a culture we know nothing about. That is the Society's goal after all: to learn everything we can, to better understand those who came before us. That is why preserving history is so important, and why it should be shared with the world, not hoarded and locked away in someone's private collection."

"Huh." Roux crossed his arms. "Well, all I know is I can't eat a history book. And if my choice was to sell a moldy old statue to some rich guy or starve, guess which one I'm taking."

Lucy snorted. "Why am I not surprised?"

"Maybe because the hardest thing you've ever had to do was choose your nail color, Snowflake," Roux shot back. "Or which bathing suit you were going to take on vacation. Talk to me when you haven't eaten in three days. Maybe I'll be impressed."

"Kids, don't make me turn this sub around." Oliver's voice, though subtly amused, was still a warning, and it stopped whatever Lucy was going to snap in return. She glared at Roux, then at Shinji, as if silently accusing him of betrayal for not jumping to her side. But even though Lucy was his friend, Shinji understood where Roux was coming from, at least a little. He and Aunt Yui had never gone hungry, but they'd never had tons of money, either. Shinji had never had designer clothes, expensive computers, or top-of-the-line anything. When they traveled, they stayed in cheap hotels and ate at fast-food restaurants. When they went shopping, Aunt Yui used coupons and bought the stuff on sale. He knew his aunt did her best, but there were times he'd wished he could get a faster computer, a better phone, or even the pair of shoes he wanted, without having to save up for it.

So, he got it. He didn't necessarily like it, but he understood. The Society wanted to preserve history, and that *was* important, but for Roux . . . he was just trying to survive. He was looking out for himself because no one else would. And in some strange way, Shinji understood and sympathized with that more than he saw Lucy's side of things.

Though Roux didn't have to be such a jerk about it.

The ship grew even larger as the *Seabeetle* crawled forward, looming above them like a sleeping dragon. As they got closer, however, Shinji began to see something strange. Small holes, three or four feet in diameter, had been bored into the side of the ship. They looked perfectly round, and the edges were smooth, like they had been cut with an extremely sharp blade.

"Hightower drones," Oliver muttered. "That's probably how they got in to search the wreck. Well, at least that makes it easier for us. We'll send in our own drone to look around. Lucy . . ." He glanced at her with a smile. "You want to do the honors?"

She gasped. "Can I?"

"Well, considering all the time you've been spending with Hayley, you probably know more about it than I do, so . . . yeah." Oliver scooted to the side, indicating the control panel. "Go for it."

"Hey, why does she get to press a button?" Roux asked as Lucy eagerly leaned forward. "I'm part of this team, too, right? When do I get to press a button?"

Lucy gave him a frosty look. "And do you know anything about maneuvering underwater drones and what you have to do to keep them buoyant while manipulating their cameras and front graspers at the same time?" she asked.

Roux blinked. "I don't think any of that was actual English," he stated.

Oliver shook his head. "That's why she gets to press the buttons," he told Roux.

Shinji felt another mechanized vibration through the floor of the sub, and a second later, something detached from its underside, swimming up in front of them. While the *Seabeetle* was shaped like a large bug, this thing reminded Shinji more of a manta ray: sleek and streamlined with two large yellow "eyes" that emitted beams of light that cut through the water. A round lens at the front was the underwater camera, he guessed.

"Camera on," Lucy muttered, flipping a switch, and the

screen in front of her flickered to life, showing the vast ocean floor and the hulking wreck from a much lower point of view. Shinji scooted behind Lucy, peering over her shoulder, as she grasped a pair of video-game-like console sticks, and the drone began to move through the water.

Now everyone crowded close, watching the screen as the drone glided effortlessly over the ocean floor toward the looming shipwreck. As it drew closer, Shinji began to feel . . . strange. As if something was watching them, being alert to their presence, and his presence in particular. His heart rate picked up, and goose bumps prickled his skin. If a long, squiddy tentacle suddenly reached out of one of those holes and grabbed the drone, he was probably going to scream.

The drone circled the ship, and they could see the holes much more clearly now. There were nearly a dozen of them poked into the hull, reminding Shinji of Swiss cheese.

"Plasma torches," Oliver said. "Definitely Hightower. They couldn't have just one drone, they had to send in a whole fleet." He shook his head in disgust. "I guess I should be thankful that they used plasma torches and not explosives. Lucy, take us in."

The drone swept through one of the holes, shining its spotlights around, and Shinji felt a chill run down his back. The images, even viewed on a small screen, were eerie. A flooded room greeted them, algae-covered pillars and rotting pipes glimmering as the light crept across walls and floors. The interior was a mess. Rotting crates and barrels lay everywhere, and debris floated in the water, spookily suspended in time.

"This must be the hold," Oliver said, gazing at the screen. "Anything of value would've been stored here, along with the supplies needed for the trip home."

"Looks like it's been tossed pretty good," Roux said.

Lucy frowned at him.

"What?"

"It's been gone through," Roux explained. "Someone trashed it looking for stuff. Man, they really made a mess, didn't they? Good luck finding anything in this."

"We don't have to find a lot," Phoebe said, watching the screen intently as Lucy sent the drone deeper into the hold. "If we can discover just one thing that can tell us more about the Natia, it will be a victory."

The feeling of being watched was getting stronger. Shinji felt more goose bumps rising along his arms as the drone glided farther into the room. Fish swarmed through the water, flashing through holes and weaving between rusty columns as the spotlight invaded their dark haven. Shinji's heart pounded as the drone circled the room, poking at empty crates, shining its light into dark crevices. He knew he wasn't in the wreck, that he was just watching the camera as it glided through the ship. But it still gave him the same eerie, tense feeling as someone feels watching a horror movie or a scary video game. Like something was going to leap out of the shadows and jump-scare him.

As the drone rounded an algae-covered post, something large and torpedo-shaped flew toward them from the darkness, making Shinji jump. Thankfully, it was not a torpedo, and as it zipped by, he saw pointed fins and the unmistakable gray-and-white body of a shark.

Roux yelped and jerked back from the screen before he remembered he wasn't in the same room with the predator. "Oh good," he said, playing it off like it was no big deal. "Now Jaws has joined the party. We're gonna need a bigger boat."

Shinji tilted his head. "He looks a little smaller than the one in the movie. Wasn't Jaws a great white?"

"I don't care what you call it; it's a fish with pointy teeth. Who cares what it is if it bites you?"

"Shortfin mako," Oliver said, watching the shark swim gracefully through the water. "Generally not aggressive to humans. Though it's strange to find one way out here."

The shark circled back, coming very close to the front of the drone, so close Shinji saw the jagged teeth poking out of its bottom jaw. As he watched it glide past the screen, a chill ran up his back. The shark seemed to be looking directly at him.

"What is it doing?" Lucy wondered as the mako circled around again, passing in front of the camera. The chills on the back of Shinji's spine intensified; the shark was definitely looking at him as it went by. He didn't know how he knew this, but he did.

"It's a shark," Roux said again. "It's probably thinking how it's going to eat the drone. Hope you guys have insurance on that thing."

"It's not going to eat the drone," Oliver said just as the shark bumped its pointed nose against the glass. It was more curious than aggressive, but it did knock the drone back and cause Lucy to wrench at the controls to keep it level. "Okay, maybe I was wrong," Oliver admitted. "Lucy, get the drone out of there. The last thing we need is for an expensive piece of equipment to end up in shark poop."

Follow, something whispered in Shinji's ear.

Shinji jerked up. The others, gazing intently at the screen as Lucy struggled with the drone, didn't seem to notice. The mako wheeled around, came right at the drone, and smacked it with its nose again, sending it tumbling through the water.

"Darn it," Lucy muttered, struggling to keep the drone upright. "Why does it keep doing that? It's like it's trying to stop me from leaving."

The shark poked the drone with its nose once more. *Follow,* insisted the voice as Shinji realized he wasn't hearing the voice in his ears; it was in his head. And he was pretty certain he knew whose voice it was.

He bit his lip. Should he say something? If he admitted he was hearing voices, especially *shark* voices, in his head, would his friends believe him? They all knew he had the power of a guardian inside him. Maybe talking to sharks was a perfectly normal thing for guardians?

Not for the first time, he wished the Coatl had given him clearer instructions.

Follow, the shark insisted again. *Now*.

Shinji sighed. "Hey, guys? I think the shark is trying to tell me something."

Silence fell as they all turned to stare at him. For a moment, no one said anything. Shinji could sense their disbelief along with skepticism and a wary amazement.

Then Roux snickered. "Is it telling you to bring it a can opener?"

"The shark is talking to you?" Phoebe's voice overrode Roux's, an eager look on her face as she peered down at Shinji. "How marvelous! Oh, this is so exciting. The guardian's power must be manifesting as we speak. How is it talking to you? Is it a different language that you are hearing, or is it more telepathic? Perhaps sharks use sonar to communicate like dolphins, though that's never been confirmed. Also, how would you be able to hear sonar, Shinji? Is that a guardian power we don't know of?"

"I don't know." He glanced back at the screen, watching as the shark circled the drone again, eyeing him the whole time as it passed. "I just know it's talking to me. It wants us to follow it."

"Follow it?" Lucy echoed, frowning. "Where?"

"I don't know," Shinji repeated with a helpless shrug. "I guess we have to follow it to find out."

Oliver sighed and ran a hand down his face. "As usual, I have no idea what magical mumbo jumbo is happening right now, but I guess we should do what the shark wants." He narrowed his eyes thoughtfully. "Well, that's something I never thought I would say."

The shark bumped the drone again, a bit more gently this time, though the voice in Shinji's brain echoed loud and clear. *Follow. Follow now.*

"All right!" Shinji said aloud. "We're following. Lead on."

He didn't know if the shark would hear him, but instantly, it wheeled around and glided toward the back of the room. Reaching the far wall, it turned and swam back a bit, as if waiting for them. Shinji looked at Lucy, who raised her eyebrows.

"Okay," she muttered, grasping the controls again. "Following a shark into a dark, abandoned shipwreck because it told us to. This is normal."

The drone moved forward. The shark waited until it was almost upon it, then spun and glided through a doorway, vanishing into the shadows.

They trailed the shark through the wreck of the ship. Or rather, Lucy maneuvered the drone through the wreck while the *Beetle* stayed put. The drone dodged beams and schools of fish, following the shark as it flowed gracefully through the water. It led them up a flooded stairway, down a tight corridor, and into a chamber that looked like it had once been the captain's quarters. Gliding to the far wall, it began swimming back and forth in front of a rotted, broken cabinet. Two heavy, waterlogged doors had been wrenched off and were lying on the ground, and the shelves inside were empty.

"What is that?" Phoebe wondered. "There's nothing inside. Why did the shark lead us here?"

"There *was* something there," Roux said, and pointed at the screen. "Look, the drawers around it have all been tossed . . . opened and rifled through. Your Hightower people have already searched the place."

"They're not *my* Hightower people," Lucy said through clenched teeth.

"Okay, so why lead us here?" Oliver wondered. "If whatever was inside is already gone, there's nothing we can do."

The shark circled the cabinet, bumping its nose into the sides, as if trying to push it over. Lucy looked back at Shinji, a question in her eyes.

"What does it want, Shinji?"

Shinji crossed his arms, frowning as he listened for the shark's voice, hoping it would clarify what was happening. But there was nothing. "I . . . don't know," he admitted. "Maybe it thinks something is still in there."

"Should I get closer?"

Shinji looked at the shark as it bashed its nose into the

cabinet again, so forcefully that a clump of seagrass came loose and drifted to the floor. "Yeah, I think it's still trying to tell us something, but it's not really talking anymore," he said. "Maybe check out the cabinet before it gives itself a bloody nose."

"Okay." Lucy sighed and tilted the controls forward. The drone glided up to the cabinet, shining its light against the back wall and into the corners. But, though he stared at the screen till his eyes started to water, Shinji couldn't see anything unusual.

"There's nothing here," Lucy said after a minute.

"No, that's what they'd want you to think," Roux said, making her frown. "Look under the drawers. There could be a button for a secret door or hidden panel."

"Are you serious?" Lucy snapped.

Roux shrugged. "It's what I would do."

The shark suddenly whirled and sped right at the camera, looking like it was going to chomp the drone into pieces. Shinji tensed, but instead of hitting the drone, the mako slammed its muscular body into the side of the cabinet. There was no sound on-screen, but the impact rocked the cabinet to the side and caused a school of fish to flee in panic. As everything settled, the entire back of the cabinet suddenly dropped away, revealing a square hole behind it. Roux let out a crow of victory.

"Ha! I was right."

Oliver gave him a single nod. "Good instincts, kiddo," he said. "I was about to suggest the same, but you beat me to it. Way to think like a pirate."

Roux shrugged, as if it was no big deal, but Shinji could tell he was proud.

Phoebe glanced down at Lucy. "Can you reach whatever is inside the hole?"

"I think so," she answered. Gazing down at the control panel, she flipped a lever, and Shinji watched as two metal clamps uncurled from beneath the drone. They were jointed, and with the claws on the end, they reminded him of crab pincers. Carefully, Lucy guided the clamps into the hidden hole at the back of the cabinet. Shinji stared at the screen, the others crowding in a bit closer in anticipation. They all held their breath while they waited for the arms to emerge. After a few moments of the drone rummaging around, Roux let out an impatient huff.

"Come on," he muttered. "Where's the treasure? What's taking so long?"

"This isn't exactly easy," Lucy said through gritted teeth. "If you're so impatient, why don't you . . . ? Wait, I got it."

The arms emerged, the clamps holding what looked like a small metal box in their claws. As it came into view, Shinji felt a surge of excitement. A mysterious, sealed box hidden behind a panel in the captain's quarters? What treasure could be inside? He hoped it was something cool.

Oliver grinned and clapped a hand to Lucy's shoulder.

"Nice job, kid," he said as Lucy gave a triumphant smile in Roux's direction. "You just saved this expedition from being a complete disaster. We might've lost the race, but looks like our instincts were right. Hightower was in too much of a hurry and missed something important." He put a hand on Lucy's arm as if gently urging her to scoot aside. "We'll get back to the ship and tell Mano the good and bad news. And . . ." He glanced at the screen, at the mysterious box held in the drone's claws. "We can see what exactly we've found down there."

"Yes," Phoebe agreed with an enthusiastic nod. "Although, technically, it was the shortfin mako shark that led us to the hidden panel through telepathic communication with our resident guardian."

"Yeah." Oliver glanced at Shinji with a wince. "Maybe we don't tell it like that."

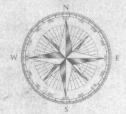

CHAPTER
TEN

Shinji, Lucy, Oliver, Phoebe, and Mano all stood around the table in the captain's quarters, staring at the small metal box in the center. Roux was there as well, and no one had said anything about making him leave. Shinji suspected they were too focused on the box and the mission to worry about the stowaway in the room.

"Ooh, this is so exciting!" Phoebe exclaimed, literally bouncing in place. "The suspense is killing me. I wonder what it is."

"We could open it already and find out," Roux suggested. "It's just a padlock, the kind the tourists use to chain up their bikes. Gimme three minutes with a bent wire, and I could pop it for you."

That was the most he had said with adults in the room, Shinji noticed. Either he was becoming more comfortable with all of them, or he really wanted to see what was in the box.

Lucy wrinkled her nose in distaste. "Is that one of your special talents?" she inquired. "Stealing bicycles?"

"Only when I'm bored." Roux grinned. "The rest of the time I try to steal mechanical rats."

Lucy glowered.

Mano cleared his throat. "I'm sure the lab has a pair of bolt cutters," he said, sensing the obvious tension between Lucy and Roux. "Let me go grab one, and I'll be right back. Two seconds."

A few minutes later, they all watched intently as Mano inserted the padlock between the jaws of the wire cutter and squeezed. The snips easily cut through the rusty bolt, and it dropped to the table with a clink. Mano nodded and gestured to Oliver with a large hand.

"Wanna do the honors, Ocean?"

Oliver smiled and glanced at Shinji, who could barely contain his impatience to see what was in the box. He suddenly couldn't sit still. His hands itched, wanting to grab the lid and wrench it open. There was a strange pull in the pit of his stomach that drew him toward the box and whatever was hidden inside. He knew, somehow, that it was important.

For a second, he wondered if it was the Coatl that was affecting him, but then Oliver chuckled and shook his head, still giving him a wry grin.

"Well, since it was Shinji's shark that showed us through the ship—wow, that's a tongue twister—I think he should be the one who gets to open it." He gave the box a nudge with his gold-headed-parrot cane, pushing it toward Shinji. "Go ahead, kiddo. This one is yours."

Shinji's heart pounded. Reaching out, he snagged the box, dragged it toward him, and pushed back the lid. Inside was a single long tube made of dark, lacquered wood. It was sealed on both ends, and the tube itself had once been painted with bright, intricate patterns, though much of it was faded and waterlogged now. Shinji picked it up, and it felt light and hollow in his hands.

"That's it?" Roux exclaimed after a moment. "That's all there is? No pirate gold? No money or jewels or treasure?"

"No," Shinji replied after thoroughly checking the box. "That's it. That's all that was inside."

Roux sighed. "Worst treasure box ever."

"What is that, anyway?" Lucy asked. "A telescope or something?"

Both Oliver and Mano chuckled. "You wanna tell them?" Mano asked, looking at Oliver. "Or should I?"

Oliver grinned. "Oh, you kids today." He reached across the table, plucked the tube from Shinji's hand, and held it up like a trophy. "Wanting to be pirates and missing something so important. Do you know what this is?" he went on, shaking the tube in the air. "It's a map case. Which means, inside . . ."

He gripped one of the seals and turned, grunting a bit, as the wood was swollen and waterlogged, but eventually it came free with a pop. He upended the tube, shook it, and a rolled piece of paper slid out into his hands.

A map.

Lucy gasped, and Roux's eyes widened as Oliver held it up. "*This* is the real treasure," he said triumphantly. "Too bad Hightower was in such a hurry and missed this little beauty. Let's see where it leads, shall we?"

Unrolling the parchment, he spread it out on the table. Everyone crowded around. It was the map of an island, as far as Shinji could tell—an irregular landmass in the center of the ocean. A dotted line led from one edge of the island to a point in the very center and was marked with a faded but very recognizable red X.

"X marks the spot," Oliver said with a thoughtful nod. "Pretty classic."

Shinji drew in a sharp breath. The map, and the red X, suddenly seemed to rush up at him, filling his vision. He saw an island with sandy beaches, thick rain forests, and a green mountain rising up from the center. He was speeding over the beach, then through the tangled vines and leaves of the rain forest, seeing flashes of color and movement from the corner of his eyes. He saw the remains of a village, thatched huts and wooden benches lying abandoned in the trees. He continued to speed through the rain forest, ducking vines and zipping between trunks, until he came to the base of the mountain that soared toward the clouds. A stone door was carved into the side of the cliff, flanked by huge pillars and covered in moss. Through the vines and vegetation, Shinji could see the carving on the stone was the head of an enormous boar, deadly tusks curving up to frame its entire face.

Shinji blinked, and the vision faded. He was back in Mano's quarters, with the map still lying on the table and Oliver's voice echoing in his ears. Nobody seemed to notice anything had happened, but he could still see the abandoned village, the stone door, and those angry blue eyes staring out at him. For a moment, he wondered if he should say anything, but then he spotted Phoebe, beaming with excitement on the other side of the table. If he mentioned anything about a mysterious door on the island, she would never leave him alone. He'd told them about the shark because he felt he had to. Admitting he was having visions of volcanoes and hearing angry voices was another story.

"How far away is this island, Mano?" Oliver was asking. "You know all there is to know about the Polynesian Triangle. How long will it take us to get there?"

Mano didn't answer. He was gazing down at the map, still lying in the center of the table. His brow furrowed, and he turned the map sideways, then upside down, as if trying to figure something out.

"Uh, Mano?" Oliver prodded. "You okay there?"

The big man shook his head. "This island," he muttered, tracing the edge of the map with a thumb. "These coordinates . . . it doesn't make sense. There's nothing there."

Shinji glanced over at Lucy, who stared back, clearly intrigued.

Now Oliver frowned. "What are you talking about?"

Mano tapped the map, where several numbers had been scribbled in the corner. "These are the coordinates to the island," he began. "But I know that stretch of ocean. There's no land there. There's nothing but open water, for miles, in every direction. There is *no* island."

"Well." Oliver peered over at the map with a faint smile. "According to this, there is."

Mano sighed. "I can get us there," he said. "Looking at these coordinates, it'll just take a day or two. Once we arrive, we can see if there's an island there or not."

"A mysterious island." Phoebe clapped her hands. "Oh, I cannot wait. This is going to be so exciting."

The journey to the mysterious, possibly invisible island took two days. During that time, Shinji tried to stay busy, hanging out in the cargo hold with Lucy and the various scientists aboard, or in his room with his laptop. All this activity was mostly to avoid Phoebe, who seemed to lurk around every corner waiting to pounce and ask him a ton of questions about the shark, its voice, and whether any other sea life had tried to contact him. But it was also to keep his mind occupied, because the closer they got to the supposed location of the island, the weirder Shinji felt. It was as if something knew he was coming, and was both impatient for him to get there and furious at everything else.

Lucy and Roux squabbled often. It was never a full-blown fight, especially if they were in the presence of any of the adults, but Shinji began to get tired of their constant jabs and pokes at each other. One evening, he was lying on his cot flipping through a comic book, when his door flew open and Lucy strode into the room.

"Roux! Where is it?"

Shinji jumped, banging his head on the low ceiling above his mattress. "Ow, Lucy!" he exclaimed, rubbing his skull as he swung his legs off the cot. "You know, there's this thing called knocking that's really popular nowadays. What do you want?"

"Where is he?"

"Who? Roux?"

"Yes, Roux." Lucy gave him an exasperated look. "Who else would I be talking about? I certainly didn't come in here looking for Oliver."

"Why do you want him? What's he done this time?"

She glowered. "My book on mythological creatures from around the world is missing," she said. "I was going to flip through it tonight, to see if there was anything about sharks and hidden islands, but it's disappeared. I know *you* didn't take it," she went on. "And there's only one thief on this ship, so . . ."

"You assumed it was Roux."

"Who else would it be?" Lucy demanded. "None of the adults would come into my room—my locked room—and take my stuff without telling me. Why are you always on his side?"

"What? I'm not!" Shinji glared at her, stung. "I just . . . I get where he's coming from, that's all. I know what it's like to be on your own. I know how much it sucks to feel that you can't trust anyone. I've seen how stupid and ugly and unfair the world can be, and how sometimes it feels like it's you against everyone else. You wouldn't see that, because . . ."

He trailed off, but it was too late. Lucy went very still, her voice dropping into the subzero range.

"Because I'm a Hightower," she said flatly. "Because my family is rich, and I never had to worry about those kind of things. Right?"

Shinji shrugged. Which was definitely not a good move. Lucy's demeanor went even colder, her expression shutting into that frosty, impersonal mask Shinji had seen on her father, Gideon Frost.

"I see. Well, forget I said anything, then. Guess I'll find it myself."

She turned and walked away without looking back, slamming the door behind her.

Shinji groaned, running his hands down his face. Lucy was mad at him again, and he wasn't entirely sure why. It wasn't like *he* was the one swiping her stuff. Maybe he would find Roux and ask if he had seen Lucy's book.

Sticking his phone in his pocket, he went looking for him.

After asking around, Shinji found Roux in the library, where Phoebe had attempted to "help" Shinji with his magic earlier. Roux was lounging in a chair with both legs dangling off the armrest, a large book propped against his knees. He didn't look up as Shinji approached, though one hand rose in a casual wave to let him know he'd seen him.

"Hey," he greeted, eyes still on the book. A very familiar book, Shinji suddenly realized. *Mythologies from Around the World*, it read on the cover.

"Hey," Shinji repeated. "Isn't that Lucy's book?"

"What? Oh yeah." Roux glanced up at him and shrugged. "With all this weird stuff about invisible islands and time bombs and talking sharks, I thought I'd better read up on some of this stuff. It's pretty crazy, actually. I didn't know you could keep fairies away with salt."

"She's looking for it," Shinji went on, feeling a stab of annoyance because Lucy had been right about Roux taking the book. "You didn't ask if you could take it."

Roux shifted in his seat. "You think Snowflake would let me borrow it if I asked? Knowing her, she'd probably say something like 'What, you actually know how to read?'" He snorted, settling himself farther into the chair. "Don't worry, I'm just borrowing it. I'll put it back when I'm done."

"No," Shinji said firmly, making Roux look up with a frown. "Look, I get it; you don't want to ask for anything because you don't think people will actually help you. But you can't break into people's rooms and just take their stuff; that's stealing."

Roux gave him a lazy, unfriendly smile. "News flash to Shinji: I'm a thief. That's what I do."

"Yeah, well, it's wrong." Shinji didn't back down. "Stealing is wrong. That's what Hightower does; they take stuff that doesn't belong to them, and they use it for their own gain."

"So what?" Roux shrugged. "Isn't Little Miss Perfect a Hightower herself?"

"That's different. She isn't like the rest of them."

"You sure about that?" Roux gave Shinji a pointed look. "I saw her with those Hightower people. I know about wanting stuff, and believe me, she wanted whatever it was they were offering."

Shinji clenched his jaw. He didn't want to think of Lucy like that, but he couldn't help it now. Lucy had told him she missed Hightower. She missed her workshop. He wondered if she missed her dad, horrible as he was.

Should he be worried about Lucy's loyalty, since even Roux had noticed?

"Just give me the book," he said at last. "I'll take it back to Lucy."

"All yours." Roux set the book on an armrest and stood, stretching lazily. "I was done with it, anyway. Tell Snowflake thanks for letting me borrow it."

Shinji bristled, but he knew the other boy was just trying to needle him, so he forced himself to stay calm. "Maybe if you asked nicely, she'd let you borrow it for real."

"And maybe if I stick my head in a shark's mouth, I won't get it bitten off," Roux said, rolling his eyes. "Not holding my breath on that one." He sauntered out the door, leaving Shinji alone with the book in the library.

Shinji sighed. Walking over to the chair, he gazed down at the large tome lying innocently on the armrest. Like many of Lucy's books, it was huge and thick. It still didn't look particularly interesting to him; there was no picture on the cover, just a weird shield symbol with the title above it: *Mythologies from Around the World*. But maybe Roux had a point. Maybe he should be more interested in this stuff. Since he was probably one of the very few living people who had actually met a mythological creature.

Reaching out, he flipped the book open to a random page. The black-and-white picture of a dragon, wings spread wide and jaws breathing fire, was the first thing he saw. No surprise there. Dragons were the subjects of one of the most common myths around the world. Shinji thought they were insanely cool, but he already knew a lot about the creatures.

He kept flipping pages, past gryphons—also cool—unicorns, Pegasus, and the Minotaur, until he came to a page with a picture of a large serpent with great feathery wings, out-stretched as it reared back in an S shape.

Shinji paused, feeling a ripple of irritation. "Well, there you are," he said, not really knowing if the Coatl was listen-ing, if it could hear him at all. "Should I keep reading, or is everything we know about Coatls wrong? I bet this book isn't going to say anything about guardians and fonts."

Shinji paused and listened as hard as he could for some-thing, anything, that could guide or help him. As usual, there was no answer. Annoyed, he started to close the book but paused. What had Phoebe said? Something about his own emotions blocking the way to his power? Whenever he'd tried calling on his magic or talking to the Coatl, he'd been frustrated or angry. And when his emotions were at their strongest, that's when his magic started to go haywire.

Clear your mind, Phoebe had urged. *To master your power, you must first master your emotions.*

He shrugged, then took a deep breath and closed his eyes. *Might as well give it a shot.* This time, he didn't try to reach for his magic or draw it out. He just concentrated on being calm, being empty. If the spirit of the Coatl still lived on somewhere inside him, he would let it appear on its own. . . .

His skin wriggled. Shinji jerked and glanced down at his arm, seeing the winged serpent tattoo ruffle its wings and look up at him.

His heart nearly stopped. The Coatl. After weeks of nothing, of silence, of wondering if the guardian of the font was still with him, it had finally—*finally*—decided to show itself.

His breath came out in a relieved puff. "About time you showed up," he whispered, though he was so happy to see it he wasn't even angry. He wished Lucy were here, but was very glad that Phoebe was not. The Coatl flicked its tongue at him. As he watched, the winged serpent slithered down his arm and seemed to spill onto the pages of the book, turning to ink as it melted into the paper. Spreading its wings, the drawing of the Coatl looked back at him, then glided to the edge of the page and disappeared, vanishing further into the book.

"Hey, wait a second." Shinji quickly turned the page, seeing the Coatl slither across the paper and then vanish at the edges again. He kept flipping pages, chasing the Coatl as it zipped past words and pictures of mythological creatures, faster than he could keep up.

"What are you doing?" Shinji wondered, turning another page, only to see the Coatl wasn't moving anymore. It sat in the center of the paper, staring up at him, then deliberately turned and wriggled up the centerfold until it came to the picture at the top of the page.

Shinji blinked. It wasn't a large picture, not like the others, some of which took up an entire page. This simple

148

drawing portrayed a pig, a wild boar, with bolts of lightning that crackled and snapped around it. He felt a chill go through his stomach as he stared at the picture. The glowing eyes. The huge tusks, reaching up to frame its entire face. There wasn't much information, barely any at all, to go with the image. The text below it read:

STORM/TEMPEST BOAR. THOUGHT TO BE REVERED BY AN EXTINCT CULTURE THAT EXISTED SOMEWHERE IN THE POLYNESIAN TRIANGLE. PERHAPS WORSHIPED AS A GOD OF RAIN AND WIND, THE STORM BOAR WAS BELIEVED TO BE VOLATILE AND BAD-TEMPERED, ITS ANGER THE CAUSE OF MANY HURRICANES IN THE SOUTH PACIFIC.

That was all the information the article gave, but the chill Shinji felt slithered all the way down his spine. The Storm Boar. The lightning-shrouded beast that roared at him in his dreams; it had to be the same creature.

"What are you doing?"

Shinji jumped at the sound of Lucy's voice, turning to find her standing a few feet behind him. He was so focused on the book and the Storm Boar, he hadn't even heard her enter the library. Tinker peered down at him from her shoulder as Lucy's eyes drifted to the book on the armrest, then narrowed sharply.

"Is that my book?"

"Um, yeah." Shinji glanced down at the open tome, but the Coatl was no longer in the corner of the page. "Roux had it. Guess you were right."

"I knew it," Lucy muttered. "I'm going to have to talk to Mano about changing the locks on my doors."

"He'll just pick them again," Shinji pointed out. "Besides, he said he was going to give it back."

Lucy just gave him a cold glare, clearly unimpressed. She closed the book with a thump, losing the page with the Storm Boar without even seeing it. She picked up the book, cradled it to her chest, then turned and exited the room without saying anything more, leaving Shinji standing there by himself. For a second, he wondered if he should track her down and apologize, but he didn't know what he'd be apologizing for.

Glancing down, he saw the Coatl tattoo was back on his arm, lifeless and unmoving once again. If Shinji hadn't seen so many strange and bizarre events by now, he might've thought he had imagined the whole thing.

"What are you trying to tell me?" he whispered. "What is the Storm Boar? Why is it calling to me? What does it want me to do?"

Apparently, one could only receive a single hint from enigmatic guardian spirits per day, because even though Shinji spent another hour in the library trying to communicate with his Coatl tattoo, it didn't answer him.

CHAPTER
ELEVEN

The journey across the ocean continued as they followed the coordinates on the strange map, trusting Mano and Oliver to know the directions at sea. Lucy eventually started talking to Shinji again but remained frosty to Roux, who never apologized for taking her book without asking. He didn't, as far as Shinji could tell, break into any more rooms, so maybe he'd taken Shinji's "stealing is bad" lecture to heart. Or maybe he just hadn't let Shinji know he was doing it.

On the morning of the third day, the skies started to darken. Black clouds formed on the horizon, looming and ominous, and the sea grew choppy, tossing the boat and causing Shinji to stumble several times as the floor beneath him rocked and pitched.

Wandering down the hall with Roux, he met Lucy at the end of the corridor. "Where's Oliver and everyone else?" he asked as, behind him, Roux grabbed a post to keep himself steady. He was, Shinji saw nervously, looking a little green. He hoped the other boy wouldn't lose his breakfast all over the carpet.

"Up on deck," Lucy replied. She looked nervous as well and braced herself against the wall as the ship rocked beneath them. "I think they went to check out the storm. From what I can see, it's a bad one."

Shinji remembered his dream, and the angry pig appearing in the roiling clouds, lightning crackling around it. It couldn't be the same storm, could it? "I want to see it," he said, stepping past Lucy. "Be right back."

"Shinji, wait up," Lucy called. "We're coming, too."

A growl of thunder went through the air as Shinji stepped onto the deck, seeing Mano, Phoebe, and Oliver at the railings. Glancing at the sky, he saw the sun was still shining directly overhead, but over the horizon, lightning flickered through an ominous wall of clouds, and a sharp gust of wind tossed Shinji's hair like it was trying to yank it out.

"Hurricane?" Oliver mused as Shinji and the others joined them at the railing. He sounded far calmer than Shinji thought he should. Especially when talking about hurricanes in the middle of the ocean.

Mano grunted. "No, not a hurricane," he muttered. "But a nasty storm nonetheless. Like I said, this area is notorious for bad weather. Most ships avoid sailing through it." He stuck a hand into his pocket, probably to grab some lucky item, and shook his head. "Unfortunately, our coordinates are smack in the center of the storm. So, we're going to be sailing right into the teeth."

The storm loomed closer. More flashes of lightning lit up the sky, and thunder boomed. Spatters of rain hit Shinji's face, and he could see huge curtains of water creeping toward them, looking almost solid as they swept forward. The waves got bigger, huge swells lifting the ship several feet before dropping it down again, making Shinji feel like he was on a roller coaster.

"All right, this is getting dangerous," Oliver said. He and Mano, Shinji noticed, were having far less trouble keeping their balance on a pitching boat, being so used to the ocean. Surprisingly, Phoebe was also keeping her feet. "You kids get below deck now," the ex-pirate ordered. "Maybe tie yourselves to something solid. The last thing we need is someone going overboard. I do *not* want to go diving into this ocean after you."

Shinji looked up at the storm, and his skin prickled. It *was* the same as the one in his dreams; the same roiling clouds and flickering blue lightning. He felt that if he kept staring at it, the clouds would part and he would see a huge boar with electric-blue eyes peering down at him from the sky.

"I want to stay," Shinji protested. If the Storm Boar did make an appearance, he wanted to see it. If only to prove to himself that he wasn't going crazy.

But Oliver shook his head. "Not negotiable, kid. It's getting too rough up here and besides"—he nodded to Roux— "I think he needs to get to the med bay before he pukes all over the deck. Ask Dr. Malcom for something to help with seasickness. At the very least, she can get him a bucket. Go on," he urged as Shinji still hesitated. "I'll call you again when it's safe."

Reluctantly, Shinji turned to go belowdecks but stopped, chills running up his spine. Something was watching them. He could suddenly feel a presence, huge and powerful, peering at them through the storm. He felt invisible eyes lock on to him.

And then something strange happened.

The ocean suddenly . . . calmed. The deck below them stopped pitching, the winds ceased, and the rain that had been starting to patter against his skin disappeared. Overhead, the sun vanished as black clouds crept across the sky, and the air turned very dark. Around the ship, Shinji could see huge waves rising and falling, sending up sprays of foam as they crashed against one another. He could hear the wind howl, saw the rain swirling through the air . . . but it never touched the ship. They seemed to be in their own private tunnel of calm, a bubble that the storm and wind and raging sea couldn't get through.

"What . . . is this?" Mano growled. He was furiously rubbing a penny between a thumb and forefinger, as if he wanted to press it into copper particles. "This isn't natural. What is happening?"

"I don't know," Oliver said, gazing over the water. "But hang on to your beards because it's about to get weirder. Look."

Shinji peered past the railing over the ocean and felt a chill go through his stomach.

A curtain of mist hung before them, blocking out the sight of the sky, the ocean, everything. It hung there, thick and opaque, shielding whatever lay within. The storm raged around it, wind and rain tearing ragged curtains away from the rest of the wall, but the fogbank didn't move.

"This is impossible," Mano said slowly. "You can't have fog in a storm like this; the wind gusts would blow it away. What is going on?"

The Storm Boar, Shinji thought. *It's calming the wind, letting us through.*

He did not voice these thoughts out loud. The adults would immediately jump all over him. Phoebe, especially, would want to know everything about the Storm Boar, and he didn't know much about it, himself. Only that he had been having strange dreams about a boar in the sky, calling to him. Oliver might be angry that he was hiding things. Come to think of it, Lucy might be mad at him, too. It was easier not to say anything yet.

Besides, this was his problem and his quest. The Storm Boar was calling *him*.

"Certainly, something unnatural is at work here," Phoebe said, and she was the only one of them who did not sound wary or confused, but excited. "I would even go so far to say that not only is this unnatural, it has magic written all over it!"

"Magic," Oliver repeated. He glanced at Shinji and raised an eyebrow, making Shinji's stomach clench. "These days, magic is typically the realm of our resident guardian."

"Oh no, this isn't coming from Shinji," Phoebe said immediately, making him slump in relief. "It's far too powerful for anything Shinji has been capable of. My guess would be this is coming from the island or something on the island. We must be very close."

"You think the island is through that?" Lucy wondered. The wall of mist loomed, towering above them. Shinji watched a tendril of fog curl around the railing like a ghostly tentacle and shivered.

"I think we're about to find out," Oliver said. "Everyone, brace yourselves."

They sailed into the curtain of mist, and the fog closed around them, muffling the sounds of the storm. The rain stopped, the thunder and lightning fading away. It was almost eerily silent now; the only noises were the soft sloshing of waves against the hull, and the thump of Shinji's heart in his ears.

"Oh yes, this is definitely unnatural," Phoebe commented, sounding ecstatic. Her voice echoed loudly in the eerie stillness, making Oliver wince. "Very spooky. Do you think anything lives out here? Sirens, perhaps? Or mermaids?"

"Let's hope not," Oliver muttered. "Shinji, Roux . . ." He turned to the pair of them. "What do we do if we hear any strange singing?"

"Um." Shinji glanced at Roux, who shrugged. "Stick my fingers in my ears and go, 'La-la-la-la-la'?" he guessed.

"Close enough."

The ship broke through the curtain of fog, and suddenly the sunlight blazed down on them. Shinji winced, shielding his eyes as he peered over the water. Behind them, he could see the ring of clouds stretching out to either side. He could even see flickers of lightning from the storm that raged on the outer edges. But directly overhead, the sky was clear. Gulls wheeled through the air, calling to one another in the shadow of an enormous volcano. A volcano in the center of a verdant island.

"Uh . . . that is not supposed to be there," said Mano, scratching his head. "There are no volcanoes recorded in this part of the ocean."

"And yet," stated Oliver with a small, wondrous smile. The huge black mountain rose from a thick canopy of trees that covered the whole island, the tangle making it impossible to see what lay farther in. "Looks like we found our Island That Isn't There."

It's the same island. The island Shinji had seen in his dreams. His pulse pounded in excitement. There was no doubt in his mind now. Somewhere on the island, the Storm Boar was waiting for him.

Shinji glanced at his two friends. Lucy met his gaze and smiled, Tinker peering down at him from her shoulder. Roux seemed at a loss for words; the sickly-green tinge on his skin had faded, and he was staring at the volcano with wide eyes.

"You think that volcano is still active?" he wondered out loud.

"Probably not," Lucy answered. Tinker scurried to her other shoulder, whiskers twitching as he gazed up at the volcano, as well. "I would guess that it's dormant. But even if it's not, what are the chances that it'll erupt while we're on the island? That sort of thing only happens in movies."

"Right." Shinji winced. "And Coatls only exist in movies, too."

"Oh my goodness, I'm excited!" Phoebe nearly squeaked. "A lost island that no one has set foot on in who knows how long. What do you think we'll find?"

Oliver stepped forward, gazing across the water. He was grinning now, Shinji saw, his whole face lit with an eager smile, as if he couldn't wait to start exploring. "Well, we're going to find out, aren't we? Mano, how close can you get us?"

The big man nodded and turned back to the wheel. "I'll see if I can find a good place to weigh anchor."

Sailing around the island, they found a small cove with shimmering turquoise waters and a pristine sandy beach stretching up into the rain forest. Gazing out at the calm water surrounding the island, Oliver shook his head.

"Man, we got lucky. Look how shallow it is here. This whole island is surrounded by reefs." He blew out a breath in amazement. "We might've found the one place where the ship could pass through without scraping the rocks."

Was it luck? Shinji wondered. Or was it the Storm Boar guiding them, leading them through the mist, through the reefs and the shoals, to this hidden cove? What would they find on the island? The remnants of an unknown civilization, maybe the Natia people themselves? Or an angry Storm Boar wanting to drive them out of its territory? But that didn't make sense—the Storm Boar wanted Shinji to find the island. It needed him to do something.

"Dr. Grant is getting a team ready to disembark," Mano said, joining them at the railing. "She's bringing a group of scientists and researchers along, in case we find anything belonging to the Natia. This could very well be the island the Natia people originated from, and they don't want to take any chances. They're planning to set up a base camp once we reach a suitable location. Depending on what they find, we might be here a few days."

"Sounds good to me," Oliver said. "I have no problems staying on a beautiful tropical island with my own private beach. If only we could somehow find a swim-up bar."

Once they were in the cove, Mano anchored the *Seas the Day* while they were still in deeper water, announcing they would all have to take a Zodiac up to the beach. The Zodiacs, a pair of motorized, inflatable rafts, were both fast and light, and had room for everyone going to the island. Shinji, Lucy, and Roux piled into one raft with Oliver, Mano, and Phoebe, while Dr. Grant and a group of six scientists took the other.

"Here we go," Phoebe called as the motors roared to life. She had her red umbrella once more, Shinji saw, and for this trip, it might actually be useful. "Last one to the island is a nuckelavee!"

Shinji had no idea what *that* was, but he wasn't going to ask.

The wind whipped at Shinji's hair as the Zodiac flew across the water, barely seeming to touch the surface as it zipped along. Below them, the ocean was so clear he could see colorful schools of fish swirling about, and the Zodiac's own shadow gliding over the seafloor. Across from him, both Lucy and Roux were grinning, their hair and clothes flying about as the raft zoomed toward the island.

The island where the Storm Boar waited.

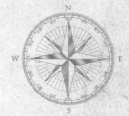

CHAPTER TWELVE

Shinji's heart continued to pound as the Zodiac reached the edge of the beach. As Mano and Oliver dragged the raft out of the water, Shinji gazed past the sand, staring at the thick tangle of trees and vegetation that crowded the edge of the beach. He could suddenly feel the island watching them.

There was a tickle in the back of his mind, the faintest hint of warning, and Shinji caught his breath. The Coatl. What was it trying to tell him? Did it want him to find the Storm Boar, or was it trying to warn him of danger?

Something brushed his arm, making him flinch and spin around. "Okay, someone's jumpy," Roux said, smirking as he and Lucy joined him, Lucy with her "emergency bag" over her shoulder. "Did you think I was a land octopus or something?"

"You're sneaky, you're always grabbing things, and you can get into places you're not supposed to be," Shinji returned. "Sounds pretty spot-on."

Roux shrugged. "I've been called worse."

Lucy gazed at Shinji in concern. So did Tinker, peering down from the top of her bag. "You okay?" she asked.

"Yeah," Shinji muttered. Guilt gnawed at him. If there *was* something dangerous in their midst, he really should be warning his friends, at least. He glanced quickly at the adults and lowered his voice. "I think there could be something on the island," he said, making Lucy's brows arch. "I feel like it's watching us. That it knows we're here."

"What is it?" asked Lucy.

"Maybe it's a volcano god, and it's angry that we're trespassing," Roux said before Shinji could answer, using a spooky tone and making no attempt to speak quietly. "And maybe the only way to appease it is to throw someone into the volcano."

"Hey, now, none of that," Oliver said, stepping in. "There will be no volcanic sacrifices on this trip. Priya would absolutely kill me. Besides, don't forget why we're here—to find signs of a lost people."

"Of course we won't be making any sacrifices," Phoebe said, appearing beside him. "But a mysterious hidden island with a lost culture and a volcano?" Shielding her eyes, she peered up at the ominous black mountain looming above the canopy. "It just *begs* for a volcano deity of some kind."

"Volcano deities tend to be very hotheaded," Oliver told her. "And easily offended. I would like to avoid having to flee the island as it's erupting with molten-hot lava."

Mano joined them at the edge of the beach, followed closely by Dr. Grant. "The team is ready," Dr. Grant announced, gazing at Mano and Oliver. Behind her, a group of six scientists and researchers approached carrying rucksacks and backpacks, but also hard black cases filled with scientific equipment. At least, that's what Shinji thought they held. "We'll follow you, until we find a good spot to set up camp."

"All right," Mano grunted. "Let's get this expedition started. Hopefully without running into any ghosts, curses, or angry island gods." He rapped his knuckles on a nearby palm, then shoved the hilt of a large machete at Oliver. "Let's go. Ocean, you're with me."

"Oh great." Oliver sighed, hefting the knife in his hand. "Hacking through a mosquito-infested rain forest. My favorite thing."

For several minutes, they pressed into the rain forest, pausing as the two men up front sliced away tangles of vines and branches to clear a trail. After a few minutes of hacking away at knots of vegetation, Oliver suddenly paused and straightened. "Hold on," he said, his voice slightly breathless, "there's a path here. Not a game trail, an actual path."

"A path?" Mano repeated behind him. "Are you sure?"

"Well, I'm pretty certain animals don't stack up rocks to make a wall, or build tiny bridges over streams. So . . . yeah, pretty sure."

"The Natia," Phoebe whispered. "We're close."

Lucy gazed nervously at the surrounding rain forest. "You don't think they're still here, do you?" she asked.

Mano frowned. "If they are, they've avoided notice for hundreds of years," he said. "It's difficult to believe no one has discovered this place, but if there are supernatural forces at work, maybe the Natia people are being protected by magic." He knocked a rhythm on the trunk of the nearest tree. "They might not even know about the outside world. If they are here . . ."

"Let's hope they're friendly," Shinji said.

"And that they don't mind us hacking through their forest," Roux added. "If spears start flying, I'm outta here."

They ventured farther into the rain forest, following the path as it twisted and snaked through the undergrowth. It was eerily silent. Unlike the jungles of Mexico, where Shinji had found the Coatl, there were no monkeys howling in the trees, no distant cries of birds or other animals, no creatures slithering or scuttling through the brush. Everything was very green and lush, with occasional splashes of color from flowers growing along the path. He did spot a few flashes of movement as small birds darted through the branches of the trees, but the island had the air of having been undisturbed since the beginning of time.

Even Phoebe seemed affected by the stillness. "This place is very peaceful," she whispered, stepping lightly along the path. "Very quiet. But not a tense quiet. You know, when you say, 'It's quiet . . . *too* quiet.' Not that kind of quiet." She paused a moment. "*Quiet* is a funny word, by the way. If you say it enough times, it stops sounding real. Quiet. Quiet."

"Quiet," Oliver said.

"There, you see? It stops sounding like a real word."

"No." The ex-pirate stopped and glared back at her. "I mean *be quiet*. There's something up ahead."

Everyone fell silent, and Mano turned, signaling Dr. Grant and her team to stop. They did, though Dr. Grant gave the captain a puzzled look as he stepped back to meet her.

"Ocean has found something," Mano said. "Wait here; we'll check it out."

Cautiously, Shinji and the others crept forward, peering through the vines and undergrowth, until they came to the edge of a clearing. At the front, Oliver suddenly put out an arm, stopping them from going any farther. Beyond the trees, Shinji could see the thatched, domed roofs of several huts scattered around the sandy soil.

Lucy gasped. "A village," she whispered. "There *are* people here."

"The lost culture," Phoebe breathed. "We found it!" She let out a squeal of excitement that startled everyone, and bounced in place. "Oh, do you know how exciting this is? The Natia civilization! A hidden people, living on this island for who knows how long. What a discovery! We should go back and let everyone know—"

"Hold on," Mano cautioned. "Let's not get ahead of ourselves. I think we should check this place out, make sure it's safe, before we turn a bunch of scientists loose on it. We don't know if the Natia are still living here."

Oliver scanned the scattering of houses with narrowed eyes. "Looks pretty abandoned to me," he said. "Still, everyone be careful. If there *are* people here, they might not take kindly to strangers tramping across their island."

Carefully, they edged into the village. Oliver was right, Shinji thought, gazing around. The place did look pretty abandoned. Weeds and vines had taken over most of the houses, crawling up walls and poking through windows. Many of the thatched roofs had large chunks missing from them, or had simply blown off. When Shinji peeked inside one house, it was a mess of clutter, broken furniture, thatch that had fallen in from the roof, and weeds growing everywhere. Whoever had lived here was long gone.

"Nothing," Lucy announced, ducking out of the hut beside him. "Just bird nests and a bunch of mouse poop."

On her shoulder, Tinker gave a squeak, and she nodded. "Yes, Tinker, I agree. Robot mice are so much better than real mice. Does anyone have any hand sanitizer?"

"All the houses are empty," Phoebe said, coming out from a hut across the path from Shinji. "I think Oliver is right; this village has been deserted. And yes, Lucy, I have hand sanitizer. Always be prepared; that's my motto."

"Let's keep searching," Oliver said. "Even if no one is here, I'd like to know what happened to this place, and where the villagers *did* go."

They continued farther into the village, passing huts of all sizes in various stages of decay. Shinji saw more signs of life and people that used to exist here: fishing poles leaning against the corner of a house, tattered nets hanging out to dry, a canoe perched upside down on a pair of logs. A few chickens scurried through the village, but they were lean and wild-looking, very different from the plump white birds he was used to. Aside from the chickens, nothing moved or made a sound. A somber silence hung over everything, and the signs that this had been a thriving village once made it even more eerie.

A chill ran up Shinji's back. He rubbed his arms to keep goose bumps from forming, looking around nervously. The village felt haunted now, like he was standing in a deserted hamlet full of ghosts and vengeful spirits. He had never really believed in ghosts, but he had never really believed in Coatls, krakens, dragons, and Storm Boars before, either.

Warily, he glanced at each of the houses, half expecting to see a figure in white staring at him from the doors or windows. There were no ghosts, of course, but his imagination continued to torment him.

A glint in the weeds suddenly caught Shinji's attention. Frowning, he paused and crouched down to examine the strange glimmer, pulling aside clumps of long grass to see what lay beneath. A strange gray-green dome came into view as he pulled back the vegetation. It was a little smaller than a basketball and definitely didn't belong in a place like this. Digging his fingers beneath the dome, Shinji found the edges and pulled the strange object free.

It was . . . a helmet, he realized. Not a baseball or football helmet, but definitely a helmet of some kind. It was old, and most of it was covered in rust, but it still had a rotting chin strap, and a greenish tint to the metal.

"Oliver," he called, trotting to catch up with the ex-pirate. Oliver turned, raising his brows, as Shinji walked up to him with the rusty helmet. "I found something. Look at this."

Oliver peered down at the object in his hands and frowned. "That's a soldier's helmet," he stated. "World War Two if I had to guess. Where did you find it?"

Shinji nodded toward the cluster of weeds the helmet had been buried under. "Just right there," he answered. "Why?"

Oliver looked uncharacteristically grim. "I don't like what that means for this place," he muttered, scratching the back of his neck with his cane. "A lot of the Polynesian islands were occupied during World War Two. Tahiti and Bora Bora were both under occupation for several years before the war ended. Not good. Soldiers and isolated communities usually don't mix well."

"Ocean!" Mano called from up ahead, his voice booming through the trees. "I think you should come take a look at this!"

Shinji and Oliver hurried to where Mano, Phoebe, Lucy, and Roux were standing at the edge of the village. All were gazing at something beyond the trees, something Shinji couldn't quite see. "What do you make of that?" Mano said, nodding to the space beyond.

Maneuvering between Lucy and Roux, Shinji frowned. A portion of the thick, tangled rain forest looked like it had been cleared. The undergrowth had grown back and was wilder than ever, but Shinji could see several stumps where trees had been chopped down, and places where the ground had been flattened. In the center of this open space, a large concrete slab sat in the weeds. It looked like a structure might've been there at one point, one that could be hastily constructed and taken down again. Piles of junk lay scattered around the concrete; Shinji saw empty shelves, loose tires, aluminum cans, even a steering wheel lying in the weeds and long grass. Atop the slab, a trio of fifty-gallon drums sat rusting in one corner, a dark brown oil stain baked into the concrete below.

"What is this place?" Lucy wondered, gazing at the piles of junk in disgust. "What happened here?"

"Soldiers," Mano explained. "I'm guessing they used this place as a staging ground for troops during the conflict. Of course, that wouldn't exactly mean good things for the people already living here." He sighed, gazing back to where the village lay, silent and empty in the trees. "Wars are terrible, but the people who get caught in the middle of them are the ones who suffer most. I guess now we know what happened to the people living here."

"We will remember them," Phoebe said emphatically. She stepped forward, her chin raised and her lips tight as she gazed around the lost village. "We have to try to learn as much about this place as we can. The Natia lived here once. This was their home. If we remember them, their stories will not be forgotten. And neither will they."

Mano gave a solemn nod. "Yes. This is what the Society does. We preserve history as much as we can. People, as well as artifacts, deserve to be remembered."

"Yeah, but . . ." Roux gazed around, his expression wary. "I know forbidden places when I see them," he said. "And this place might as well have a bunch of NO TRESPASSING signs tacked up on every tree. What if we wake up a bunch of angry ghosts that don't exactly want us on this island?"

"Worry not." Phoebe pulled a small glass container out of her pack, holding it up triumphantly. "I have salt!" she announced. Roux blinked in confusion, and she raised a finger. "You see, if we're targeted by any angry ghosts, all you have to do is stand inside an unbroken salt circle and you should be fine. Or . . ." She tapped her chin with a knuckle. "Was that the fae who don't like salt?"

"Both," Roux said, and they all glanced at him in surprise. "It works on fairies and ghosts. Or you can also burn sage to keep ghosts away." He blinked at the amazed stares surrounding him. "What? I can read, you know."

"Unbroken salt circle," Mano mused, tapping his chin. "I'm going to have to remember that."

Oliver scratched his head with his parrot cane. "I guess we should let Dr. Grant and the others in on this now," he said. "Before they come looking for us and explode with excitement. Phoebe, round up the research team and tell them we'll be basing here. Ask them what equipment they'll need to get started."

Phoebe gave an excited squeak and bounded off. Oliver shook his head and glanced at Mano. "You and I should probably start looking for a place to set up some kind of camp," he said. "I'm guessing close to the village, but far enough away that we're not in danger of disturbing anything. I've known a few scientists; sometimes they get so excited about their research, they don't notice their camp is right next to an ancient burial site or a sacred temple. I'd like to avoid angry spirits or restless dead if at all possible."

"What should we do?" Shinji asked.

"Oliver!" Phoebe called before he could answer, her voice echoing somewhere inside the village. "Dr. Grant is here. She wants to talk to you right now!"

Oliver cursed under his breath and tapped the golden parrot beak against his temple several times. "Ugh, who put me in charge of this expedition? That was a terrible idea," he muttered. "Kids, you just . . . stay out of trouble."

He walked away with Mano, leaving Shinji and the others alone. They looked at each other uncertainly, until Roux shrugged.

"Okay, then. See you guys later."

"Where do you think you're going?" Lucy wanted to know.

The other boy gave a conspiratorial grin as he backed away. "Me? Nowhere. Just going to look around for . . . stuff."

"Don't you dare steal anything from this village," Lucy warned in a vehement tone. She pointed a finger at him, as if wanting to stab it through his face. "Did you hear what Oliver said about sacred temples and burial sites? If you take anything, you might anger the spirits."

"Trust me, you don't have to worry about that," Roux said. "There are places you steal from and places you don't. An abandoned village in the middle of a jungle, in the middle of a forbidden island, in the middle of a freak storm, in the middle of the ocean . . . is *not* one of the places you steal from. I've seen horror movies." His nose wrinkled, and he shook his head. "I'm not going to touch *anything* in this village. I like to avoid curses and angry ghosts, thanks."

"Then where are you going?" Shinji asked.

"Wow, suspicious much?" Raising an arm, Roux gestured to the adults milling through the village behind them. "I'm just going to look around. We're on a mysterious island surrounded by weird fog that we found because a *shark* pointed us to a treasure map. I mean, how can you not want to check this place out? I thought you two were part of this super-special *explorers* club." He shrugged. "But if you're scared, I'll go myself."

"You know, you don't have to be such a troll." Lucy tossed her braid back and gave him a superior look. "We were going to come anyway. Also, talk to me about being scared when you're hanging from a giant spider's web."

Guardian. This way.

Shinji froze. It wasn't that he heard any actual words, whispering to him in his head or calling to him from the trees. It was more a sensation, a feeling, that something was watching them. He turned and caught a flash of two pinprick blue eyes gazing at him from the ferns at the edge of the jungle. His heart leaped to his throat, but before he could even take a breath, the eyes vanished.

Roux was shaking his head, and from his dubious expression, he was about to make a comment about giant spiders when Shinji brushed past him and walked toward the edge of the jungle.

"Uh, okay, I guess we're exploring now."

"Shinji?" Lucy called as they hurried after him. "What are you doing?"

"I thought I saw something," Shinji muttered. As he walked to the edge of the trees where he had seen the eyes, his breath caught. A small path, barely more than a game trail, snaked away into the jungle until it vanished from sight.

"Ooh, a path," Roux exclaimed, rubbing his hands together. "Maybe it'll lead to an ancient burial ground or hidden temple."

Lucy, peering over Shinji's shoulder, hesitated when she saw the trail. "Oliver told us not to wander off," she said uncertainly.

"No, he didn't," Shinji said. "He told us not to get in trouble."

She glared at him. "You know what I mean."

Shinji took a breath. He couldn't see the eyes anymore, but he knew something was still watching him. Waiting for him. Only him. Because he was the guardian. The others didn't get it; he was the one with the magic and this responsibility he still didn't understand. He just knew when something called, he had to respond.

"Shinji," Lucy warned as he stepped onto the path.

"I won't go far," Shinji said without looking back. He kept moving forward, brushing ferns and branches aside, and heard Roux immediately step onto the trail. After another moment, Lucy followed.

The trail didn't go far, though Shinji had to duck branches and shove more vines aside to get through. Pushing his way through a large clump of ferns, he stumbled from the path into a small clearing. It wasn't large, but it was secluded and quiet, completely isolated from the village and the rest of the camp.

Shinji blinked. In the center of the grove, lying in the dirt, covered in moss, vines, and vegetation, was an airplane. A tiny airplane, with a front propeller completely bent and rusted in the grass. A single cockpit sat behind the propeller with the glass smashed in. One wing lay snapped and broken in the dirt, and a large gash rent one side of the plane nearly in half.

"Whoa," Roux said, eyes wide as he edged into the clearing. "Okay, that's way better than a haunted burial ground with creepy dolls and spiders."

Lucy walked forward as well, squinting up at the wrecked plane. "I wonder what kind it is," she said. "It certainly wouldn't belong to any of the villagers. How did it get here?"

"Maybe it crashed," Shinji guessed. He glanced at the trees overhead and saw that several large branches were broken and snapped, though the destruction seemed to have taken place a long time ago. "It probably belonged to the soldiers who were here. Oliver and Mano are definitely going to want to see this. . . ."

He trailed off, a chill again creeping along his spine. It

was back, that feeling of eyes on the back of his neck. Something was there, in the forest. Tracking them.

Behind Shinji, a twig snapped in the trees, and the bushes rustled. Shinji whirled around, muscles tensing, and heard Lucy gasp. Something was coming, pushing steadily through the ferns and undergrowth. Something . . . big. Not elephant size but not squirrel size, either. Backing away, Shinji held his breath as whatever was coming paused at the edge of the ferns, then stepped into the open.

His stomach dropped. A pure-white boar stood at the edge of the trees, watching him with pale blue eyes. It wasn't huge, but its tusks curved up from its bottom jaw, razor-sharp and deadly, and a bristly mane ran down its back. Shinji froze as the boar stared at him, those pale blue eyes meeting his own. Calmly, it turned and walked away a few steps, then paused and looked back at him once more, its gaze intense.

Shinji's heart pounded in his ears, his stomach cartwheeled inside him. This was it! The Storm Boar, or maybe a messenger of the Storm Boar. It had finally appeared to show him what to do.

"Shinji," he heard Lucy whisper behind him. "Don't move. We should wait until it gets farther away and then try backing up."

"I think you're supposed to climb a tree if it charges," Roux added unhelpfully. "If we can outrun it, that is. I wouldn't try to play dead."

Shinji barely heard them. The eyes of the boar, pale blue and intelligent, stared into his. They filled his vision, as depthless and eternal as the ocean. For a few seconds, he couldn't look away.

Show me, he thought at it. *Where is the Storm Boar? What does it want me to do?*

"Shinji?" Lucy said again. "What are you doing? Come on, let's get out of here."

"It wants me to follow," Shinji told them. The boar continued to stare at him, and he took a step forward. "I have to go."

"Wait!" Lucy grabbed his arm. "You can't just take off into the forest without telling anyone," she hissed. "Especially after a wild pig. We should go back to the camp and let Oliver know what's going on."

Shinji pulled his arm free. "You guys go," he told her, still gazing at the boar. He could feel its impatience, urging him on, and backed away from her. "Go back to camp. Tell the Society what happened. But I have to follow the boar."

"Why?" Lucy demanded.

"Because I've been having visions of this place," Shinji snapped, frustrated. "I've seen this island before, in my dreams. There is something trapped here; it keeps calling to me, wanting me to free it. I think the boar appeared to lead me to the place I'm supposed to go. Just like the shark, showing us to the hidden map. And since I'm a guardian, I'm the only one who can do this. That's why it came for me."

Roux blinked, staring at him like he was insane, but Lucy's eyes narrowed sharply.

"You've been having visions?" she repeated. "Of this island? When? How long has this been going on?"

Shinji felt a thump of guilt in his chest but shrugged. "It doesn't matter. A few days."

"And you didn't tell me?"

"Why? So you could tell Oliver and Phoebe about it?"

Lucy's eyes filled with hurt. Shinji was sorry the moment he said it, but he didn't back down. "I'm the guardian," he went on, wishing he could make her understand. "The Coatl sacrificed itself to grant me the magic of the font. Whatever happened on this island, I have to fix it. The Storm Boar has been leading me here from the beginning. I can't turn back now."

"You don't have to do it by yourself," Lucy began, but Shinji turned and walked across the clearing without bothering to answer.

"Shinji," she said, her voice tense.

The white boar didn't wait for him to get close, but immediately turned and slipped into the undergrowth, vanishing from sight.

"Shinji!" Lucy shouted after him.

Without stopping to think, he followed.

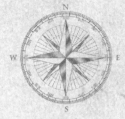

CHAPTER THIRTEEN

Lucy and Roux hurried after him. "This is crazy," Lucy hissed as they caught up. "Following a wild pig into the forest. We're going to get so lost."

"At least it'll be interesting," Roux added, sounding far more nonchalant than he should have. Or maybe he was trying to act like he wasn't affected. "Talking sharks, sirens, and magic ghost pigs. Maybe we'll run into a unicorn next."

"You don't have to come," Shinji insisted. "I don't need help. Go back to the others and let them know what's going on. Tell them I'm fine; I'm just doing guardian stuff."

"Stop it." Lucy glared at him as she shoved a wayward

lock of blond hair behind one ear. "One, I'm not leaving you alone out here with a spooky wild pig, even if you are supposed to be following it," she snapped. "Two, I still can't believe you didn't tell anyone you were having visions. What do we even know about this Storm Boar? Is it a guardian like the Coatl? Why is it trapped? How do we know we're even doing the right thing setting it free? Did you think about any of this, or are we just going in a random direction because a wild boar told us to?"

"You know, maybe this is why I didn't tell you anything," Shinji muttered. "You ask too many questions."

"And you don't ask any!" She made a disgusted motion, prompting Tinker to squeak in protest from her shoulder. "You think you have to do this all yourself. And now we're following a wild pig through a rain forest without any grown-ups knowing where we are, maybe running into something dangerous, just because you want to be a guardian. If my dad heard about this, he'd tell me how dumb it was to rush head-first into something without knowing anything about it."

He felt irritation flare inside him. "Go back to Hightower, then," he snapped, whirling on her. "If you miss it so much, you should just go home. You can have your workshop and all your inventions, and you won't have to worry about me dragging you into danger anymore."

Silence fell. Shinji and Lucy stood there, Shinji flushed and angry, Lucy with her expression gone cold and icy.

After a few moments, Roux gave an uncomfortable cough.

"Uh, hey, guys? The boar isn't stopping. Maybe we can have this fight when we're not in the middle of the forest?"

Shinji looked up and saw the white boar's hindquarters still walking away from them through the trees, its short, bristly tail flicking from side to side. He glanced back at Lucy, but she wasn't looking at him anymore.

"Fine, go follow your pig, then," she said in a cold voice. "I'm still not leaving you out here alone. But if something happens, it's not my fault."

Guilt gnawed at Shinji. Why had he said that? That was the second time he had thrown Lucy's upbringing back in her face. But there was no time to talk about it now; the boar wasn't stopping and had nearly disappeared into the undergrowth. Suddenly afraid that if he lost sight of the boar it would disappear, Shinji jogged after it. He would apologize to Lucy later; right now, the Storm Boar was counting on him.

He had to find out what it wanted. He had to get *something* right.

They continued through the rain forest, following the pale form of the boar along game trails and narrow paths. Nothing stopped them or got in their way. The trail, though it wound lazily through the thick undergrowth, was mostly clear. Shinji saw more birds and insects, but no larger wildlife. Except the white boar keeping just within their sight several yards ahead.

Evening started to fall. The shadows around them

lengthened, and the forest grew dimmer the farther they went. The white boar was easily visible, though, almost seeming to glow as it slipped through the shadows, like a ghost in the night.

"It's getting late," Lucy said, gazing nervously at the sky, which was now a deep, bright orange. "Everyone back at camp is going to be worried about us. Maybe we should text them, just to let them know we're okay?"

"I suppose," Shinji said. He was glad that Lucy was talking to him. She was still angry but seemed to have put their argument aside for now. At least they weren't marching through the woods in complete, awkward silence. "Just don't tell them where we are."

"No worries there," Lucy muttered. "I don't *know* where we are."

"I'm surprised they haven't called you," Roux put in. "Knowing that Ocean guy, I would've expected your phones to be buzzing every two seconds."

That *was* strange, now that Shinji thought about it. He'd been in such a hurry to follow the white boar, he hadn't given Oliver, Phoebe, and the rest of the expedition a second thought. Of course they'd be worried if the three of them vanished without a trace, and were probably out searching for them, now. Given that, it was weird that Shinji's phone hadn't made any noise at all.

"Oh no," Lucy murmured, and he heard the alarm in her voice. "Shinji, check your phone."

He did. The screen was completely blank. There were no bars, no buttons, nothing but an empty blue screen. It wasn't just that there was no signal; the phone was utterly bricked.

"Guess your white pig doesn't want us calling for help," Roux said.

Lucy bit her lip and tugged the end of her braid. "I don't like this," she said. "Something about this whole thing feels off. Shinji, are you *sure* you don't want to go back?"

Shinji shook his head. He didn't know how to explain it. Ever since he had been given the magic of the font, he'd felt lost. Like he was supposed to do *something*; he just didn't know what. Now, for the first time, he had a clear picture. The Storm Boar needed his help, and he was going to answer that call.

"I can't," he told Lucy, who just sighed in resigned exasperation. "I can't go back. I have to keep going."

"Probably a smart move, since we have no idea how to go back even if we wanted to," Roux said in a voice filled with false cheerfulness. "The trail disappeared a long time ago. In other good news, I think we've reached the volcano."

Shinji looked up. Through the branches overhead, he could see the steep side of the mountain rising into the air, and his skin prickled. The volcano. The center of the island. If he was an ancient mythological creature who had gotten itself trapped somehow, that's where he would be. It was the only place that made sense.

Besides, he could suddenly feel . . . something, coming

from the volcano. It was very faint, barely noticeable, but if he really concentrated, he could feel it, pulsing like heat waves against his skin.

Anger.

Shinji shivered. He remembered the voice in his dreams, bellowing at him from the clouds. He remembered the furious blue eyes glaring down at him. If the Storm Boar was this mad, was it a good idea to bring his friends into its lair?

But then again, if he had been trapped for who knew how long, he would be angry, too. He would just have to make sure the Storm Boar didn't attack his friends. Once he set it free, it would calm down. It would be less ferocious and more . . . peaceful.

He hoped.

"Look at that," Lucy said, nodding to something in the bushes. A small shrine had been constructed at the edge of a game trail. It was a simple altar made of stone, with wooden bowls and clay pots sitting atop it, though all were empty. "What do you think those are?"

"Offerings to the volcano?" Shinji guessed with a shrug. "Or maybe to the Storm Boar."

A glimmer of white caught his attention. The white pig was walking steadily up the mountain, following a narrow path that wound up the side of the cliffs. Roux followed Shinji's trail of vision, then sighed.

"Following a ghost pig to the top of a volcano. Yeah, this

sounds like a great idea. If you get the sudden urge to jump off the cliff into molten lava, be sure to tell us."

Lucy's lips thinned. Shinji knew she wanted to protest or urge him to turn around, but she didn't say anything, and they continued to follow the boar.

Up the side of the volcano.

The path up the mountain started off easy, but as they got higher, the trees and vegetation began to disappear, the air grew thin, and the trail turned rocky and steep. Soon they were all panting and gasping for breath. Shinji stumbled once and fell, cutting open his palm as it hit the jagged black rock of the volcano. Lucy silently handed him a roll of gauze from her emergency travel pack, and though she didn't say *I told you so*, the implication was clear.

Finally, as the sun began to set, they reached the top. Standing at the edge of the mountain, Shinji gazed down into the caldera and felt his stomach drop. The bottom of the bowl was filled with bubbling magma, glowing a bright orange against the coming twilight. Columns of smoke writhed up from the surface of the lava lake, billowing into the air. Even standing at the top of the volcano, Shinji could feel the heat from where he stood, radiating against his skin, like looking at the sun on the hottest summer day.

The white pig was still moving away from them, following a narrow switchback trail that wound its way down the side into the caldera. Into the heart of the volcano.

Roux drew in a slow breath. "Oh man, we should not be here," he muttered, staring wide-eyed at the burbling lava. His nonchalant attitude was starting to fray a little, alarm and fear showing through the cracks in his bravado. "That is definitely not a dormant volcano. You guys *sure* you don't want to go back?"

"I can't go back now," Shinji replied, feeling his forehead start to bead with sweat. A trickle of moisture ran into his eyes, and he blinked it away. "I have to keep going. We're close. I can feel it. Really, you guys don't have to come. I'm not asking you to walk into lava with me. You can go back to camp and let Oliver know what's going on. I'll be fine."

"Yeah, sure." Roux shook his head, the mask of flippancy falling into place again. "Like we're going to leave you on the edge of a freaking pit of lava. Besides, there's no way I'm going back to tell that Ocean guy I watched you walk into an active volcano. That sounds like a great way to get myself thrown overboard."

"We came all this way," Lucy added, staring at the bubbling lava beneath them. "We're not leaving now." She turned a fierce glare on Shinji. "So, *you're* just going to have to make sure we don't step on the wrong stone and make the whole island erupt or something."

"Yeah," Shinji muttered. "No pressure."

Very carefully, they descended the path into the caldera. Shinji hugged the volcano wall as tightly as he could, trying not to look down. The heat was intense. Pebbles and dirt broke away from his shoes as he shuffled along the edge, the rocks tumbling down the ravine until they hit the surface of the lava pool.

About halfway down the side of the volcano, the narrow trail widened a bit until it became a rocky ledge. At first, Shinji thought he saw the mouth of a cave along the volcano wall, but when he got closer, he realized it was a huge stone door sitting beneath a rocky overhang. The door was old, covered in soot and ash, but the carved head of the enormous boar peered out at them.

Shinji's eyes widened, his stomach twisting with both excitement and recognition. It was the same door as the one he had seen in his vision. Whatever was calling him waited on the other side. He tensed as they got closer, expecting the carved eyes to flash open, pinning him with an electric-blue glare, but the boar's head remained stony and lifeless as they approached.

"Well, I'd say we're definitely in the right place," Roux said, frowning as he gazed at the stone door. "So, how do we get through?"

The white boar was nowhere to be seen, as if it had ghosted its way right through the mountain. Lucy glanced at Shinji. "When we were at the Coatl's temple, there was a door like this," she said. "Remember? You just had to press your hand against the stones to get it to open."

Shinji shrugged. "Yeah, I guess I can try that," he said.

Raising his arm, he stepped up to the door and firmly pushed his palm against the rough surface.

Nothing happened.

"Huh," Roux said. "Maybe the ghost pig has a different doorbell."

Shinji dropped his arm. "Any other bright ideas?"

"Hmm," Lucy mused, looking thoughtful as she continued to stare at the stone barrier. "What if you show the door your tattoo?" she said. "I'm thinking it might react to seeing a guardian. Try that."

Feeling a little silly, Shinji raised his arm again, this time pointing the Coatl tattoo directly in front of the boar's head. But there was no reaction; the stone eyes remained stone, and the door remained firmly shut.

"Press the tattoo against the door," Lucy suggested. "Maybe that will work."

Shinji tried. It didn't.

"Ooh, use your head and head-butt it open," Roux chimed in. "Just bend over and run into it as hard as you can."

Shinji did not take that suggestion.

"What if there's a certain kind of knock?" Lucy wondered. "Like a secret pattern or a code to make the door open. Do you remember anything like that in the Coatl's temple? Or maybe from your vision?"

Before Shinji could reply, Roux stepped forward. "Okay, look," he said in a voice of exaggerated patience. "This is silly. Sometimes, doors are locked. Sometimes, valuable junk is guarded by high-tech security and really good dead bolts. But sometimes, doors are just left open. And you never know unless you turn the knob. Maybe we should just push on it and see if it opens before we try any secret knocks or impossible passwords."

"It's a huge stone door that leads to an ancient creature of mythological power," Lucy pointed out. "Why do you think we can just walk inside?"

Ignoring her, Roux turned and put both hands against the stone surface, then glanced at Shinji. "Come on," he said, "help me out. Let's see if Mr. Ghost Pig guards his valuables or not."

"You're not going to just push the door open," Lucy insisted as Shinji stepped forward and put both hands against the stone like Roux had done. "It probably weighs, like, fifty tons. Plus, this is the entrance to the territory of a giant boar. Giant boars aren't known for being helpful, or nice. It's not just going to swing open if you try to—"

"Push," Roux said.

Shinji and Roux pushed. For a moment, nothing happened. It felt to Shinji like they were pushing against the side of a mountain. But then something gave way, and the door made a grinding, groaning sound as it swung slowly back. Through the doorway, a narrow stone tunnel wound its way into the darkness.

Lucy clucked her tongue. "Huh. First time for everything, I suppose."

Shinji stared into the passageway. He could feel something deep within the mountain and knew that once he stepped through the door, there was no turning back. Lucy and Roux stood beside him; could he really ask them to follow him down into the unknown?

"Come on," Roux said, as if reading his thoughts. "Are we doing this or not?"

"Yes," Lucy added. "We've come this far and opened the door. Might as well keep going. Tinker . . ." She raised her hand, and the mechanical mouse hopped into it. "Illuminate," she whispered, and Tinker's eyes flashed as two thin yet oddly powerful beams of white light emerged from them, shining into the dark passage. Lucy raised her arm, and the mechanical mouse leaped off her hand onto Shinji's shoulder, weighing almost nothing as he crouched there, shining his light into the darkness of the tunnel.

"Let's go," Lucy told Shinji, gesturing down the passageway. "We'll follow you."

Shinji nodded and took a deep breath. With Tinker's light showing the way, they stepped through the door into the side of the volcano.

CHAPTER
FOURTEEN

The passage didn't go very far. Shinji and the others had only taken a few dozen steps into the tunnel before it ended in a long stone stairwell, descending into the darkness. Torches jutted out of brackets on either side of the tunnel, flames flickering brightly. No one asked how that was possible; the force in the mountain was obviously waiting for them. Without hesitation, Shinji and the others started downward, heading deeper into the volcano.

At first, the atmosphere in the stairwell was damp and cool. However, the farther they went, the hotter the air became. Shinji was sweating again, moisture trickling down his forehead and running into his eyes, making them sting.

Finally they reached the bottom of the stairs, where another short stone passageway continued into the mountain.

"Man, it's like an oven in here," Roux said, wiping his brow as they walked down the tunnel, Tinker's eye beams lighting the way. "And what is that smell?" He waved a hand in front of his nose. "Ugh, that's nasty. Who had too many beans for lunch?"

"It's sulfur," Lucy told him, wrinkling her nose. "So don't even look at me. I wonder how close we are to the actual lava."

The tunnel ended, opening up into an enormous cavern. Large cracks snaked along the floor, venting steam into the air. Spikes hung from the ceiling, not made of stone, but shiny, black, and wickedly pointed, like obsidian. They reminded Shinji of huge shark teeth, dangling ominously overhead.

"Ugh, I feel like we're in a mouth," Lucy muttered.

"A mouth that really needs toothpaste," Shinji added.

Roux snickered. "And a breath mint—"

There was a crunch that seemed to echo through the chamber, and Roux's foot disappeared as a portion of floor crumbled beneath him. Roux yelled and flailed his arms, trying to keep his balance as more cracks appeared in the rocks at his feet, revealing an ominous red glow beneath. He teetered a moment, then started to fall.

Lucy lunged, grabbed Roux's wrist, and yanked him forward just as the stones he'd been standing on crumbled and dropped into the bubbling pool under the surface of the rocks. Panting, Lucy and Roux swiftly backed away from the hole, joining Shinji, who let out a sigh of relief.

"That was close!" Lucy gasped as Roux leaned against a rock and slid down into a sitting position. His face pale, he stared at the hole he'd almost fallen into, as if just realizing how close he'd come to a very painful death.

"Are you guys all right?" Shinji asked.

Roux nodded, wiping sweat from his eyes. "I haven't had a bath in a month," he muttered. "I do not want my first one to be in lava." He glanced at Lucy, giving her a wry smile. "You have good reflexes for a rich tourist girl," he said almost begrudgingly. "I would've expected you to let me fall."

Shinji crossed his arms. "You have a weird way of saying 'Thanks for not letting me fall into lava and melt to death.'"

"Sorry." Roux held up both hands. "I didn't mean it like that. It's just . . . I don't know anyone else who would've bothered to help me." He shrugged, glancing at Lucy. "So, uh . . . thanks. For not letting me fall into lava and melt to death."

"It's fine." Lucy waved him off, though she gave Shinji a quick smile. "Don't worry about it. When you're a member of the Society of Explorers and Adventurers, you have to be ready for anything. Sharks, snake warriors, rickety bridges over ravines . . ." She glanced at Shinji with a wry grimace. "You're not the first person I've saved from falling to their death while on a mission for SEA."

Shinji held out a hand and pulled Roux to his feet while Lucy gazed around the cavern. "This must be a lava tube or something," she mused, watching steam writhe out of a crevice and coil up toward the ceiling. Glancing at the ground, she gently tapped the rocks with the toe of her boot. "I bet the whole floor beneath us is magma."

"Oh, that's great," Roux said, staring at the other side of the cave, which now felt like a million miles away. "So, how do we get across?"

"Very carefully." Lucy grimaced. "As Scarlett would say, 'No one think heavy thoughts.'"

With the utmost care, they tiptoed across the cavern. Shinji found himself holding his breath every time he put his foot down, ready to freeze or leap back should the floor crumble under his shoes. Sometimes, he could hear the lava, slowly churning and bubbling right below them, and sweat ran down his face from more than the heat.

After what felt like hours but was really only a few minutes, they reached the other side of the cavern. The ominous burbling of lava under their shoes faded, and the temperature got a little cooler. Once they were in yet another tunnel, Shinji took a deep breath of not-quite-stifling air, though it still felt like he was breathing through a hair dryer.

Tinker's eye beams continued to light the way as they walked, and eventually they came to yet another cavern, though this one wasn't quite as large. Stone pillars seemed to march down the center of the chamber, leading to a flight of stone steps. At the top of the stairs sat the massive head of a stone boar, jaws open in a silent bellow, fangs and tusks jutting up like stalagmites. Two doors sat within the boar's mouth, a sullen red glow pulsing through the cracks and spilling over the stones. Shinji's stomach dropped, and his heart beat faster when he saw it.

"This is it," he whispered. "The heart of the volcano. It's on the other side of those doors."

"What is?" Roux asked. "Also, are you seriously going to walk right into that pig's open mouth?" But Shinji was already moving, hurrying across the rocky floor. The boar head loomed before him, towering and ominous, the eyes seeming to glare down at him as he jogged toward it.

Yes, whispered a voice in his head. *Come forward. Free me.*

With a low rumble that shook the ground, the huge doors in front of them swung open. Dust and smoke billowed out, and a wave of heat hit Shinji in the face. Startled, he stumbled to a halt at the edge of the open jaws, watching the doors continue to swing slowly outward, until they hit the sides of the cavern wall with a rumbling boom.

Shinji's heart pounded. Stone tusks rose into the air on either side of him, the maw lined with teeth that looked like they would easily crush him to pulp if the jaws decided to come to life the second he stepped inside. At the back of the pig's mouth, the open doors beckoned, that sullen red glow making the jaws look almost bloody.

"Shinji." Lucy's voice echoed quietly beside him. She

gazed at the open doorway, her face bathed in the red glow beyond. "Are you *sure* you want to do this? We don't know what's inside. We don't know what will happen if we go forward."

"I think I agree with Lucy." Roux, gazing up at the snarling mouth of the boar, shook his head. Too uneasy to even realize he'd called Lucy by her name for the first time. "That is not the face of a happy pig."

"We're with you, whatever happens," Lucy assured Shinji. "But are you absolutely sure you have to do this? There's still time to turn around and go back."

Shinji stared through the doorway. He couldn't see anything beyond the frame but that eerie red glow. He could still *feel* it, though. The presence that had been calling him. The voice that had been invading his dreams. It was there, just on the other side. Waiting for him.

Carefully, he stepped into the open jaws, between the long, curving fangs. For a split second, his imagination saw the mouth move, the jaws coming to life and snapping shut like a bear trap. But the statue remained stony and lifeless, and after a tense heartbeat, Shinji relaxed. Behind him, Roux gave a loud exhale that showed he really thought Shinji might get crunched and swallowed like a bug.

Shinji glanced at his friends from within the boar's jaws and smiled grimly. "You guys coming or not?"

Lucy groaned. "If we don't get eaten, remind me to punch you later," she growled.

"Noted," Roux added. "I'll hold him down for you."

For the first time ever, the two shared a real smile. Shinji tried not to read too much into the reason behind it.

With Lucy on one side and Roux on the other, Shinji walked through the open jaws of the Storm Boar and into the heart of the volcano.

CHAPTER
FIFTEEN

Hot. It was insanely hot. Beyond the tunnel, the air glowed red, and Shinji could hear the slow burbles and churning of molten lava. Which was not surprising, given the enormous magma lake sitting in the center of the cavern. The entire chamber was a huge lava bowl, with a narrow ledge circling the rim. As Shinji stepped through the door, he could feel pulses of magic coming from the center of the bowl, threaded throughout the whole room. Shinji heard Lucy gasp as she, too, realized where they were.

"The heart of the volcano," Lucy whispered, staring at the bubbling magma. "It's . . . a font!"

A font, like the one they had found in the Coatl's temple.

A place where magic bubbled to the surface, affecting the land around it. These fonts had once dotted the world, though there were far fewer of them now than there used to be. The magic of the fonts granted good fortune and prosperity to those who used them, but they were also guarded by mythological creatures of great power. Guardians.

"Wait." Shinji jerked up. "Then that means . . . is the Storm Boar the guardian of the font?"

Another guardian. Of course. That made sense. If the volcano was a font, strange and magical things would happen around it, affecting the outside world. The weird storm, the creepy fog, the invisible island no one had found . . . it was all because the magic of the font was protecting this place. And the Storm Boar was its guardian.

But then why was the Storm Boar trapped here? Why did it need Shinji's help?

Even more confident, he stepped farther into the room, looking around carefully. Along the wall surrounding the chamber, pictures and images had been carved into the rough stone, creating a mural that circled the whole room. Shinji saw images representing men and women, the ocean, the volcano, and several large pictures of a giant boar. They might have told a story if he focused on them, but the creature in the center of the room demanded all his attention.

In the very center of the lake, a single flat rock rose out of the magma. Four stone torches had been placed at every corner, burning with bright flames. Standing in the middle of that rock, watching them all with a baleful glare, was an old white boar with electric-blue eyes.

Shinji stared in shock. Even after they had seen the white pig and followed it here, he was expecting something different. It wasn't the same pig, but it certainly wasn't the Storm Boar from his visions. He thought the Storm Boar would be gigantic, surrounded by lightning and rumbling thunder. He thought it would be angry. But the creature in the center of the molten lake did not look like the fearsome guardian of a font. There were no strands of lightning snapping along its hide, no booming voice in his head, no earthshaking fury. Apart from its unusually colored eyes and coat, it could have been just an ordinary pig.

"Wait, *that's* what you've been looking for?" Roux sounded as surprised as Shinji felt. "It's just an old pig. Don't tell me we came all this way for a barely alive piece of bacon."

"Something is wrong," Lucy whispered. She raised an arm, fingers splayed, toward the center of the lava pool, where the boar waited. "I can feel the magic of the font, especially coming from the torches, but it stops when it hits the platform," she said. "Like there's an empty space where the magic *should* reach but doesn't."

Shinji narrowed his eyes, staring at the boar. For a moment, his vision blurred, and a shimmering dome of magic covered the platform, pulsing with energy. The torches at the edge of the platform flared and snapped, and each time they did, the dome flickered brightly.

"There's a barrier," Shinji muttered. "Covering the platform. I think it's keeping the magic from the Storm Boar."

The Storm Boar's electric-blue eyes locked with his, and Shinji felt his stomach twist. *Free me,* a voice in his head rumbled. *The barrier put here by the betrayers keeps me from the magic of the font. The idol calls me, and I will have its call returned. Break the seal, guardian. Snuff out the torches, and set me free.*

Shinji took a deep breath. This was why he was here, why he had come. This was the moment he would prove himself worthy to be a guardian. Almost of its own accord, his hand raised toward the platform and the boar trapped within. He could feel magic everywhere, coming from the font, from the torches, from inside him.

"Clear your mind," he whispered to himself. "Let the magic flow through you."

A breeze began to swirl around his fingers, growing stronger and faster every second. His breath caught, and the magic sputtered a bit, but instead of trying to hold on to it, he simply let it go. The wind grew stronger, tugging at his hair and making the torches around the platform dance and snap. Inside the barrier, the Storm Boar bellowed with excitement.

"Shinji!"

Something grabbed his arm, making him jump. The magic fizzled, and the wind died away. Shinji blinked and turned on Lucy, who stared back with a half-fearful, half-worried look on her face.

"Shinji, wait. I don't know if this is a good idea."

He scowled at her. "What are you talking about? This is why I'm here."

"Look at the pictures on the walls," she said, pointing to the crude murals surrounding the chamber. "They tell a story. The people here, the Natia, once worshiped the boar." She nodded to the first sketch, showing a crowd of people with their arms raised to a great boar overhead. "They had an idol of the boar that was kept in a special place in the village. See? That's a picture of it on the pedestal."

On the platform, the Storm Boar was growing angrier, snorting, tossing its head and pawing at the ground. Shinji could feel its impatience and felt his own impatience rise up in response. "What's your point?" he snapped at Lucy.

"My point is maybe we shouldn't mess around with things we don't understand," she shot back. "Maybe we should go tell Oliver, Phoebe, and everyone else, and see what they think about this!"

"Yeah, I'm gonna have to agree with Snowflake," Roux added, and the fear in his voice made Shinji pause. For the first time, he sounded terrified. His face was pale, his eyes wide as he stared at Shinji. "You know, I was okay with the talking sharks and mystical islands and ghost pigs and all the weirdness that's happened ever since I snuck onto your crazy ship. But now we're standing in the center of a volcano and Shinji is throwing around magic like a freaking Sith

Lord." Roux scrubbed his fingers through his scalp, making his hair stand on end, and gave a sharp gesture with both hands. "I'm done," he said. "I'm out. Weirdness level is max. Let's get out of here and go get the adults before this pig decides it wants to eat us for lunch."

Now even Roux was against him. Shinji clenched his jaw. "You don't get it, do you?" he snapped at them both. "This is the reason I've been having visions. This is how we even found the island in the first place! The Storm Boar called me here because I'm a guardian and I'm the only one that can help it. The whole point of me coming to this island was to free the Storm Boar. There's no way I'm stopping now!"

Yanking his arm from Lucy's grasp, Shinji whirled back to the platform and raised an arm, calling his powers to life once more.

Wind swirled through the chamber, snapping at the torches, making shadows dance wildly along the walls. It tore at his hair and clothes, swirling dust and pebbles around the room. Lucy and Roux shielded their eyes, staggering away from Shinji as the gale whipped through the room and rushed along the walls.

With a howl, the flames atop the torches were snuffed out. Inside the barrier, the Storm Boar raised its head and roared as, with the sound of breaking glass, the shimmering dome of energy shattered, magic fraying apart and vanishing into the air. Shinji felt a rush of power flood the place as the

Storm Boar stood. For a moment, his vision went white, and he felt himself falling.

The soldiers pushed through the door, indifferent to the pleas of the gathered priests and worshipers. They had already finished with the rest of the town, breaking into homes, taking everything of value. But the temple should have been safe. The soldiers had been here before, treading upon the holy spaces with a casual disdain and indifference, but they had never given the relics of the people more than a casual glance.

This time was different. Something in the set of their shoulders, in the blend of determination and fear on their faces said louder than words that, as the soldiers made ready to depart the island for the final time, even the holy ground of the temple itself would not be spared.

An elder pushed himself to his feet and moved to block the door, placing his aged body between the soldiers and the sanctity of the temple. It was a wasted effort. A rifle butt rose and fell, and the elder crumpled, unconscious, to the ground.

Orders were barked, the foreign tongue that had become so familiar to so many of the islanders during the occupation, demanding payment, claiming that a debt was owed. Payment? For what? For a protection that was never asked for? For building their supply depots on sacred ground and scaring away the fish with their massive ships and smoke-belching engines? For bringing the ugly realities of war to their shores?

Others were standing now, shouting angrily, but the headman was there, counseling peace, speaking against resistance. His passivity earned a sneer from the officer, and another order was barked. The men moved toward the alcoves where the sacred idols rested. They showed no sign of hesitancy, no sign of remorse as they grabbed the carefully worked statues—statues crafted of precious metals and glimmering stone—from their altars, shoving them unceremoniously into rucksacks. And then they were before the main altar, the altar where the idol of the Storm Boar rested. Where it had sat, going back longer than any in the room, or their grandparents, or *their* grandparents before them could remember.

The soldiers hesitated now, and well they should, for even these soldiers, so out of tune with the island and its ways, even they could feel power radiating from the idol. The relic that represented the pact between the people and the island guardian. The headman stepped forward now, hand raised, pleading with the men not to take the relic. Tragedy would befall the island and everyone on it, he warned. If the idol was stolen, they were all doomed.

The soldiers hesitated, looking uncertain. But the officer shouted once more, and one man, perhaps braver, or maybe stupider, than the rest, reached forth a trembling hand and tumbled the sacred icon into the open backpack of another.

A terrible tremor shook the island, dust falling from the ceiling of the temple, raining down like ash as the island voiced its displeasure.

YOU HAVE BROKEN THE PACT, boomed a deep voice that seemed to come from the earth itself. *THE PROMISE BETWEEN THIS ISLAND AND HUMANKIND HAS BEEN DEFILED. NOW KNOW MY WRATH!*

The soldiers, faces locked in masks of fear and uncertainty, turned and ran.

But with them went the sacred idol and the treasures of the people.

And the Storm Boar was angry.

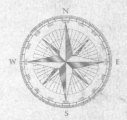

CHAPTER SIXTEEN

With a gasp, Shinji opened his eyes, seeing the chamber and the white pig in the center of the lava pool. The white pig was growing, becoming bigger by the second. Lightning strands flickered to life along its hide, and the air grew sharp with the smell of ozone and rain. The boar was now the size of a grizzly bear, but it kept growing, towering over them with no signs of slowing down. Its bristly fur was now a blinding white, its tusks longer than Shinji's arm, and its eyes were the electric-blue-white of a lightning strand.

"Shinji." Lucy knelt beside him, her eyes wide with fear. "Are you all right? What's happening?"

"I . . ." Staggering upright, Shinji clutched at his hair,

trying to make sense of the images he'd just seen. Horror filled him as he realized what he had done. Lucy had been right. In freeing the Storm Boar, he had put everyone in danger.

"I know what happened," Shinji whispered, pulling away from Lucy. He felt sick, but the immediate threat of the angry Storm Boar shut out everything else. "Let me go; I have to talk to the Storm Boar before it destroys the whole island."

"What?!"

Thunder boomed, shaking the ground. Sinji, Lucy, and Roux lost their balance and fell, sprawling to the stones, as the massive Storm Boar raised its head and bellowed. Rocks came loose from the walls, plummeting down and landing with loud splashes in the lava. The mountain beneath them shuddered, long rumbles coming from deep within the earth.

"If you're going to do something, do it fast!" Roux called, shielding his face as a melon-size chunk of rock landed with a crash a few feet away. "Before this angry sausage brings the whole mountain down on top of us!"

"Storm Boar!" Shinji scrambled to his feet, throwing out a hand, and the huge pig turned to glare down at him. It towered over Shinji, a mountain of bristling fur and siz-zling lightning strands. "Listen to me!" he called up to it. "I know you're angry, but the people who are responsible for this aren't here anymore. Those men who took your artifacts are long gone."

The Storm Boar roared, so loudly the ground shook again. More rocks plummeted into the lava, causing splashes of red-hot magma to splatter everywhere. Roux yelped and scrambled away as drops of lava rained down near him. Lightning flashed from the Storm Boar's hide, striking the walls and causing several explosions of rock and stone. In the magma pool beneath the boar, the lava surged up, waves crashing against the sides and spilling over the edge. Cracks opened up in the ground, growing wider as the entire mountain continued to shake and tremble.

Run, whispered a voice in Shinji's head. He was unsure if it was the Storm Boar, the Coatl, or his own instincts, but he didn't question it. Leaping back, barely dodging a rock as it smashed into the floor, he spun and saw Lucy still on the ground, staring up at the boar as it squealed and thrashed about. Rushing over, Shinji grabbed her arm and pulled her to her feet.

"We've got to get out of here!"

"Oh, you think?" Roux snapped, staggering up beside them. His eyes were wide, his hair standing on end as lightning flickered and sizzled around them. "What was your first clue: the rising lava or the giant rampaging lightning boar?"

"Come on!" Lucy cried, and they fled the chamber, through the jaws of the boar statue, as the real Storm Boar's furious squeals and bellows rang out behind them.

I caused this, Shinji thought as they burst out of the room and began running. Rocks and bits of the ceiling rained down around them, plinking off the stones and stinging his skin. *If the Storm Boar destroys the island or hurts anyone else, it'll be my fault.*

The mountain continued to shake. Lucy tripped and fell once, crying out as she struck the bottom of the stairs. Both Shinji and Roux immediately whirled, caught her by the arms, and pulled her upright.

"Tinker!" she gasped, looking around wildly. "Where's Tinker? I lost him."

A squeak caught their attention. Tinker was racing toward them over the rocks, his body a metallic blur against the dark stones. Pebbles pelted down around him, and he dodged from side to side as he scampered.

"Come on, Tinker!" Lucy cried, holding out her hand.

A shadow fell over the mouse as he lunged forward, and a huge chunk of rock dropped from the ceiling. It was too big and too fast for Tinker to dodge, and Lucy gasped as it plummeted toward him.

Shinji acted without thinking. He raised an arm, and a gust of wind rushed across the floor, catching Tinker and blowing him out of the way just as the rock smashed into the stones. The mouse reached Lucy and raced up her arm. She clutched him to her in relief.

Roux caught Shinji's eye as they started running. Lucy had been too concerned with Tinker's safety to notice, but Roux had seen Shinji use his magic again. But there was no time to question it. Massive chunks of rock dropped from the ceiling and crashed to the ground, causing tremors beneath their feet. The noise was deafening. Shinji, Lucy, and Roux wove through the cavern, breathless, and ducked into the tunnel.

With a roar, the ceiling behind them collapsed, filling the entrance with stones and blocking the way back to the cavern.

"Man, this Storm Boar isn't playing around." Roux gasped as they staggered away from the blocked exit. "What's got him so riled up?"

Lucy looked at Shinji, who flushed. He still couldn't believe he had been so easily manipulated. He thought he'd been doing something right, something only a guardian could do, and now the whole island, and everyone on it, was in danger because of it. Lucy's eyes narrowed. "You know something," she said. "You said something about men and artifacts. What happened, Shinji?"

A muffled roar sounded through the mountain behind them. Shinji gritted his teeth. "The soldiers who came to the island stole something when they left," he answered shortly. "They took a bunch of ancient artifacts that were sacred to the village and sailed away with them. One of them was the idol that represented the pact between the Storm Boar and the Natia people. And now he wants it back."

"So, I was right," Lucy said, and Shinji clenched his jaw. He couldn't argue or say anything in his defense. This whole mess *was* his fault, because he had been too stubborn, too convinced that he was doing guardian things, to listen.

"Yeah," Shinji growled. "You were right, and I was a moron. Go ahead and say it."

But Lucy sighed and did not say *I told you so*, like he expected. "So, what do we do now?" she asked instead.

A massive rumble went through the ground under their feet, and the tunnel walls began to crack. A stone came loose from the ceiling and nearly crushed Shinji's foot when it fell.

"Talk later," Roux said. "Run now!"

They broke into a sprint, aiming for the end of the tunnel, as the cracks in the walls got wider and the floor began to split apart. Bursting from the passageway, they stared in horror at the chamber before them. The floor was now riddled with lava pools, gaping red pits where the ground had fallen away to reveal the magma below. As they stared around in dismay, one of the obsidian spikes on the ceiling came free, plunging to the ground and sending chips of flinty rock flying in every direction.

"What now?" Lucy asked, looking at Shinji. "The floor could give way if we try to walk on it, or one of those spikes could hit us if they come loose."

"Well, we can't stand here," Shinji replied. "We have to find a way across."

"Okay." Roux took a deep breath and stepped forward. "Follow me," he said. "I'll try to find the safest way across. It'll be fine, just like sneaking around the harbor warehouse at night and avoiding all the cameras and security guards."

"Roux, wait." Lucy held out her hand, a worried frown on her face. "What if you fall in?"

He gave a crooked little smile. "Then you'll know not to step in that spot."

Before Shinji could reply, Roux darted into the cavern, giving them no choice but to follow. He moved quickly, skipping over cracks, skirting the edges of magma pools, his gaze constantly sweeping the ground in search of the best paths. Several times, he stopped, shaking his head, and headed off in another direction. Shinji could only guess that it was too dangerous or the floor was too unstable to keep going.

But Roux was so focused on watching the ground, he forgot about the dangers overhead. With a crack, an enormous obsidian spike suddenly broke from the ceiling and fell, aiming right for the top of his head.

"Roux, look out!" Shinji cried, and lunged, tackling the other boy around the waist and shoving them both out of the way. The stone barely missed them, crashing to the ground and punching through the floor to the lava beneath. Shinji and Roux hit the ground at the same time, and Shinji felt the stones beneath him crumble. He tried to scramble to his feet, but the ground under his shoes gave way, dropping him and Roux into the hole.

As Lucy screamed, Shinji lashed out wildly and felt his hand connect with the stone wall. At the same time, his shoes hit solid ground, and he pressed himself back against the rock. Somehow, he had landed on a narrow outcropping several feet down. Maybe ten feet below him, lava steamed and bubbled, blasting his face with heat. A portion of the ledge he stood on crumbled, dropping into the bubbling magma below. Looking up, he saw the bottom of Roux's feet, legs swinging wildly as the other boy dangled from the edge.

"Roux! Shinji!"

Lucy's face appeared, peering anxiously down at them. Reaching over the edge, she grabbed the back of Roux's shirt and pulled. Grunting, Roux kicked his legs, scrabbling and clawing at the ground, and managed to drag himself out of the hole.

Panting, both Lucy and Roux gazed down at Shinji, their faces pale. Shinji peered back, flattening himself against the narrow ledge as hard as he could. "Can you climb?" Roux called down to him.

"Are you crazy?" Shinji responded. The outcropping barely offered enough room for his feet, and beyond it was a sheer drop into molten-hot magma. "I can't climb a straight wall. Is there a rope or a branch you can toss down?"

Roux gazed around the cavern and shook his head. "No, there's nothing here," he said. "You're going to either have to climb or jump."

"Shinji!" Lucy cried, pointing down wildly. "The lava is rising!"

Heart in his throat, Shinji peered down and saw she was right. The magma was rising, creeping steadily closer to the ledge, swallowing rocks as it came.

"Shinji!" Roux yelled, and lay on his stomach, holding his hand out to him as far as it would go. "You're gonna have to jump!" he called as Lucy did the same, lying down and reaching out a hand. "Jump, grab hold, and we'll pull you out."

Shinji's heart crashed in his ears, but there was no other choice, and no time for anything else. The lava was only a few feet from the bottom of the ledge and climbing ever closer. As quickly as he could without losing balance, he turned around so that he was facing the rock wall, with Lucy and Roux directly above him. Gazing up at their pale faces, Shinji shook his head.

"I can't jump that high," he called, making Roux's jaw tighten.

"Well, it's either jump or go for a magma swim," he called back.

"Shinji, come on," Lucy urged, looking like she was almost in tears. "The lava is almost there."

Shinji's back blazed with heat. He didn't want to look down to see how close the magma was. Instead, he crouched on the ledge and jumped as high as he could, holding out both arms to the hands reaching for him.

The tips of his fingers brushed theirs, and both grabbed for him. But then his fingers slipped through their grasp, and Shinji dropped back onto the ledge, nearly losing his balance as he did. For a second, he teetered on the narrow outcropping, flailing his arms wildly, as Lucy screamed.

Pressing himself into the rock, Shinji closed his eyes. His heart pounded, but he reached inside himself, calming his mind as Phoebe had once told him to do, and searched for the power within.

Opening his eyes, he jumped.

There was a rush of wind through the cavern, and a strong gust caught Shinji just as he leaped into the air. He felt his clothes snap as the gust lifted him up, and for a split second, he felt like he was floating.

Then hands gripped his wrists tightly, fingers clamping over his skin, and the wind died away. Gasping, Shinji glanced up to see Roux and Lucy holding his arms as they all dangled over the edge of the pit. Looking down past his feet, Shinji watched the red-hot magma spill over the ledge he'd been standing on and swallow it completely. A magma bubble popped, lava droplets landing inches from his shoes.

"Pull me up!" Shinji yelped, swinging his feet wildly. "Guys, pull me up!"

"Hang on," Roux gritted out as he and Lucy pulled. Rocks scraped Shinji's knees and chest, tearing a hole in his shirt, but the other two dragged him over the edge and onto solid ground again.

"Too close," Lucy panted as Shinji finally got his feet under him, staggering away from the hole. His legs shook, and he nearly collapsed to the rough stone beneath him. "Are you all right, Shinji?"

"Yeah," Shinji rasped. Looking up, he met their pale, worried faces and suddenly realized that the two of them had just saved his life. Another few seconds, and he might have been half submerged in molten lava. "Thanks."

Before either of them could answer, a red glow blossomed in the air behind them. With an ominous burbling sound, the lava reached the edge of the hole and spilled out of it, crawling slowly toward the three like a giant ooze.

"We can hug it out later—let's get out of here!" Roux said, and they sprinted across the cavern, which was quickly spilling over with lava. Magma bubbled up from cracks and crevices and spread across the floor, following Roux, Lucy, and Shinji as they raced toward the exit. Rocks continued to rain from the ceiling and crash around them, and they had to leap over streams and pools of lava that flowed into their path.

"There's the tunnel!" Lucy gasped, pointing across the floor to the passage that had led them in. "We're almost out!"

As she spoke, the cavern shook, and another huge spike dropped from the ceiling right above the exit. It crashed to the ground, blocking their way, and a rain of smaller rocks followed, piling up in the tunnel. Shinji and the others skidded to a stop in front of the huge stone, and Roux let out a curse.

"Oh, come on! You gotta be kidding me!"

"Help me move it," Shinji said, stepping to the side of the stone and putting his shoulder against it. The other two followed, and he took a deep breath. "Push!"

They pushed, grunting and straining against the rock, but it barely moved. Rocks and chunks of ceiling pelted down around them, and the lava oozed ever closer, but the stubborn boulder refused to budge more than a few inches.

"This isn't working," Lucy panted as they finally slumped in defeat. "We're not strong enough."

"Is there another way out?" Roux wondered, looking desperately around the collapsing cavern. But the only other tunnel Shinji could see was the one back through the lava. Unless they could swim through molten rock, there was no escape.

The slowly rising carpet of magma crept closer. Now it was just a few yards away, and the half circle of rock they were standing on was shrinking by the second.

Suddenly the boulder moved. They spun, wide-eyed, as the enormous rock shook, rocked from side to side, then with a slow grinding sound, rolled out of the way, revealing a familiar face on the other side.

Lucy gasped. "Mano!"

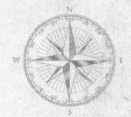

CHAPTER SEVENTEEN

Shinji sighed in relief as Mano peered in at them. Then Oliver's face suddenly appeared as well, his expression relieved and exasperated at the same time.

"You know, I admit I've done some crazy things," he said, stepping aside so they could all dart through the doorway. "But this . . . this might top them all. What in the name of Poseidon's beard were you *doing* at the bottom of the volcano?"

"Um . . ."

"Ocean," Mano snapped, taking a step away from the door. "The lava is still flowing while you stand there and gab," he pointed out. "This thing is going to blow any second now!"

They hurried down the passageway, feeling the tremors of the volcano ripple through the ground. "Where's Phoebe?" Lucy wondered, Tinker clinging wildly to her shoulder as she kept up with Mano. "And how did you guys even find us?" The big man gave her a split-second glance.

"Ocean is an expert tracker," Mano replied, looking faintly puzzled that she didn't know. "He was able to find your prints at the edge of camp and follow them until we found the path up the volcano."

"I'm no Maya," Oliver added behind him, "but I've been on enough expeditions with her, trekking through jungles and rain forests. After a while, you pick up a few things."

"As for Miss Mystic, we left her studying some 'important documents' at the base camp when we went looking for you. She seemed very intent and focused on her work, so we thought we wouldn't bother her. Of course, this was before the whole island started shaking and the volcano started to smoke."

"Let's hope she's still at camp," Oliver muttered. "And didn't decide to come looking for us."

"I've already radioed Dr. Grant and the rest of the team," Mano said, tapping a walkie-talkie strapped to his belt. "They're evacuating now. We just need to get these kids to the *Seas the Day* before the volcano explodes."

Bursting out of the tunnel, they reached the caldera

and the winding path up the mountain. As he gazed down, Shinji's heart leaped to his throat. The lake of magma was much closer, bubbling and steaming like a pot on the stove. Below them, the volcano shook and continued to rumble, and clouds of white smoke billowed into the air.

"Everyone!" cried Lucy, and pointed above them. "Look!"

Shinji looked up. In the skies directly above the volcano, a massive swirling cloud was forming, like a miniature hurricane. Slowly but surely, it grew bigger and bigger, darkening the sky. Flickers of blue-white lightning danced through the clouds, and thunder rumbled ominously overhead.

With an answering rumble below, the volcano trembled.

"That's not good," said Shinji.

"You have such a gift for understatement," Oliver said. "Let's go."

Oliver took the lead, and they hurried up the narrow, winding trail as quickly as they could. The volcano continued to shake, and rocks tumbled down the sides to plunge into the sea of magma at the bottom. Once, the path in front of Lucy abruptly gave way, a good chunk of rock sliding down the side of the volcano into the waiting lava. Lucy almost went with it, and Shinji's heart nearly stopped, but Mano grabbed her arm before she could fall and pulled her back from the edge.

A vicious blast of wind tore at Shinji's hair and clothes as he reached the top of the volcano. Lightning flashed, and a boom of thunder made him flinch. Glancing up at the sky, he could almost see the Storm Boar's face in the swirling clouds.

"There's the ship!" Oliver called, pointing out to sea, where Shinji could just make out the *Seas the Day* floating in the water. "And there's the camp. Let's get down there before they change their minds and leave without us."

They sprinted back to the village. The camp was in a state of organized panic when they arrived. Scientists scurried to and fro carrying expensive equipment, frantically packing everything away. Mano and Oliver strode forward, shouting instructions, pausing to help those in need. Overhead, the swirling storm clouds grew until they covered the whole island. Gusts of wind tore at the tents, sent smaller items tumbling over the ground, and caused everyone to stumble, fighting the winds.

"This storm certainly isn't making things easy," Oliver said, bracing himself against the gusts whipping around him. His coat flapped wildly as he held on to a tree trunk, observing the nearly empty camp with Shinji, Mano, and the others. "I think we're just about done here, don't you?" he said. "I'm all for leaving things exactly as we found it, but I'm also a fan of not getting covered in lava."

"Shinji! Oliver!" a familiar voice rang out, and a moment later, Phoebe came flying down the path toward them. Her arm was raised, and her hair streamed behind her as she ran.

"Oh, thank goodness you found them!" she gasped, skidding to a halt in front of Shinji. Doubling over, she pressed her hands to her knees and sucked in air for a few seconds, trying to speak and breathe at the same time. "I found . . . the elder's . . . journal . . ." she panted. "It told . . . the history of the village. Their rituals, daily lives, and their relationship with the guardian spirit of the island. They called it . . . the Storm Boar. According to the elder, the Storm Boar was sealed away in the volcano to prevent some great catastrophe from happening, and it's likely still there, waiting to get its revenge. Shinji . . ." Phoebe straightened, giving him a very serious look. "Whatever you do," she continued in a solemn voice, "*do not* release the guardian of the island. Very, very bad things will happen if you do."

Everyone looked at Shinji. He winced. "Um . . . about that . . ."

A thunderous boom rocked the island as, behind them, the volcano exploded.

Plumes of smoke billowed upward as jets of fire shot into the air, blazing red against the darkening sky. An eerie glow appeared at the top of the volcano, reflected against the storm, as lava began pooling down the sides of the mountain, trailing bright crimson scars over the surface. Shinji's blood ran cold.

Mano raised his head. "Time's up. Everyone, get to the boat!" he bellowed, his deep voice rising easily above the howling wind. "Leave the rest behind; we don't need it! Just go, now!"

The few remaining scientists stopped what they were

doing and hurried off, running into the rain forest and disappearing into the trees.

Mano let out a sigh and nodded. "All right," he muttered, scanning the camp one last time. "That's everyone out safely. Now it's our turn."

Phoebe suddenly straightened with a gasp. "Oh!" she cried, as if just remembering something. "The journal. Be right back!"

"Phoebe!" Oliver shouted as Phoebe turned and sprinted toward the village. "Where are you going?"

"The elder's journal!" she called over her shoulder. "I left it in the chieftain's house! Keep going; I'll be right there!"

"Wait!" Oliver called, but she was already gone. Oliver scrubbed a hand down his face. "Mystics," he groaned. Glancing at Mano, he gestured at the forest with his parrot cane. "Take the kids to the ship," he told the captain. "I'll be right back."

As Oliver took off at a run back toward the village, Shinji gazed past the houses into the forest, seeing an ominous red glow through the trees, creeping ever closer. He glanced at Roux and Lucy, and both gave grim nods. Before Mano could say anything, they all sprang forward, following Oliver and Phoebe into the village.

"Kids!" Mano bellowed. "Get back here."

They ignored him. Sprinting into the village, Shinji spotted the chieftain's house easily; it was the largest hut near the very center. Wind tore at the thatch roofing, blowing it away in chunks, and the whole hut shook as the island trembled. Shinji vaulted up the rickety steps and ducked through the doorway, Lucy and Roux right behind him.

"Phoebe," Oliver was saying as they came in, "we have to go. What are you looking for?"

"A book!" Phoebe glanced up from under a table. "I left the journal on the table right here. Or I thought I did, anyway. Where did it go?"

"There's no time for this," Oliver insisted, then noticed Shinji and the others as they stepped into the room. "And everyone is here now. Great. Priya is never going to let me take you anywhere ever again." He tapped his forehead several times with the golden parrot beak and sighed. "Well, since you're all here, start looking for this book. Apparently, we can't leave without it."

There was a breath of wind across Shinji's face. Not the angry, violent gusts from the storm outside, a quieter, gentler breeze that wafted across the floor. It fluttered the pages of a book half-hidden beneath a shelf, and Shinji blinked.

Kneeling down, he pulled out an old leather book. The pages were handwritten in a language he didn't recognize, but at the bottom of one page was a black-and-white drawing of a familiar boar, its head raised in a silent bellow as it called lightning down from the sky.

Shinji's heart leaped. "Phoebe," he called, scrambling up from the floor. "I think I found it."

"Oh yes!" Phoebe rushed up to him, taking the book

from his hands. "That's it!" she exclaimed. "The elder's journal. This could contain vital information to help us face whatever is to come next. Good job, Shinji."

"Great, so we can go now?" Oliver strode across the room and peered through the door. His eyes widened. "Yeah, we need to go," he ordered, turning to glare at them all. "As in *now*. Right now. Come on!"

They rushed outside, and Shinji's stomach twisted hard with fear. Lava had spilled from the forest and was oozing steadily toward them over the ground. The huts at the edge of the trees had already caught fire, the thatched roofs ablaze as magma pooled beneath them. Shinji could feel the intense heat burning his face as the deadly carpet slithered over the ground, consuming everything in its path.

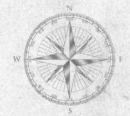

CHAPTER EIGHTEEN

"**M**ove!" Mano roared. "Get to the ship, now!"

Shinji's legs burned as he ran toward the beach, smelling smoke and hearing the crackle of fire behind him. The black raft still waited in the sand, but the waves had reached all the way up the shore and were pounding the beach. The ocean had turned gray and choppy, and far out to sea, Shinji could make out the ship bobbing up and down on the waves.

Thunder roared as Mano and Oliver dragged the raft into the ocean, fighting the waves that came crashing to shore. A wall of water hit Shinji in the chest as he scrambled into the raft, drenching his clothes and blasting seawater up his nose. Coughing, he hunkered down as Mano started the engine, and then they were zipping away from the beach, bouncing over the ocean as they headed toward the ship. Shinji turned and looked back at the island, watching lava stream down the volcano, the storm swirling madly overhead.

I caused this. This is my fault.

The raft caught a gust of air on a huge wave, coming down with a jolt that clacked Shinji's teeth together. Around them, swells rose and crashed, and the rain beat against Shinji's skin as the raft struggled toward the ship. Finally they reached the side of the boat, bobbing wildly on the choppy water, and scrambled up the metal ladder onto the deck.

"Raise anchor!" Mano shouted as soon as they were aboard. "Everyone, belowdecks. We're getting out of here."

Oliver, gazing up at the sky, shook his head. "Yep, that's a hurricane," he muttered, and quickly followed Mano across the deck. "And there's a ring of very sharp rocks between us and open water. Do you have any idea of how we're going to get out of here without smashing the ship into the reef?"

"Quickly," was the answer as they all ducked into the pilothouse. "Besides, aren't you an expert on extraction, Ocean? I mean, that's your claim to fame, right? You've done this before."

"Piloted a ship through a hurricane?" Oliver grinned and scratched the back of his head. "Once or twice," he admitted. "Not *safely*, you understand. I can't promise to have it back in one piece."

"I'll risk it." Mano nodded to the wheel at the front of

the room. "Take the helm, Ocean," he ordered. "I'm trusting you to get us through this."

Oliver nodded. Striding to the wheel, he took a deep breath and put both hands on the spokes, closing his eyes momentarily. Phoebe gave a confused frown.

"Oliver, what are you—"

"Shh." Oliver didn't open his eyes. "I'm establishing a connection with the ship," he murmured. "All ships have different personalities, quirks, dislikes, and little foibles. The more you understand them, the easier it is to navigate. This one"—he tilted his head to the side—"is a little bit finicky about storms."

Phoebe still looked confused, but Lucy was nodding, as if that all made sense. Then a flash of lightning turned everything outside white, making Roux flinch. "Well, can you maybe convince the boat to get us out of here alive?" he asked Oliver.

The ex-pirate opened his eyes and grinned. "I'll do my best."

The ship surged forward, cutting through the waves. Rain beat against the windows, and thunder rumbled overhead. Between the rain, the wind, and the flashes of lightning, it was difficult to see anything. Shinji didn't even know if they were going in the right direction.

"Come on, girl," Oliver muttered, his face intense as he turned the wheel. "You can do it."

A wave rose up, crashing against the side of the ship.

It rocked violently, causing everyone to lose their balance. Shinji braced himself against the wall as the ship bobbed dangerously from side to side. Lucy cried out, and Oliver clutched the wheel tightly, trying to keep the vessel upright.

The boar doesn't want us to leave, Shinji realized. *It's trying to sink the ship.*

He rushed out onto the deck. Wind and rain tore at his hair, shrieking in his ears. Another wave crashed against the hull, splashing over the deck and drenching him completely. The boat lurched to the side, and Shinji grabbed the railing to keep his balance.

He could feel the magic in the storm around him, in the waves and driving rain, even in the lightning that flashed through the sky. It felt . . . angry. But he could also feel the power in the wind swirling past him, and that felt more familiar. The rain and lightning belonged solely to the Storm Boar, but the wind . . . that was the realm of the Coatl. *His* magic.

"Shinji!"

Lucy appeared beside him, shielding her face from the rain and wind as she joined him on the deck. Roux was right behind her, grimacing as the rain beat down on them all. "What are you doing?" she cried, her voice nearly lost in a growl of thunder overhead. Another wave crashed into the ship, soaking them with cold seawater.

"I think the Storm Boar is trying to push us into the rocks," Shinji said. "It's trying to smash the ship on the reef."

Lucy paled. "Can we do anything?"

Shinji turned back, facing the storm. "Maybe I can."

Gripping the railing for balance, he closed his eyes as he'd seen Oliver do, and reached out for the magic.

This time, it was harder. Much harder.

Shinji could feel the anger in the storm whipping around them. He tried calming his mind, using his own magic to push back against the howling wind and slashing rain. But the Storm Boar was too powerful, his fury too great; Shinji tried pushing against the storm, only to have it tear his own wind magic to pieces.

"What are you kids doing?" cried someone behind them. Phoebe's voice. She held her bright red umbrella in both hands, braced against the wind as she stepped close. "Shinji, it's not safe out here. If you get washed overboard by the storm, Oliver would never forgive himself. What are you doing?"

"He's trying to use magic to get us through the storm," Lucy replied.

A wave slammed into the ship, and it bucked, nearly tearing Shinji's hands from the rails. Phoebe struggled to hold on to the umbrella as it was nearly torn from her grip. "I can't do it," Shinji gritted out. "The Storm Boar is too strong. I can't hold it back."

"Oh," Phoebe said, finally getting control of her flapping umbrella. "Well, you can't hold back the storm, Shinji—that's a given. Your magic is the power of wind. When the wind encounters something immovable, it doesn't go through; it moves around it. Don't try to fight the storm; go around it.

That . . . somehow made a lot of sense.

Shinji opened his eyes. The wind blew in his face, stinging his cheeks and forehead with rain. The fury of the Storm Boar raged around him, but he ignored it and looked inside himself instead. Taking a deep breath, Shinji raised a hand.

Don't go through. Go around.

The rain stinging his face suddenly stopped as Shinji changed the wind's direction, swerving around the gusts instead of pushing back. As the wind swirled, he felt the ship lurch forward, no longer fighting the storm. Rain poured and lightning continued to flash, but the *Seas the Day* moved steadily forward, aided by the wind instead of being hampered by it.

"Yes," Phoebe cheered quietly beside him. "See, Shinji? You're doing it."

"I think we're gonna make it," Roux muttered just as something scraped along the ship's hull, making a terrible grinding sound. Shinji froze and Lucy let out a gasp as the entire deck shuddered beneath them. Phoebe staggered, and as she did, the gale finally tore the umbrella from her hands. The bright red parasol caught the wind, soared swiftly over the water, and went spinning away into the darkness.

"Oh dear," Phoebe said, hand over her eyes as she gazed mournfully after it. "Athena's knots, that was my favorite umbrella. Hopefully it will come back like last time." The ship shuddered again, and she grabbed the railing. "I think we clipped a rock," she announced. "Mano is not going to be happy about that. But keep going, Shinji," she urged. "I can see the edges of blue sky. I think we're almost out."

Shinji gave the wind a final push, and the ship surged forward. They struggled through the rain and waves crashing against the hull until, very suddenly, they broke through the edge of the storm. The ocean calmed, the rain let up, and the sun blazed down on them as they sailed into tranquil waters.

Shinji let out a breath and slumped against the railings, breathing hard as the magic left him. Lucy let out a cheer.

"You did it! We're out."

"Oh, Shinji, I'm so proud!" Phoebe beamed at him. "You learned how to harness the magic of the Coatl! You took my lessons to heart after all."

Panting, Shinji gazed back at the island. The volcano still raged, spewing smoke and fire into the sky. Above the island, the enormous, swirling mass of clouds was still growing. Lightning flashed, streaking from the sky to crackle into the surging waves. Shinji was super happy not to be beneath those roiling clouds anymore.

"That is definitely a hurricane," Phoebe commented, following his gaze. "But at least it's staying in one spot. I guess the Storm Boar doesn't want anyone coming back."

"That's fine with me," Roux said. "I don't wanna go back, either."

Phoebe sighed. "A pity, really. If I had only known about the guardian and the font earlier. I would have loved to study both a bit more."

Tired, shaken, and completely drenched, they went back to the pilothouse, where Oliver still stood at the front. He, too, looked tired, his coat rumpled and his hair sticking up from the wind. But, standing in front of the wheel, his hands resting easily on the spokes and his gaze on the ocean, he reminded Shinji of a pirate more than ever before.

"Nice sailing, Skipper," Phoebe said as they crowded inside. "I was afraid we were going to hit the reef, but you somehow found the one tiny spot we could squeeze through."

Mano snorted. "We did hit the reef," he grumbled. "If my boat has a hole in it, Ocean, you get to pay for repairing it."

"I barely scratched it," Oliver protested. "You try steering a ship in the middle of a hurricane and see how well that goes for you. Thank goodness the wind was with us at the end there. It felt like I was steering right into it for a while."

Lucy and Shinji exchanged a look, and they both grinned. "So, what now?" Lucy asked. "We came all this way to beat Hightower to the ship and discovered an island with a font, but now there's an angry guardian that's been released and a hurricane in the middle of the ocean. What are we going to do?"

"Well, I'll tell you what we're *not* going to do," Oliver said. "We're not going back to that island."

"But what about the Storm Boar?" Shinji asked.

Oliver frowned. "What about it?"

"I . . . released it," Shinji said reluctantly. "Shouldn't we try to . . . put it back?"

"Put it back?" Phoebe cried. "Of course we can't put it back; it's a guardian that has been magically sealed away for who knows how long. I would be a little cranky, too."

"I don't think there's a return policy on guardians, kid." Oliver shook his head. "And I'm not qualified to do that kind of magic juju. Besides . . ." He nodded back to the island, and the massive storm raging over the volcano. "There is no way I'm taking you kids anywhere near that island right now. We barely got clear the first time. What we're going to do is head back to the Society and tell Priya what happened. They'll need to know about this."

Shinji set his jaw. He understood what Oliver was saying; none of them knew how to work the type of magic that had imprisoned the guardian. And even if they did, they probably couldn't return to the island without being smashed against the reef or swallowed by lava. But he was responsible for releasing the Storm Boar. The guardian was obviously angry, and in his rage, he had destroyed a whole island. This mess was Shinji's fault, one hundred percent. But . . . maybe there was a way to make things right again.

"What about the idol?" he asked.

They all stared at him. He winced under their combined glares.

"What idol?" Mano asked in a low voice.

Shinji bit his lip. "Something was taken from the island," he explained. "The soldiers that were stationed there took a sacred idol that represented the pact between the Storm Boar and the people of the island. That's why he's so angry."

"Really?" Roux asked. "I thought it was because he was locked up for so long. So, is the boar mad because he was trapped in the volcano or because the idol was stolen?"

"Also, who sealed him in the volcano in the first place?" Lucy added. "Surely not the villagers; why would they seal away their own guardian?"

"Wait!" Phoebe cried. "I think I read about this in the elder's journal. Hang on." She opened the leather book, flipping rapidly through pages, until she paused and pointed a finger to the book. "Yes, listen to this. The final entry."

Shinji felt a chill slide up his back as she started reading.

The Storm Boar has awakened, and we are lost. Its wrath is terrible, and the very ocean has turned on us. I do not know what has become of the strangers who took the idol. I do not know what became of their ships. I only know the skies have turned violent, the wind is unbearable, and the rain is flooding our crops. We have tried appeasing the Storm Boar, but our offerings have been ignored. The Boar wants only one thing: the sacred idol that we were supposed to protect. The pact between us and the guardian. The pact was broken when we allowed the idol to leave these shores, and the storm is the result.

This cannot go on. I fear we must abandon the island; it is a cursed place now. But we cannot leave while the sea rages around us. Our ships would sink in the storm. There is only one course of action left to us, though I tremble to even put it into words. May the gods forgive us, but . . .

We must seal away the Storm Boar.

Our elders know the ancient ritual. And the magic of the font will grant us the power needed to do such a thing. Once this is done, we will leave the island and never return. Even if the Storm Boar is sealed away, the island will not forgive us for this blasphemy. The horizon beckons, and we will seek our new lives beyond it. And if the Boar ever escapes, gods help the ones who set him free.

Silence fell as Phoebe looked up from the journal, a somber air descending on the room.

"So, the people sealed away the guardian," Lucy ventured in a quiet voice. "And now that's he's free, he wants his idol back." She observed the storm raging over the island and wrinkled her nose. "Is he really just going to throw a giant temper tantrum until the statue is returned?"

"Well, on the bright side," Oliver said, "at least the boar isn't chasing the idol down itself. So, we have a little time.

Don't worry, kid," he went on, giving Shinji an encouraging grin. "We'll go back to headquarters, let Priya know what happened, and she'll be able to call on some Storm Boar expert who will know what to do. I'm sure the Society has one of those."

"I hope so," Shinji muttered. Guilt and shame ate at his insides. He had released a vengeful guardian on a peaceful island. He had nearly gotten everyone killed. All because he had ignored Lucy's and Roux's warnings and had tried to do everything himself.

"Once we're farther away from the island, I'll contact Priya," Mano announced. "And don't worry, Ocean, I'll explain everything that happened. Better that she hears it from me and not you."

"Uh, yeah." Oliver grimaced. "Probably for the best. She still hasn't forgotten that whole debacle in Cambodia."

"Hey, guys?" Roux said. Standing at a window, he stared back toward the island, his gaze pointed toward the sky. "Not to freak anyone out, but I think the hurricane is moving."

"What?" They all turned. The ominous mass of darkness hovered over the volcano. Shinji watched the clouds swirl and the lightning flash, but the storm was so massive, he couldn't tell if it was staying in one place or not.

Suddenly there was a blinding flash of lightning that lit up the whole sky. In that flash, Shinji could see the split-second outline of a huge boar in the clouds, eyes blazing electric blue as he raised his head and roared with thunder.

And the storm began to move.

"It's coming," Mano breathed, taking a step back. "The hurricane is coming. Step aside, Ocean," he said, moving in front of Oliver and putting a hand on the wheel. "You've done your part, but I need to get my ship out of here. If that storm catches up, this boat is sunk."

"Is the Storm Boar after *us*?" Lucy asked, staring out the window with wide eyes as Oliver relinquished the wheel to the captain. "Why is it chasing us? We don't have the idol."

"Hmm, I don't think the Storm Boar is coming for us necessarily," Phoebe said, also gazing out the window at the approaching hurricane. "But I do think he is looking for the idol. The question is, where is the idol now? We know the soldiers took it from the island. Where did they go? How far away did they get? Is it on another island? Oh dear." She blinked, as if just realizing something. "That could be a problem if whatever island it's on is inhabited."

"To put it lightly," Mano said. "There are dozens of islands scattered through the South Pacific, many of them inhabited. If they get hit by a hurricane, the damage will be catastrophic."

"Yeah," Oliver agreed with a sigh. "Looks like we're going to have to find that idol ourselves, before the big angry sky pig wrecks every island he comes to. Shinji? You're our resident guardian. Any ideas?"

"I don't know," Shinji said in frustration. "It's not like the Coatl has given me any clues." There was a sick feeling in the pit of his stomach. He remembered the Coatl's statue, and the quest to return it to the font in the guardian's temple. This felt the same, except the Storm Boar wasn't waiting around for someone to return the idol to him. He was going to get it himself, and destroy anything that got in his way. "The idol could be anywhere," he said, "and there's no way to track it down."

"Hmm . . ." Phoebe tapped her finger against her chin, looking thoughtful. "Maybe there is," she mused. "Everyone, follow me."

CHAPTER NINETEEN

They trailed Phoebe back inside the ship, down into the library, where she had first tried to help Shinji tap into his powers. Where Shinji had gotten his first glimpse of the Storm Boar. As they entered the room, Shinji felt the ship starting to rock a little more beneath them. As if the waters outside were becoming choppy from the approaching storm.

"All right, Shinji, have a seat," Phoebe said, pointing to the same spot on the floor as last time. There was no cushion, but Shinji sat cross-legged with Lucy and Roux to either side. Phoebe settled herself in front of him, and Oliver hovered in the corner, watching.

"What are you trying to have the kid do exactly?" the ex-pirate asked.

"The guardians are connected to one another through the magic of the fonts," Phoebe replied. "If Shinji can tap into the power of the Coatl, we might be able to learn . . . *something*. Something about the Storm Boar, and maybe how to stop it."

Oliver's jaw tightened, his fingers nervously rubbing his parrot cane. "Messing around with magic isn't a good idea," he said. "Messing around with magic on a ship is, to paraphrase Mano, especially bad luck. You can't control it, and if anything goes wrong, it goes *very* wrong. The Mystics know that better than anyone."

"I know." Phoebe sighed. Glancing up, she gave Oliver a serious look. "I know, Oliver. Trust me, I know. I am aware of my family's . . . foibles. But there is an angry guardian bearing down on us in the form of a hurricane and threatening everything in his path. I'd say things have already gone very wrong. What we need to do is make things right again. And to do that, we need to know what the Storm Boar is after, and where it is now."

"And you think you're going to find that out with magic?"

"I'm not. But Shinji might be able to. Anyway, it's worth a shot!" She rubbed her hands together and gave Shinji a smile. "All right, Shinji, this will be just like last time. Close your eyes, relax, and try to establish a connection with the

Coatl. Breathe deep, in and out. In and out. There is no hurry, no stress, no pressure—"

"Except an angry mythological boar chasing us from the middle of a giant hurricane," Roux offered.

"Thanks. Not helpful." Shinji clenched his fists on his knees, feeling his heart start to pound. He had to do this. Everyone was watching him, but it was different this time. Before, he was just trying to figure out his magic and what he could do with it. Now a lot of people were counting on him. An angry guardian was on the rampage, and it was his fault for releasing it. For feeling like he had something to prove. He had to make things right, but he couldn't do that on his own.

I need your help, he thought to the magic inside him. *Please, the Storm Boar is going to hurt a lot of people if we don't do something. What does he want? How do we stop him?*

For a moment, nothing happened. The room was silent, the floor rocking slightly beneath him as he breathed in, and out, and in . . .

There was a ripple of color and light, and everyone flinched back as something appeared in the air before them. Shinji blinked, wincing as an image formed overhead, like a video game hologram, transparent and flickering. Lucy gasped, and Roux let out a yelp of surprise, scrambling backward like a scuttling crab.

"What the heck? What's happening right now? Did Shinji just turn into a projector?"

"Hush," Phoebe said, sounding excited and breathless herself. "The Coatl is showing us something."

Roux fell silent. Above them, the image blurred for a moment, then grew clear. Shinji saw a large ship, sailing through the waves toward the distant horizon. Overhead, the sky was black with clouds, and the ocean was beginning to writhe and froth in the sudden wind.

There was a crackle of energy, and a bolt of lightning streaked from the sky, slamming into the highest point of the ship. Shinji flinched as sparks flew, and all the ship lights flickered once before winking out.

A shadow fell over him. He looked up, into the clouds, and his blood froze as the head of a massive boar emerged from the darkness, eyes blazing blue against the night. It raised its head and roared, and a huge wave rose out of the ocean, towering over the ship. It roared again, and the wave came crashing down. For a few seconds, there was nothing but foaming water and raging sea. When everything settled, the boat was nowhere to be seen.

Beside Shinji, Lucy drew in a sharp breath, startling him. He had nearly forgotten she was there. "So, the Storm Boar sank the ship," she whispered. "And the idol was on it."

"Looks like it," Roux muttered. "Which means we're not getting it back anytime soon. That idol is probably still sitting at the bottom of the ocean."

The view suddenly dropped straight down, and Shinji winced as they plunged into the ocean. They continued sinking deeper into the depths, passing fish, sharks, even a whale, until they reached the seafloor. There, lying in the sand, was the ship they had seen struggling through the waves. A strange ripple crossed Shinji's vision, and the vessel seemed to age several decades, becoming covered in sand and rust. As if it had been sitting on the ocean floor for many years.

Staring at it, Shinji felt an odd sense of déjà vu, as if he had seen it before. . . .

Lucy let out a gasp. "Wait, that's the ship we found earlier!" she said. "When we were in the *Seabeetle*. It's the same one, I'm sure of it."

"If it's that same ship that we came here to find," Oliver began, "then . . ."

A spotlight suddenly cut through the water, shining over the hull of the shipwreck. Wincing, Shinji turned as a long, sleek shadow emerged from the gloom; a submarine much larger than the *Seabeetle*, cruising toward the shipwreck like a giant metal shark. The sub glided past them, and Shinji could see the words printed on its pristine hull: SS *Sea Plunderer*.

"Hightower," Lucy said in a cold voice. "Of course. So, Hightower has the Storm Boar's artifact."

And if Hightower had the idol, they weren't going to give it back. Even if it could help stop an angry, raging Storm Boar.

So, what were Shinji and his teammates going to do now?

The vision panned upward, rising through the ocean, until Shinji found himself flying through the clouds at top speed. Ocean, forest, and then cities flashed by beneath him, too blurred to see clearly. When it finally slowed, he could see a crowded skyline, with tall buildings and towers silhouetted against a mottled gray sky.

"That's . . . Los Angeles," Oliver muttered. "Why are we in LA?"

No one answered. For several minutes, they flew along the coast, past buildings and bustling interstates, until they reached an isolated harbor. As they approached, Shinji could see a tall barbed-wire fence surrounding the perimeter, with a security checkpoint at the gate and NO TRESPASSING signs posted everywhere. Ignoring the gate guards, they glided through the fence, swooped over the harbor, and finally came to a large warehouse at the end of the dock.

Here, too, the doors were sealed tight, with lights and very visible security cameras panning back and forth above the entrance. But neither the cameras nor the doors could stop them as they glided insubstantially through the walls and found themselves in an enormous warehouse. Numerous aisles stretched before them, with boxes, crates, and all manner of weird items crowding the shelves. But Shinji didn't have time for a closer look as the vision swept forward, weaving through the narrow aisles like a mouse running a maze.

As they zipped through the tight corridors, Shinji caught

a glimpse of something down another aisle. Something bright and metallic. For a second, he thought it was some kind of four-legged robot, but he only caught a split-second glimpse of it before it was gone.

Suddenly the vision slowed, coming to a stop at the end of an aisle. As Shinji looked up, the vision seemed to focus in on a single box, nothing big or fancy, just a simple lockbox in the center of the shelf. As he stared at it, he could sense something important within. Something that hummed with magic. It had to be the Storm Boar's artifact.

Return the statue to the heart of the storm.

With a flash of light, the images before them disappeared. Shinji, Lucy, Phoebe, and Roux were left staring at one another, surrounded by shelves full of books, blinking and wondering what had just happened.

"Okay," said Oliver from the corner, making everyone glance at him in surprise. "I would like to emphasize my statement that magic is weird and dangerous and I don't like it, cool as that was." He scratched his head with his cane and leaned back against a shelf. "So, we know where the idol is. Some Hightower warehouse very close to Los Angeles. And knowing Hightower, they're not going to just give us the statue if we ask for it."

Lucy snorted. "Not unless you pay them a few billion dollars," she replied. "And even then, they might not sell just because you're with SEA."

"So, what do we do now?" Shinji asked.

"The only thing we can do." Oliver pushed himself off the wall and flourished his cane with a grin. "We break in and take it."

Shinji's brows rose. "But . . . isn't that stealing?"

"Technically, yes." The ex-pirate didn't look very troubled about that fact. "But there's no time to negotiate, is there? That hurricane is coming fast. We need to get the statue as soon as we can."

"Think about what will happen if we *don't* return the idol," Phoebe added. "Lots of people are in danger. We must return the idol, before the Storm Boar's wrath destroys anything else."

Shinji nodded. *Return the idol to the heart of the storm.* Easier said than done. Getting into Hightower wouldn't be simple, but if it meant fixing what he'd caused and stopping the Storm Boar, he would try his best. "So, we have to sneak into a Hightower warehouse, find the artifact, break it out again, and then sail *back* into the hurricane to give the statue to the Storm Boar," he said, just to make certain he understood what the stakes were. "Sounds like fun."

"Sounds impossible," Roux said cheerfully. "When do we start?"

"Right now." Phoebe stood up, a determined look crossing her face. "I'll tell Mano what we've learned. We'll need to set a course for Los Angeles right away. Operation Stop the Hurricane begins now. Lucy, I'll need you to tell me everything you know about Hightower's operations. Roux, I hear you're good at getting into places you're not supposed to be. Polish up those skills. Shinji . . ." She turned on him with a fierce stare. "We're probably going to need to call on the Coatl's powers once or twice at the very least. I need you to be ready to unleash your magic at the drop of a hat, because our lives may depend on it. Can you do that?"

"Sure," Shinji replied. "No pressure or anything."

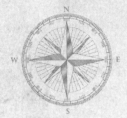

CHAPTER TWENTY

Shinji stood in his tiny room, facing the desk against the wall by his bed. An upside-down paper cup stood in the very center, away from everything else. Taking a breath, Shinji slowly raised his hand, feeling the magic stir inside him. Carefully, he sent out a very light breeze, trying to lift the cup into the air without blowing it across the desk or onto the floor. This was one of Phoebe's new exercises for him: staying in control and using just enough magic to raise the cup. If he lost control of the wind and hurled the cup into the walls or floor, he would have to start over.

The paper cup wobbled as the breeze nudged it, but didn't

rise. He tried again, to the same effect. The wind wasn't strong enough to lift it into the air, and Shinji frowned.

"Come on," he muttered, and gestured sharply. There was a gust of wind, and the cup suddenly blew across the desktop, tipped over on its side, and rolled onto the floor. Shinji winced.

"Magic problems?"

He jumped. Roux was leaning casually against the door-frame, amusement in his eyes as he watched. Shinji hadn't even heard him open the door.

"Working on it," Shinji said. Bending down, he picked up the cup and replaced it in the center of the desk. "What have you been doing?"

Roux shrugged. Despite his ever-present smirk, he looked tired. Dark circles crouched under his eyes, and his longish hair was even messier than normal. "Studying the layout of the warehouse with Mano," he replied. "One of the scientist people was able to pull up a satellite view of the area." He shook his head. "It's gonna be tough. Not a lot of good entry or exit points. Probably cameras everywhere. If it was just up to me, I wouldn't try it. Too risky."

"Lucy is supposed to be working on something to help with that," Shinji said. Another pang of guilt struck him as he remembered his argument with Lucy on the island, when he'd told her to go back to Hightower. She hadn't said anything about it, but he still felt bad and wished he could take it back.

"Really?" Roux yawned, then shook himself with a grin. "Well, if she ever invents a remote control to turn security cameras on and off, I'd definitely want to borrow it. Oh yeah," he added as Shinji rolled his eyes. "That Ocean guy wants to talk to you."

"Oliver does? Why?"

Roux shrugged. "I didn't ask. I just said I would tell you. Better hurry, though. He sounded impatient."

"What about you?"

"*I'm* not the one in trouble. For once, anyway." The other boy plopped down on the floor and put his feet up on Shinji's suitcase. "Tell Ocean I said hi."

Shinji left his quarters and went looking for Oliver, finding him in the break room. The ex-pirate was sitting on the couch and watching the small television in the corner. Over the past two days, the storm had grown even bigger and was on track to slam into the western coast, according to the news. Fortunately, the smaller islands were out of the hurricane's path as it swept north, so at least Shinji and his group were spared the Storm Boar's fury. But for the people on the West Coast, the news warned, they needed to prepare for the worst.

"Everyone who *can* get out of the way of this thing should do so now," a weather reporter said, standing in front of a map of the western United States. Behind him, an enormous swirling mass of clouds crept ever closer to land. "Mandatory evacuations have been issued for all of coastal LA," the reporter went on, "especially those right on the water. Bottom line, if you can get farther inland, you should do so, and soon. Meteorologists are predicting record storm surge, and winds of a hundred and fifty miles per hour or more. You do not want to be close to the water when this storm hits. Get off the coast, get out of the way of the storm if you can. If you can't, then make sure you're prepared. Water, flashlights, batteries, stock up on all of those. Power outages are expected for most, if not all, of the city once the hurricane makes landfall."

"What a mess," Oliver commented as the news station switched to an image of a clogged highway, with several lanes of vehicles at a near standstill. All trying to flee the city. "It'll get even worse if that storm actually makes landfall, though. This could end up being an enormous humanitarian disaster."

Shinji wrapped his fingers around the back of a chair at the break room table and squeezed. *Because of me. I released the Storm Boar. I caused this.*

"By the way," Oliver said, turning to Shinji, "I had a little chat with Lucy this morning. I wanted to know what happened when the three of you left the base camp and went up to the volcano. She didn't want to tell me everything, but I was able to piece the story together well enough." Oliver studied his reflection in the golden head of his cane, looking thoughtful. "So, you decided to follow a white pig to the top of the mountain to release the Storm Boar, huh?"

Shinji winced. "Yeah," he said again. "That was my fault. It was stupid; I get it. I should've listened when she told me it was a bad idea."

"Kid, trust me, I know all about rash decisions." Oliver shook his head and smiled. "Ask any member of the Society, and they can regale you with tales of Oliver Ocean's dumb choices. But the same can be said of everyone in SEA. From Phoebe to Mano to Priya and myself. We're explorers and risk takers. Danger is just part of being an adventurer. *But*," he added, pointing the parrot beak in Shinji's direction, "there is one thing that we all agree on, and that is we are stronger together than we are alone. Individually, I'm just one person. But, as part of the Society, I have access to almost unlimited knowledge, skill sets, talents, and information. If I can't do something myself, I can always count on the Society of Explorers and Adventurers to back me up. We're a family, and our job is to support one another. Do you see what I'm getting at?"

Shinji swallowed hard. "I think so."

"Good." Oliver leaned back and put his feet up on the coffee table. "Last I saw, Lucy was in the electronics lab," he said, gazing at the television again. "And according to Mano, we'll be at the drop point in about two hours' time. I would track her down and get everything out in the open before then. We don't need any hard feelings once we get into this crazy heist. It'll only be a distraction."

"Yeah," said Shinji, trying not to sound as nervous as he suddenly felt. "Understood."

A few minutes later, Shinji found Lucy in the electronics lab as Oliver had said, huddled over a computer and busily typing away. Tinker sat beside the keyboard, copper ears twitching as she worked. The mouse looked up and squeaked happily at Shinji as he came in, but Lucy didn't seem to notice.

"Hey," Shinji greeted, sliding onto the stool beside her. A quick glance at the computer screen showed a long line of code that was complete gibberish to him. "Whatcha doing?"

"Making it easier for Tinker to talk to other machines," Lucy muttered without looking up. "So, if we need to turn off a camera or silence an alarm, he'll be able to hack into the system more easily. I think I've almost got it now. . . ." She tapped a few more keys, then sat back with a sigh. "Okay, Tinker," she said as the mouse sat up on his haunches, whiskers quivering. "Connect Shinji."

Shinji's phone immediately buzzed. Pulling it out of his pocket, he glanced down at the screen and saw a new text had come in from "Unknown number."

Hello, it read. It is Tinker.

Shinji's jaw dropped to the floor.

"Now he'll be able to talk to us if he needs to," Lucy said as Shinji closed his mouth and blinked in amazement. "You can try talking to him, too. Give it a shot."

"Um," Shinji said, "how, exactly?"

"With your phone," Lucy explained in an overly patient voice. "Just text him."

Shinji shrugged. "Okay," he muttered, and started typing words on his screen. Hello, Tinker, he texted back. Can you really understand me?

The mouse's red eyes flickered to green for a moment, and he cocked his head. Shinji's phone buzzed again.

Language: English. Font: Default Roboto. Yes, the sentence has been communicated clearly. Hello, Shinji Takahashi. I can understand you.

"Are you serious?" Shinji whispered, a huge grin spreading over his face. Lucy nodded with a smug smile of her own. Shinji looked down at his phone. "So, what if I asked him something like this . . . ?"

"Don't make it too complicated," Lucy warned, but Shinji's fingers were already moving, flying across the screen as he texted.

So, Tinker, are you a mouse or a robot? What do you really think of Lucy?

Lucy frowned at Shinji, but Tinker's eyes flickered green for several moments as he seemed to consider this question. Finally Shinji's phone buzzed again.

I am Tinker, it read. I am aware.

A pause, and then: Lucy is ♥

"I told you he was smart," Lucy said, smiling like a proud

parent at Tinker. "He's going to help a lot with all the security we're going to run into at Hightower. At least with all the electronic things."

"That's awesome," Shinji said. He paused a moment, staring at his phone, then took a breath. "I'm sorry I told you to go back to Hightower," he said quickly. "I didn't mean it. And I should've listened to you when you said we should tell the others. I just . . . I felt I needed to free the Storm Boar, to prove I was a good guardian. I thought that's what I was supposed to do. But I was just fooling myself, and I made things even worse. So . . . yeah. I'm sorry."

"It's all right," Lucy replied softly. "I get it. My dad always made me feel like I wasn't doing enough. That I had to do more with my talents. I'd work harder, I would try to do better, but I felt like I was always disappointing him." She, too, paused a moment, as if gathering her thoughts, then added, "Shinji, you know I'm never going back, right? No matter what they offer me. Hightower has money and power and the latest technology and fancy toys, but when I'm with you and the Society, I feel like I'm doing something that matters. Helping people and preserving life. The important stuff. That's worth more than any magic or new tech Hightower can offer. That's why I'm staying with SEA."

"Yeah." Shinji nodded. "I get it. Besides, we're a team."

"We're a team," Lucy agreed with a smile. "You, me, and all of the Society of Explorers and Adventurers."

"Aw," said a new voice as Roux slipped into the room like some kind of ragged ghost. "What about me? Can I be part of the super-special team, too?"

Lucy rolled her eyes, but she was still smiling. "Don't be stupid," she said. "I thought you were part already."

Roux, shockingly, blushed—clearly surprised. He looked like he was about to respond, but at that moment, Phoebe appeared.

"Ah, there you three are," she said, pausing at the door. She had changed out of her normal sea-green coat and was now dressed in black from head to toe. "We are about two hours from Los Angeles, which means only an hour from the drop-off point at Hightower Campus. Oliver and Mano want us on the bridge to go over the plan one last time. And then Operation Stop the Hurricane will really kick into high gear!" She punched the air as she said this, then looked back at them with an eager smile. "This is so exciting! Is everyone ready?"

"Does not throwing up from nerves count?" Shinji asked. One hour. Now that it was finally time, things felt much more real than before. "I wish I hadn't eaten that last chicken wing."

"Oh, you'll do great," Phoebe assured him. As if this was a basketball game or a presentation he had to make for school. Not a daring heist that involved sneaking past Hightower security, breaking into their warehouse, and stealing a magical artifact that would stop an angry guardian from destroying a city. "We have a foolproof plan, and I have complete faith in everyone's unique talents. What could possibly go wrong?"

Roux visibly winced. "Famous last words," he muttered. "Why does everyone here like to tempt fate?"

Oliver appeared in the doorway, looking serious for once. He still wore his long coat but, like Phoebe, had changed into darker pants and a black shirt. The golden head of his parrot cane glimmered brightly in the crook of his arm as he gave them all a somber look.

"We have a problem."

CHAPTER TWENTY-ONE

Shinji and the others walked into the captain's quarters, where Mano was glowering at the map spread out on the table before them.

"Of all the bad luck," he grumbled as they entered. "I don't know how you're going to pull this one off, Ocean."

"What's going on?" Shinji asked.

"We were going to bring the *Seas the Day* in as close as we could to Hightower Campus," Mano replied, tapping the map with a thick finger. "And then you five were going to take a Zodiac the rest of the way to the beach. Unfortunately, we ran into a hiccup. I just got word that two of Hightower's ships have anchored in the cove behind the property. The *Sea Plunderer* being one of them."

"Oh no," Lucy said. "That means we won't be able to get very close without alerting Hightower that we're coming."

Mano nodded gravely. "Even the Zodiac might be spotted if you try to take it in with those ships sitting there," he said. "It's small and fast, but it's not invisible. And it makes a lot of noise."

"We're going to have to risk it," Oliver said. "We don't have a choice. That hurricane is coming. We have to get that statue from Hightower, one way or another, and we have to do it tonight."

Invisible. Shinji jerked up. "Wait," he exclaimed. "Invisible. What if we used the *Seabeetle*? It can walk along the ocean floor and travel beneath the Hightower ships."

"That . . . might actually work," Oliver said. "With the storm coming, Hightower certainly wouldn't be paying attention to anything going on *below* them. We'll just sneak past, nice and quiet, and they'll never know." He gave Shinji an approving nod. "Good thinking, kid. We'll make a pirate of you yet."

Moments later, cold spray was blasting Shinji's face as he climbed into the hatch of the waiting *Seabeetle*, gritting his teeth as the ship bobbed wildly beneath him. Lucy, Phoebe, and Roux were already inside, pressed against the seats as the sub swayed in the rising wind. Just outside the hatch, Oliver turned to face Mano.

"This is where I leave you, Ocean," the big man said. "I would come along, but if that hurricane hits us, it'll be a disaster for everyone on this ship. I'm taking her farther up the coast to try to outrun the storm. I'm sorry I won't be able to join you, but I'll knock on every wooden surface I can and throw a whole canister of salt over my shoulders for your good luck."

Oliver nodded. "It was great catching up, Mano. We'll have to do this again sometime."

Mano snorted. "You mean getting lost, nearly sinking, running for our lives from an erupting volcano, and trying not to get smashed into a reef? Just like old times."

He pulled Oliver into a crushing hug, then grinned at the rest of them. "Good luck, all of you," he told them as a gasping Oliver dropped through the hatch into the pilot seat. "Miss Mystic, I'm not too proud to say I was wrong about you. In the future, you are welcome aboard my ship anytime. Shinji . . ." He gave Shinji a nod and a grin. "Until we meet again. Don't let Ocean get you into *too* much trouble."

The *Seabeetle*'s hatch was sealed, and with a shuddering whine, the crane began lowering them into the roiling water. The waves sloshing against the glass were much stronger than before. Shinji gritted his teeth as the sub rocked from side to side, the *Seabeetle* creaking a bit in protest. But then they were below the surface of the ocean, and the darkness of the sea closed around them like a shroud.

"No lights this time kids, sorry," Oliver said as they descended into the pitch-black water. "The water in the cove isn't very deep, and we don't want Hightower to see spotlights gliding underneath them, so we're going to have to do this in the dark."

"Tinker," Lucy whispered, holding out her hand as the mouse crawled into her palm. "Light."

Tinker gave a soft squeak, and then his entire tiny body began to glow, the metal becoming brighter and brighter, until he resembled a mouse-shaped lightbulb in the center of Lucy's palm. Oliver looked down with a wince and shielded his eyes.

"A little too bright there, mouse. Could you turn it down a few notches?"

Another squeak, and Tinker's light dimmed to a softer, less blinding output. Roux shook his head with a rueful smile.

"I really need to get one of those," he muttered.

They traveled across the ocean floor in near silence. Tinker and the glowing luminescence of the *Seabeetle*'s console were the only light within the sub, and it lit everyone's faces with an eerie glow. Outside the glass, Shinji couldn't see anything but darkness, and his pulse hammered in his ears. "We're coming up on the ships now," Oliver murmured, staring at a circular radar screen. Two white dots blipped into view each time the radar pulsed. "At the depth we're at, they shouldn't see us, but just in case, I'm turning everything off until we're past."

"Tinker," Lucy whispered, and the mouse immediately dimmed to a barely noticeable glow. They crept along without speaking, in near pitch-darkness, the soft beeps from the radar the only sounds in what felt like an endless void.

"Almost there," Oliver whispered. "Just a few . . . more . . . steps . . ."

Suddenly, without warning, the inside of the *Seabeetle* flashed with light. All the screens lit up, and outside, the spotlight flashed on, cutting through the darkness. A school of silvery fish zipped away in the sudden illumination, and Oliver let out a startled curse.

"What the heck?" Quickly he and Lucy hit several switches, shutting everything down. The headlights vanished, the screens turned off, and the *Seabeetle* was plunged into darkness again. It only took a few seconds, but to Shinji, it felt like a spotlight was shining directly on them for entirely too long.

When it was dark once more, everyone froze, holding their breath. Waiting to find out if Hightower had seen them. But as the seconds ticked by, no alarms were raised. The ships above them didn't move, and Shinji's muscles began to unclench.

"All right," Oliver said at last. "I think we're in the clear. I don't think they saw anything."

"Then let's get out of here," Roux hissed, "before anything else happens."

Oliver nodded, and the *Seabeetle* crept forward again, scuttling over the sand and continuing into the dark.

"Well, that was unfortunate," Phoebe commented. For the first time, she seemed nervous, staring back the way they had come, a slight frown on her face. "That couldn't possibly have happened at a worse time, could it? Maybe . . ." She paused, biting her lip. "Maybe I should stay behind for this mission. There are enough capable hands here to get the job done, and you certainly don't need anything unlucky or unexpected happening again; this mission is too important."

"Stay behind?" Lucy echoed. "Where? We can't turn around and go back."

"Oh, just leave me with the *Seabeetle*." Phoebe waved her hand airily, though her expression seemed sad. "Don't worry, I'll find my way back somehow. I always do."

"No." Shinji shook his head. He saw Oliver, watching him in the reflection of the glass, and set his jaw. Mystic curse or not, Phoebe had been the one who had helped him with his magic. If it hadn't been for her, he would still be struggling to control his power. It was weird that she knew so much about magic and had been stuck with a curse that made things go haywire around her, but that wasn't her fault.

"We're a team," he said. "None of us can do this alone. We need everyone here to make it work."

"Kid's right, Phoebe," Oliver added, surprising Shinji. In the glass, the ex-pirate's reflection was somber, but he gave Phoebe a faint smile. "We're up against Hightower, a hurricane, and a giant mythological Storm Boar. We're gonna need all the help we can get."

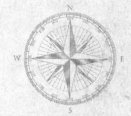

CHAPTER TWENTY-TWO

Waves sloshed over the *Seabeetle* as it finally crawled out of the ocean onto the beach.

"Well, here we are," Oliver said, pushing the hatch open. A rush of wind blew into the sub, tugging at Shinji's hair as he peered through the glass. The beach they had landed on was tiny, barely a strip of sand at the base of a rocky coastline. Shinji gazed up the jagged outcroppings, and his heart started to race. At the top of those cliffs was the Hightower Campus, where, locked inside a warehouse and surrounded by security, the Storm Boar's artifact waited.

Oliver stared up the rocky slope as well. "Hope you guys are ready for a climb. And, kiddo . . ." He turned to glare at

Shinji with a faint smile. "If you could refrain from falling or sliding back down the cliff, that would be great. I know you enjoy those near-death experiences, but there's no Maya and no safety harnesses this time."

Shinji rolled his eyes. "Geez, fall down a cliff once and they never let you forget it."

Carefully, they started up the slope. At least it wasn't a sheer vertical cliff like the one they'd had to scale in Mexico, where if Shinji hadn't been attached to a safety harness he would've been a splattered pancake on the ground. This one, although rocky and treacherous, could still be climbed without special gear or equipment. Roux led the way between large rocky outcroppings, following a sandy trail as it wound back and forth, until they reached the top.

"Okay," Oliver said, peering out from behind a rock. "We made it all the way without anyone falling to their deaths. Good first step; what's next?"

Phoebe, peeking out from the other side, nodded to something ahead of them. "Probably that," she said.

A tall barbed-wire fence rose up from the dirt and weeds about thirty yards away. Coils of razor wire ran along the top, and the fence itself was made of chain link. Beyond it, Shinji could just make out a cluster of low, flat buildings across an open gravel field.

Oliver, gazing at the metal barrier in front of them, gave a snort. "It looks so pedestrian," he commented. "Knowing

Hightower, I was expecting something a little . . . more. Lasers and electrical fields, that type of thing."

"That's probably what they want you to think," Roux said, eyes narrowed. "I wouldn't let down my guard, though. This is just basic stuff to keep out the normal riffraff. If you're protecting something valuable, one of the best methods is to hide it in plain sight. A super-fancy, high-tech fence just attracts attention, and lets everyone know you've got something to steal."

Oliver stared at Roux for a few seconds, then shook his head with a wry grin. "You're quite the conniving little scoundrel, aren't you?"

Roux shrugged. "I prefer the term *opportunist.*"

"So, how do we get inside?" Phoebe wondered. "If I could find a branch of suitable length, I could pole-vault over. Oh, but there don't seem to be any trees around here. Or if I stood on Oliver's shoulders, maybe we could boost Lucy over the top. Oh, but then we'd have to figure out how to get rid of the barbed wire. Maybe we could dig a hole big enough for Shinji or Roux to wiggle under. Yes, that might work." She turned on them with a slightly crazed smile. "Which one of you is smaller?"

"We could do all of that," Oliver said as Shinji and Roux eyed each other uncertainly. Reaching into his coat, he pulled out a pair of wire cutters. "But these would probably be faster."

The snips easily cut through the wire fencing, making a hole large enough for all of them to slip through. Ducking through the crack, Shinji straightened and gazed around warily. Now that they were past the first barrier, he felt much more exposed. Like there were Hightower eyes watching them from every angle. Nervously, he glanced at the flat, open area leading up to the cluster of buildings on the other side of the lot. There weren't a lot of places for them to hide should something unexpectedly appear.

"All right, we're officially in," Oliver whispered as Lucy was the final person to slip through. "Now all we have to do is find the right warehouse, get the artifact, and hightail it back the way we came. Easy, right?"

"Sure," Roux muttered. "Also, not trip over any alarms, get spotted by any cameras, run into any security guards, or alert any motion detectors. Easy."

"Tinker," Lucy whispered, and held the mouse up in her hand. "Can you sense any cameras or alarms around here?"

The mouse sat up on his haunches, nose to the wind and ears twitching. For a few moments, he stayed like that, like a meerkat scanning for predators. Finally he dropped back to all fours, and Lucy gave a decisive nod.

"Tinker doesn't detect anything. At least, not close by. I think it's safe to move closer."

Oliver nodded. "Okay, then," he muttered. "Here we go. Remember what we talked about. If you see anything, don't yell or make any sudden moves. We don't want to attract even more attention."

"What about the secret signal?" Phoebe broke in. "We could still try that. I don't think you gave the idea a fair shake when I first suggested it."

"I told you, I still have no idea what a whippoorwill sounds like," Oliver said. "And even if I did, I'm not going to whistle like one. We'll have to send signals the old-fashioned way."

"Oh well, I suppose that's for the best. They're not native to this area, anyway."

"What? Then why would you suggest it?"

"Oh, please, do you think your average security guard would hear the call of a whippoorwill and think, *That's weird. I didn't think whippoorwills were native to this area of the country?*"

"I still think *ka-caw ka-caw* was fine," Shinji added.

"Impractical," Phoebe said immediately. "There are no crows awake and flying around in the middle of the night. Whippoorwills are nocturnal; the males specifically sing at night to defend their territory or attract mates. Though, according to folklore, hearing a whippoorwill call near your house was an ill omen and a sign of impending death."

"Oh, right, and that's so much better than *ka-caw ka-caw.*"

Oliver was tapping his parrot cane against his temples

again. "We're wasting time," he groaned. "Lucy, is it still all clear?"

"Yes."

"All right, then, let's go, before these two start arguing about screech owls."

They started across the lot, toward the cluster of white buildings in the distance. Shinji still didn't like how exposed he felt, out in the open, with nowhere to hide or obstacles to dart behind. At least it was dark; the clouds blocked out the moon and stars, and there were plenty of shadows to skulk through as they made their way toward the Hightower complex.

And then they ran into the real barrier.

Roux had been right; the simple barbed wire had just been for show. Once across the empty lot, a tall, high-tech security gate stretched away to either side, circling the compound. This one was made of black iron bars, with white stone pillars every twenty or so feet. There were no coils of barbed wire at the top, but the metal signs hanging from the fence read THIS AREA IS PROTECTED BY VIDEO SURVEILLANCE, with a picture of a security camera beneath it. Farther down, Shinji could see a security checkpoint near the road, the white guard station sitting in the light of a streetlamp. The whole fence and the area around it was also brightly lit; if anyone walked into that light, there would be nowhere to hide.

Shinji and the others crouched in the shadows a safe

distance away, staring at the iron barrier between them and Hightower.

"Pretty fancy gate," Roux muttered. "Doesn't look electrified, though. Which is good, 'cause I didn't really want to have my eyeballs jolted out of my head."

"Oh, I doubt the current would be high enough for that," Phoebe said matter-of-factly. "The worst that would happen is that you might go blind."

"We can probably climb it," Shinji said. "It's not that tall."

"Not without tripping every alarm and alerting every camera in the area," Roux shot back. "Those signs aren't there for show."

Shinji glared at him. "I meant *after* we disable whatever is watching the fence. Lucy can do that. Right?" He glanced over his shoulder at Lucy.

"Give me a second." Stepping forward, she knelt and put Tinker on the ground. "He'll have to get closer to talk to any electronics in the area, but he's tiny. A camera will have a much harder time spotting him than if Shinji lurched up to the fence."

"Since when do I lurch?"

She ignored him. "Tinker," she whispered to the mechanical creature, "we have to somehow get through that fence. You know what to do?"

Tinker's copper ears moved back and forth like mini satellite dishes. With a tinny squeak, he darted forward and immediately vanished into the scrub and dead grass.

Stepping back, Lucy pulled out her phone, the glow of the screen illuminating her face. "I should be able to talk to him," she muttered, her thumbs moving across the surface. "If he sees anything weird or dangerous, he'll let me . . ."

She trailed off, making Shinji tense. "What's going on?"

"Tinker says there are things moving around on the other side of the fence," she said, frowning. "Not cameras or sensors. Bigger things."

"Security guards?" Oliver wondered.

"He's not sure," Lucy replied, still frowning in confusion as she texted. "But he knows what people are; if they were guards, I would expect him to say so."

"Maybe they're killer robots," Roux joked.

"They're not killer robots," Lucy said without looking up. "But they're small. And they're . . ." She blinked, and her eyes got wide. "Flying?"

"Flying," Oliver repeated. Shinji jerked up with a gasp.

"Drones," he whispered. "I bet Hightower has drones patrolling the perimeter."

As he spoke, something appeared, gliding along the fence line. It moved silently, two pairs of propellers pushing it forward like a ghost. A large camera eye scanned back and forth as it came toward them.

"Everyone, get down," Oliver hissed. "Lucy," he went on as they all flattened themselves to the dirt. "Call Tinker back, now."

Lucy nodded, and Shinji held his breath, watching as

the sleek flying machine glided down the fence line, its four propellers whirring silently as it came.

"Okay," Oliver muttered as the drone continued on like a giant metal insect. "Drones. Great. That's not extravagant at all, Hightower."

Roux watched the flying machine turn the corner of the fence and disappear from sight. "It looks like it's on a set patrol route," he observed. "So, even after the cameras get disabled, we're gonna have to time it so that the drone doesn't spot us as it circles around."

"That's what I figured," Oliver said. "This might be a bit tricky, but hey, what's life without risk? Lucy, can Tinker disable the cameras?"

"Working on it," Lucy muttered, staring at her phone again. After a few moments, she shook her head. "Tinker can override the cameras around this area, but not for long," she said. "He can give us maybe a minute, two at most. After that, we run the risk of alarms going off."

"We're going to have to time this perfectly, then," Oliver said. "Roux, have you got the pattern down?"

"I think so," Roux muttered, and pointed to one of the posts along the fence line. "When it crosses that spot *there*, that's the time to start running. And we'll have about thirty seconds to get over the fence and get outta sight."

"Here comes another one," Shinji pointed out.

"On my signal, then," Oliver said, raising a hand. "Lucy, tell Tinker to disable the cameras . . . now."

Lucy's fingers furiously moved over the screen, and she nodded. "Done."

Shinji tensed as the drone passed in front of them, feeling his heart pound in his chest. Beside him, Roux drew in a slow breath, hunching down in order to be able to spring into action.

"Man, I hope this thing isn't electrified," he muttered.

"Go!" Oliver barked.

Shinji leaped forward as everyone else did the same. Sprinting up to the fence, he watched as Phoebe vaulted gracefully over the bars like a gymnast, then leaped for the top himself. Thankfully, there was no jolt of pain or buzz of electricity as his fingers curled around the top. But when he pulled himself over, one of the pointed black tines caught the back of his shirt. As he dropped to the other side, Shinji was jerked back and hung there, his toes barely touching the ground. He let out a yelp and twisted around, yanking at the snag, but the fabric wouldn't budge.

"Shinji!" Oliver had already vaulted over and was starting to sprint away with the others, but froze when he saw Shinji hanging from the tines. "Keep going," he told Phoebe, and hurried back to the fence. "Man, you are good and stuck, aren't you?" he muttered through gritted teeth, tugging at the snag. "How did you manage this?"

"Practice," Shinji said sarcastically. Phoebe joined them, and Shinji saw Lucy and Roux coming back as well, worried looks on both their faces. *Keep going*, he wanted to tell them. *Don't worry about me.* But that would be futile; if he was caught, Hightower would know they were here. It would be over for all of them.

A spotlight appeared around the corner, gliding over the ground and getting brighter. Shinji's heart raced, and his stomach threatened to leap up into his throat.

"Oliver!" Lucy whispered, her voice frantic. "The drone is coming!"

Oliver cursed under his breath but didn't stop trying to free the snag. The drone was close to them now; all it would have to do was turn the corner of the fence, and they would all be caught in the glare.

Abruptly, Phoebe swooped down and snatched something from the cement: a brown glass bottle that still looked half full of something. As the light swept closer, she hauled back and threw the bottle into the air. It sailed over a building, came down, and Shinji heard the crash of broken glass when it hit the concrete.

Immediately, the spotlight whirled around, heading in the opposite direction. At that moment, Shinji felt the fabric of his shirt tear away from the fence, allowing him to drop to the ground.

"Go!" Oliver snapped, and they took off, sprinting toward the closest building before the drone could turn toward them. Darting around a corner, they huddled together and pressed their backs against the wall, breathing hard. Tinker scampered across the pavement with a glint of bright metal, leaped onto Lucy's arm, and crawled up to her shoulder. Shinji tensed, waiting for an alarm to sound, for drones to descend and flashing lights to go off, letting them know the jig was up. But as the seconds passed in silence, he started to relax.

Oliver let out a gusty breath, wiping his brow with the back of a coat sleeve. "Well, that was fun," he muttered. "Shaved a few years off my life, though it's nice to know fancy, high-tech robots are just as gullible as humans. Still, I vote we not do that again."

"Ah, the old tricks are still the best ones," Phoebe said exuberantly. "I knew my high school softball skills would come in handy for something. In all seriousness, though, Shinji . . ." She turned to him with a smile. "I always consider tearaway garments for important missions. That, or skintight outfits. There is a reason Priya always wore cat suits when in the field."

"Wait, Priya? Wore cat suits? Our Priya?" Lucy asked.

"Oh yes. They were her signature style," said Phoebe.

Oliver cleared his throat. "Anyway, we're inside the fence," he murmured, looking around at the sprawl of unmarked structures around them. "We just have to find the right building. And avoid the hundred or so security cameras that are probably stuck everywhere."

"You know what's also weird?" Roux commented as Oliver peered around a wall. "No guards. Where are all the security guards? You'd think a place like this would be crawling with them."

"You have to pay human guards," Lucy answered. "Machines never get sick, or need vacations, or ask questions. Whenever they can get away with it, Hightower would rather have automatons do the work." Reaching up, she scratched Tinker between the ears, and he gave a happy squeak. "Good news for us: we probably won't run into any human security guards patrolling the site. But who knows what else Hightower has set up around here."

"Hmm. Well, we'll just have to avoid whatever it is, then." Phoebe peered around the corner, eyes moving back and forth as she scanned the property. "The coast looks clear. And according to my photographic memory, I believe the warehouse is in that direction. Follow me."

She started to move out of cover, when Oliver grabbed the collar of her coat and pulled her back with a yelp.

"Oliver, what—"

He put a finger to his lips, just as a beam of light cut through the darkness several yards away. A second later, a drone appeared, but this one did not fly. Instead, it moved across the ground on four jointed metal legs, looking like some kind of large, metallic bug. As it came to the wall of a building, it didn't go around the barrier, but dug its legs into the brick and scuttled up the side like a real insect.

Everyone pressed back into the wall, holding their breath and staying as still as statues, until the drone had skittered up the building and moved on.

"Oh good," Shinji whispered when it was safely gone. "Spider drones. That's always fun."

"Hence the other things I was talking about," Lucy said. "Those are Hightower security drones. There's probably a bunch of them that patrol the property, not just the outer fence like the fliers. And no, Tinker certainly can't disable them. They're way too high-tech."

Roux peeked around the corner with Oliver. "So, we're gonna have to sneak past them the hard way," he mused. "Without being spotted." Glancing over his shoulder, he shot a dubious look at the rest of them and grinned. "I'm pretty sure I've got this; I don't know about the rest of you."

Oliver snorted. "You're not the only scoundrel in the party, kiddo. I've snuck into my fair share of shady docks and warehouses. *And* out again. Granted, none of them were patrolled by spider drones, so we're just going to have to be careful. And keep looking up."

"Hang on," Shinji said. "I think I have an idea. Lucy, Tinker can talk to us now, right? Can *he* track the drones and tell us when it's safe to move?"

She blinked. "That's actually a good idea," she said, sounding amazed that he had come up with it. Shinji tried not to be offended. "Tinker, do you think you can do what Shinji suggested?"

Tinker twitched his ears, regarding them both with glowing eyes. After a moment, Shinji's phone buzzed.

Tinker understands, the text read. *Shinji does not have to ask Lucy. Tinker can hear you.*

"So, is the rat really going to help us?" Roux wondered as Shinji stared at his phone. With a blip, another text came through.

Tinker will help, it said. *Tinker will not even tell rude boy to go sit on an electric fence.*

Lucy, also gazing at her phone, let out a cough that sounded like a stifled laugh. Holding up her hand, she let Tinker crawl onto it, then lowered him to the ground. The mechanical mouse sat on his haunches a moment, nose and ears scanning the sky. Then he darted off with a flash of copper and was gone.

"Follow Tinker," Lucy said, returning her attention to her phone. "He'll let us know when it's safe to move. Right now, he says wait, a drone is on its way back."

Oliver shook his head. "If anyone asked me what I'd be doing this week," he muttered, "my answer would not have been *waiting for a robot mouse to tell me when it's safe to dodge Hightower security drones.* But here we are."

One of the drones walked by along a wall, its legs making faint clicking sounds on the bricks, its spotlight eye shining over the ground. Shinji clenched a fist at how spiderlike it really was.

Beside him, Phoebe let out a breath. "Hightower does have some interesting technology," she mused.

"This is nothing," Lucy replied. "You should've seen some of the projects they wanted me to work on. Tinker is the only artificial intelligence that successfully combined tech with real magic, but some of their other inventions got really close. Hopefully we won't run into any of them here."

"Why not?" Shinji wondered. "What kind of things were they working on?"

"One word," Lucy told him. "Spiderguns."

Everyone shuddered. "Oh great, that's going to be in my head forever." Oliver sighed. "An army of mechanical killer spiders crawling across the ceiling toward me, how fun. I can't wait to see what other nightmare surprises they have waiting for us."

Both Shinji's and Lucy's phones buzzed. Drones have passed, the text read. Safe to move in 2.7 seconds. Also, Tinker has found the structure SEA team is looking for. Sending coordinates now.

"Tinker's found the warehouse," Lucy said.

She started to say more, but suddenly the wind shifted. A warm blast of air hit Shinji's face, smelling of rain and dust. Thunder rumbled in the distance, making his stomach clench.

"Okay." Oliver nodded with a wary glance at the sky. "Storm's coming, and we're running out of time. Let's get that idol and get the heck out of Dodge. Hopefully without running into a spider army."

CHAPTER
TWENTY-THREE

Following Tinker's instructions, they dodged a pair of drones and finally reached the warehouse that had appeared in the Coatl's vision. Shinji recognized it immediately: a squat, nondescript building with no windows and four large loading bays at the back. The metal doors were extremely thick, and tall enough for a T. rex to walk through without bumping its head.

"Hmm, no windows," Roux muttered, gazing up at the front of the warehouse. "And we'll probably need explosives to get through those doors. Anyone have any C-4 lying around?"

"Tinker is sensing lots of cameras and alarms around the area," Lucy said, phone in hand as she stared at the screen.

"He can try to start disabling them, but it might take some time. And if the alarm senses him, it'll be over."

"What if we went in through the roof?" Phoebe mused, craning her neck to stare at the top of the building. "If we could get up there, we could rappel down through the skylights. Oh, wait." She snapped her fingers. "Darn, I left my rappel cables in my other bag. Double darn, I didn't think to call the Society and have them send over any equipment. My lipstick grappling hook would've been perfect for this heist."

"No fun Society toys this go-round, sadly," Oliver said. "But I have another idea. This way."

They circled the building, where a single, normal-looking door sat at the front entrance.

"There's probably an alarm," Oliver went on, glancing at Lucy. "But I'm guessing Tinker can turn it off, at least long enough to walk through the door. I admit, plastic explosives always sound fun, especially against Hightower, but I don't have any on me this time. And rappelling in through the roof may look cool in the movies, but with our luck, Shinji will fall out of his harness and land on his head on the concrete."

"Hey," Shinji protested. "Again, that was not my fault. My harness was too big."

Oliver just grinned. "Whatever, kiddo. All I know is that you and heights don't get along. And walking through a door sounds much easier than swinging in through the skylights. Lucy, can your mouse unlock this thing and turn off any alarms?"

"He can try."

"Well, darn." Phoebe sighed as Lucy began texting instructions to Tinker. "There go my hopes of rappelling down *Mission: Impossible* style."

"Got it," Lucy whispered a few moments later. "Tinker is in. The door is unlocked and the alarms are disabled, but only for a minute."

Oliver nodded. "Let's go, then."

They hurried across the lot and up to the warehouse, with Shinji arriving at the door first. He tensed as his fingers reached for the metal handle, half fearing a gate would come crashing down or laser beams would chop them all to bits as soon as he touched it. But nothing happened. Nothing, except the door swung back, and they all crowded through the frame.

Just inside the door was a small reception area, a white counter on the back wall and a large sign that said TOWER CORP displayed prominently above it. The entire room was spotless and pristine and very Hightower.

"Don't stop here," Oliver ordered, nodding to a camera over the desk. Shinji's stomach clenched, but the light below the lens was dark. Tinker had turned it off. "We need to get to the back. Lucy, are all the doors unlocked?"

"He's working on it now," Lucy replied. There was a beep by the door in the corner, and she nodded. "Okay, door unlocked but . . ." She paused, frowning at the screen. "He says there are more things moving around in the warehouse."

"More drones, probably," Oliver said, striding across the room. "We'll deal with them when we get there. Come on."

He bashed his shoulder into the door, and it flew open. They followed a short hallway past three or four small, neat offices, until they came to yet another door. This one wasn't locked, and as it swung back, Shinji's heart leaped into his mouth.

A huge warehouse stretched away before him, the ceilings soaring overhead and the racks and shelves that seemed to go on forever. Hundreds of aisles ran the length of the room, filled with everything you could imagine, and even things you couldn't. Crates and boxes crowded the shelves, along with rugs, paintings, vases, old computers, ancient-looking books, and items Shinji didn't even have a name for, all fighting for space. Finding one small box in this huge, sprawling sea of junk would be impossible if they didn't know where to look.

He saw the others gazing around in amazement, too. "Wow," Oliver muttered, picking a dusty smoking pipe off the shelf. "How old is some of this stuff, I wonder?"

Phoebe suddenly let out a gasp, plucking the item from his hand. "This is an original pipe from Duke Monocle's private collection," she exclaimed, holding the pipe at arm's length. "And it's just collecting dust in this old warehouse. Ugh, Hightower, what are you doing?"

"So, it's valuable, then?" Roux asked, sidling up beside her. "How much do you think it's worth? Tens of thousands? Hundreds?"

"Don't get any ideas," Lucy warned with a scowl.

"Oh, come on," Roux protested, and waved a hand at the sprawling warehouse around them. "Look at this place. I bet they don't even know where half this stuff is. No one would know if something mysteriously disappeared."

"I would know," Lucy said firmly. "We're not Hightower. We don't take what doesn't belong to us. Besides, we didn't come here for this."

"Technically, this stuff doesn't belong to Hightower, either," Roux pointed out. "So, what's the difference?"

There was a flash, and a moment later, a deafening boom of thunder made the whole warehouse shake and caused the windows to rattle. Everyone, including Shinji, jumped.

Phoebe winced and immediately replaced the pipe on the shelves. "Well, that was a timely reminder," she said. "Lucy is right; we have far more important things to worry about."

"That's what we like to call an understatement," Oliver said, and turned away. "Come on," he urged. "Let's find that idol and return it to the storm, before that hurricane flattens the city with us in it."

A deep growl suddenly echoed through the warehouse, making everyone freeze. As silence fell, Shinji could hear footsteps racing toward them. Except, they didn't sound like normal footsteps. They sounded . . . metallic, clanking over the concrete and getting steadily closer.

"Something is coming," Roux warned, looking like he

wanted to bolt away and dive out a window. Oliver drew his cane.

"Kids, get behind me," he snapped as a pair of large shadows came bounding out of the aisles toward them. Lucy gasped, and Shinji's heart dropped as the creatures stalked forward. They looked like dogs, big Doberman pinschers, except they were made of metal like Tinker. Their bodies were of black iron, their skulls were sleek metal, filled with rows of razor teeth. Their eyes glowed red as they came forward, growling.

Lucy let out another gasp. "I remember these things!" she exclaimed as they all swiftly backed away. The dogs followed, snarling and baring their metal teeth. "There was a blueprint for a robot guard dog that landed on my desk last year. The lead inventor wanted to know if I could program them so that lasers could shoot out of their eyes."

"Please say you did not," Oliver said, keeping his cane between himself and the snarling dogs. Beside him, Phoebe had sunk into some kind of martial arts stance, arms held out like a ninja.

"No," Lucy admitted, much to Shinji's relief. "Lasers were too hard to figure out. But . . . um . . . there was something else. . . ."

The dog closest to Oliver stepped forward, growling. Its glowing eyes blazed red as it faced the ex-pirate, who kept the golden head of his cane pointed at it. *"Intruders,"* said a very robotic, mechanical voice. *"Surrender now."*

"Oh, they talk," Oliver said. "That's charming."

"Surrender now," the dog went on, still baring its teeth at Oliver and Phoebe. *"Put down your weapons. Or we will be forced to dispose of you."*

"Dispose of us?" Roux echoed. "No thank you. That sounds painful."

"Also, what weapons?" Shinji added. "We don't have any weapons, unless you count a wooden cane with a parrot head as a deadly weapon."

Lucy shook her head. "Don't bother talking to them," she whispered. "They're not intelligent. They can't make informed decisions. They're just following a protocol."

"Surrender," repeated the dog in its flat, robotic voice. *"Lower your weapons or we will dispose of you. You have five seconds to comply."*

"Kids," Oliver said as everyone tensed. "Listen to me. The mission doesn't change. We'll keep these things occupied. You find the idol and get out. Don't worry about us."

"Five . . . four . . ."

"What?" Shinji exclaimed. "No way we're leaving you."

"Three . . . two . . ."

"We'll be fine. Just go."

"One."

With a roar, the dogs attacked. Jaws gaping, they lunged, and Oliver and Phoebe leaped forward to meet them. Oliver's cane lashed out, smacking a dog in the head. There was a loud, metallic clank as the golden parrot connected with the canine's metal skull, but the dog didn't seem to notice. It snapped at Oliver viciously, and he barely spun away.

Phoebe dodged the attack of the second dog, then stepped forward and punched it in the ribs with a loud *Hi-ya!*

"Ow!" she yelped, shaking her hand as she danced away. "Note to self: Punching metal creatures is rather inefficient, and hurts quite a lot. Oliver!" she called, still retreating from the attacking metal Doberman, "this doesn't seem to be working. I suggest we try something else."

"I'm open to suggestions," Oliver said, scrambling away from the first robot dog. He swung at it with his cane, and the dog's teeth clamped down on the parrot head. "Hey! No, bad dog—let go of that. That's mine."

The dog growled, tugging at the cane. Suddenly there was a crack, and the robot backed away with the golden parrot head clutched in its jaws. Oliver groaned and threw up his hand.

"Oh, come on, that was my favorite cane. I'll have you know that it's a one-of-a-kind golden Duncan parrot head, not a chew toy."

The dog growled. Spitting out the head, it lunged at Oliver again, who leaped atop a stack of crates to avoid it. Scrambling to the top of the pile, he bumped into Phoebe, who had done the same thing. "Oh, hey, fancy running into you here," he said, stepping back as the dog leaped at him, jaws snapping at his feet. "Come here often?"

Phoebe kicked a dog in the nose, sending it crashing

back down to the floor. The robot dog didn't seem fazed or hurt in any way as it bounced to its feet. It continued to leap at them, metal jaws snapping with hollow clanking sounds.

Shinji peered out from behind the stack of pallets where he had retreated with Lucy and Roux. "We've gotta help them," he said, clenching his fists in frustration as he watched the battle. "Lucy, those dogs are partly electronic, right? Can you get Tinker to hack into one?"

"Not from here," Lucy said, sounding frantic as she watched the scene in the center of the room. Oliver and Phoebe had retreated to the highest crate and were fending off leaping dog attacks with kicks and a broken cane. "Maybe if he was closer, like if he could physically get onto one, but those dogs are jumping around so much, there's no way he'll be able to do it."

"Wait," Roux said. "So, you're saying your rat needs to be touching a dog to have a chance of stopping it? Like sitting on its back?"

"Exactly," said Lucy.

Roux grinned. "No problem. I can get him there."

Lucy gave a suspicious frown. "How?"

"I'm good at avoiding stuff." He held out a hand, palm up. "Just trust me, okay?"

"Trust you. With Tinker."

"Yeah." Roux rolled his eyes. "Come on, it's not like I'm gonna run off with him now. Do you want to help Oliver and Phoebe or not?"

"You'll never get there. You're going to get yourself and Tinker mauled."

There was an angry bark, and Shinji looked up. One of the dogs had crawled onto the top of the stack of crates next to Oliver and Phoebe's and was balanced precariously on the edge. It snarled and snapped at Oliver's cane as he swung at it with the broken end. While Oliver was fighting the dog, Phoebe ducked around him and gave the crate a resounding kick. The box teetered, then toppled off the stack, taking the dog with it. Crashing to the ground, it broke open on the concrete. Coils of wire and computer cables spilled from the broken box onto the floor.

Shinji straightened. "I have an idea," he said, whirling on the other two. "I think I can trap a dog, at least one of them, and make it easier for Roux to get Tinker to it. But we have to do this now. And only if Roux has Tinker. Lucy?"

The dog leaped upright with a howl of fury and lunged at the crates again. But this time, it started attacking the boxes at the base of the stack, crunching through the wood with metal teeth. The second dog, when it saw what the first was doing, started munching through the crates as well. As more and more boxes were destroyed, the stack Phoebe and Oliver stood on began shrinking rapidly. Shinji's stomach clenched as the crate Oliver was standing on tipped to the side and nearly fell. He managed to hop to another before the box toppled, but their mountain wasn't going to last much longer.

Lucy's lips tightened, her face going pale. "Fine," she said. Holding up her hand, she let Tinker crawl onto it, then held the mouse out to Roux. "Be careful with him," she warned.

"I will." Roux held out his hand like Lucy, palm facing up. Tinker considered a moment, ears twitching back and forth as he gazed at the offered hand. After only a second, though, he leaped lightly from Lucy's palm to Roux's. Lucy winced as Roux's fingers closed over the mouse and he stepped away. "All right, ra—er, Tinker. Let's go play with some robot dogs."

Shinji held out an arm. "On my signal," he said.

Stepping forward, he took a deep breath and half closed his eyes, searching for the power inside him. Raising his arm, feeling the magic stir once more, he opened his hand.

A blast of wind rushed past him, whipping at his hair and snapping his clothes. From the corner of his eye, it almost had a golden tint, as if he was calling on the essence of the Coatl itself. It swirled into the room, stirring dust and rattling the items on the shelves. A vase tumbled to the floor with a crash, causing the dogs to stop and look up. Their glowing red eyes locked on Shinji.

"*Intruders*," the dogs said in their robotic monotone. "*Surrender or we will dispose of you.*"

"Shinji, what are you doing?" Oliver called as the dogs growled and broke away from the crate pile, stalking toward him. "We told you to run. Get out of here, all of you!"

Shinji ignored him. As the robot dogs came forward, he shaped the wind into what he wanted and sent a miniature tornado into the center of the room.

The wind shrieked through the air, picking up debris and flinging it everywhere. Roux ducked behind a pillar as a broken ceramic chunk flew past him and smashed against the wall. He shouted something to Shinji, but his voice was lost in the gale.

Shinji gritted his teeth, struggling to maintain control over the swirling winds. It was like trying to hold on to a flailing octopus, with the tentacles going everywhere at once. The whirlwind picked up more pieces of debris and flung them here and there, but it also caught the pile of cables and computer wires from the broken crate. The tangle rose into the air and began swirling around the robot dogs. It wrapped around their legs and bodies, entangling them in a net of wire and rope. They snarled and snapped at the cables, tearing through them with metal fangs, but for the moment, they were distracted.

"Roux," Shinji said through clenched teeth, "now!"

Roux sprang forward. The dogs spotted him and immediately began snarling and trying to attack. But the knot of wires slowed them down. Roux dodged out of the way of one lunging dog, spun around its haunches, and stuck Tinker to the middle of its back. He quickly leaped back to avoid the snapping jaws as the dog whirled around and bit at him.

"Yes!" Shinji cheered just as the power rushing through him sputtered out. The winds died and the whirlwind vanished, sending cables and broken pieces of wood clattering to the floor. Shinji swayed on his feet, then collapsed to the cement. For a few seconds, he knelt on his hands and knees as he waited for the dizziness to fade and for the room to stop spinning.

A growl echoed above him. Panting, Shinji raised his head . . . and came face-to-face with one of the robot dogs. Coils of wire and cables were still wrapped around it, dragging along the floor, but it didn't seem slowed by them any longer. The canine stared down at Shinji with baleful red eyes. Its metal jaws opened, showing rows of glittering steel fangs. It tensed to lunge, and Shinji braced himself for the attack.

Something slammed into the dog from the side, knocking it away. It tumbled over the concrete in a cloud of sparks before smashing into a pile of crates. Wide-eyed, Shinji looked up as the second robot dog stepped between him and the first. Tinker crouched on its back, his eyes flickering a neon green, and Shinji noticed that the dog's glowing red eyes had turned green as well.

With a snarl, the red-eyed dog leaped to its feet and lunged, and the dog Tinker was controlling sprang forward to stop it. The two metal creatures slammed into each other in the center of the room, and it sounded like a pair of cars colliding on the highway. Metal screeched, iron crumpled, and fangs clanked harmlessly off steel hide as the robot dogs began fighting.

"Shinji." Oliver was suddenly beside him, dragging him to his feet. "Whatever that was, it was crazy," he said as Shinji stumbled, leaning on his arm for balance. "I don't know why I expected the three of you to do what you were supposed to do, which was to find the idol and get out. Are you all right?"

"You're welcome," Shinji rasped sarcastically, earning a snort from Oliver. The robot dogs were still fighting, but it was impossible to see if they were doing any damage to each other. He just heard metal teeth scraping off metal bodies, but at least the dogs weren't coming after him and the others anymore.

With a squeak, Tinker scampered across the floor. Lucy bent down to help him, and he leaped into her palms. "Come on," she said as she rose. "Tinker was able to reprogram the first dog. It'll keep fighting the other one until they're deactivated. That should give us enough time to find the statue and get out."

"Well, I must say I am impressed," Phoebe said as they jogged away from the dogs, heading farther into the warehouse. "The three of you make quite the team. And, Shinji, that was you calling on the Coatl's powers, wasn't it? How exciting! It seems my meditation techniques are working."

"Yeah," Shinji replied, and shrugged. "Breathe in, breathe out. Easy."

Of course, it wasn't that easy, but Shinji understood his magic a lot more now than he did before. And it was only possible through the help of his friends. Once he stopped trying to do everything himself, things made a lot more sense.

"That's great and all," Roux said, "but we still have to find that idol. If you haven't noticed by now, this place is huge. It'll take forever to find it."

"Oh, don't worry about that," Phoebe told him, and tapped her finger to the side of her head. "Remember when I said I had a photographic memory? All we have to do is go to the end of this aisle, turn left, follow that aisle, turn right, turn right again, walk three aisles over, turn left, duck under the stairs to the upper level, walk four more aisles, turn down the aisle marked 'underwater accoutrements,' turn left at the split, and then go all the way to the end. The lockbox will be on a shelf at the end of the aisle. See? Easy-peasy, right? Anyone could find it."

"Um. Sure." Oliver winced. "We'll just follow you."

CHAPTER TWENTY-FOUR

A few minutes later, they stood in a narrow aisle, staring at the shelf at the end. A single lockbox sat in the center of the metal frame, nestled between rusty tubes and a box filled with copper buttons. The lockbox blended perfectly with the other items on the shelf. If they hadn't been following Phoebe, they would have walked right past it. A bulky iron padlock hung from the door, covered in dirt and rust.

"Huh," Oliver commented, looking skeptical as they stared at the tiny safe. "You know, considering this is holding a sacred idol for the possession of which a mythological creature is going to flatten a city, I was expecting something a little . . . grander. So, who's going to open it?"

"It's not electronic," Lucy said. "Tinker won't be able to unlock it."

Roux chuckled. "Good thing you guys have me, then."

Digging into his pocket, he pulled out an ordinary-looking wire that had been twisted around into a bent pick.

"Padlocks are easy," he muttered, sticking the pick into the keyhole. "I used to practice on the bikes chained up around town. Combination locks are a little harder, but you just gotta get the feel for them." He grunted, frowning as he fiddled with the padlock. "Problem is, this thing is so rusty, finding the right angle is . . . Ha. Got it. As Phoebe would say, easy-peasy."

With a faint click, the lock opened. Shinji held his breath as the door swung back. Inside, the safe was empty, except for a small, stone statue, carved in the likeness of a boar. An odd thrill went through him. It was definitely the idol he'd seen in his vision—the one the soldiers had stolen.

Roux wrinkled his nose.

"That's it? That's what the Storm Boar is throwing a temper tantrum about? A hunk of rock shaped like a pig?"

"It's not the size," Phoebe said. "It's what it represents. Clearly, that idol is the physical representation of the connection between the people of the island and the Storm Boar. Obviously, it is very important to him."

"Well." Oliver sighed. "We'd better get it back to him, then. Shinji, why don't you grab the idol so we can get out of here?"

Shinji hesitated, remembering a tiny novelty shop in Africa, and the statue of a winged snake on a dusty shelf. "The last time I grabbed an idol, I got stuck with a magic tattoo," he said. "I don't know if I can deal with two guardians."

"Oh, I'm sure you'll be fine," Phoebe assured him. "This is a completely different situation. Back then, the Coatl wanted you to return his stolen idol to the temple. Now the Storm Boar wants you to return his stolen idol to the heart of the storm."

"How is that a different situation?" Lucy asked. "It's almost exactly the same!"

"Oh." Phoebe paused, thinking about that. "You're right! Well . . ." She glanced at Shinji and smiled. "I'm sure you'll be fine."

Shinji grimaced. "Okay, fine." Looking at the idol, he started to reach for it, but before he could grab it, Roux's hand shot out, quicker than he could respond, and snatched the figurine from the safe.

"There," Roux said triumphantly, holding it up. "I've got it. Now can we . . . ?" He stiffened, eyes going wide, before he started jerking and spasming wildly. "Aaagh!"

"Roux!" Phoebe cried as Lucy screamed. Shinji's stomach twisted hard, and he started to reach for the statue, to snatch it out of Roux's grip. Maybe if he grabbed it instead of Roux, the power of the Storm Boar wouldn't affect him as much.

But then Roux abruptly stopped shaking. Raising his head, he gave them all a mischievous grin. "Got ya."

Lucy punched Roux in the shoulder. Shinji would've done the same, but he knew how much Lucy's punches hurt. "Don't *do* that!" Lucy scolded, though she seemed to be holding back a smile.

Oliver actually snorted a laugh, shaking his head. "Hilarious," he said begrudgingly. "Shaved a few years off my life, but nicely done. Now, can we get out of here, please? Before we get attacked by any more drones, cameras, robot dogs, or security guards shooting lasers from their eyeballs?"

Before Shinji could answer, the lights overhead flickered. A moment later, a growl of thunder shook the very walls around them, making Shinji's skin prickle.

"Storm's coming," Oliver muttered, sounding much graver now. "All right, everyone, let's get serious. We really are nearly out of time."

Shockingly, they made it outside and back over the fence without any further problems, though Tinker did have to warn them about the drones still flying around the yard. Outside, the wind had picked up, smelling of rain and the coming storm. Above them, the sky was pitch-black, but over the ocean, lightning flickered ominously against the horizon. As Oliver had said, the storm was on its way.

"So, the Coatl told us that we have to deliver the statue into the heart of the storm," Phoebe said, gazing out toward the ocean. "But we don't have a ship anymore, and I don't think there's time to procure a new one. Not to mention, I can't think of any ship captain who would be willing to sail their vessel in a hurricane. Well, except for Oliver."

"A ship is too slow," Oliver said. "By the time we could get close enough, the storm would already be here. We're going to have to fly. . . ." He grimaced, his face going slightly pale. "And there's only one person I know who's crazy enough to fly right into the heart of a hurricane."

"Oh no," Lucy said, her eyes widening. "Please say you're not talking about . . ."

"Afraid so," Oliver went on. "And I've already called her, so we need to get going. There's a private airfield a couple miles up the coast. She and *Rhett* are waiting for us there."

"Hello, everyone!" Scarlett greeted, waving enthusiastically as they approached. Her bright red hair snapped, the ends of her scarf whipping about in the gale. Behind her, the rusty, hulking form of *Rhett* sat on the runway, propellers moving very slightly in the wind.

"So, Shinji, Oliver tells me you need someone to fly into a hurricane," Scarlett said as they all crowded in front of the plane. "I thought he was joking at first, but apparently there was this angry guardian that was freed and now it's going to destroy the city unless a special statue is returned, or something?"

"Pretty much," Shinji said, and held up the idol. "I have to take this thing into the heart of the storm and . . . give it back there, I suppose."

"You?" Scarlett blinked at that and shot Oliver a look that was suddenly alarmed. "You didn't mention Shinji was coming along for this ride, Ocean," she said. "Granted, I have no problems flying into a hurricane myself, even if *Rhett* has never done it before. But if Priya knew you were taking kids into this storm, she would absolutely kill you."

"I know," Oliver groaned. "Don't remind me."

"Shinji must come," Phoebe said. "This is not an ordinary storm. It's likely we'll need his guardian powers to get the idol where it needs to go."

Shinji met Scarlett's gaze. "I have to do this, Scarlett," he said firmly. "I caused this storm. I have to be the one to fix it. But . . ." He glanced at the others, at Lucy and Phoebe, Oliver and Roux, and took a breath. "I'll need everyone's help to get me there."

"And if Shinji's going, I'm going." Lucy lifted her chin in her don't-mess-with-me stance. "I'm a member of SEA. If this doesn't show everyone that I'm not with Hightower anymore, I don't know what will."

Everyone looked at Roux. "What about you, kiddo?" Oliver asked. "We're about to fly right into a hurricane. If you want to sit this one out, no one will blame you."

"Yeah." Roux sighed. "That would be the smart thing to do." He glanced at Shinji with a wry grin. "But you don't bail on your team in the last five minutes of the game."

"I see. Well, if everyone is decided, then I guess we're going to be flying into a hurricane," Scarlett said, returning to her frenetic cheerfulness. "I've never flown directly into a hurricane before, but *Rhett* and I are up for a challenge, isn't that right, big guy?" She patted the side of the plane affectionately, and Shinji heard a clunk inside, as if something had fallen off. "He's ready if you guys are. I'm going to guess time is of the essence?"

"When is it not?" Oliver sighed as Scarlett wrenched back the plane door with a rusty screech, making everyone except Phoebe cringe. "Here we go again," Oliver muttered as they all climbed aboard the plane. "Should I go ahead and strap that parachute on right now?"

"Oh, I got rid of that," Scarlett told him with a casual wave. "I didn't see the need for just the one; there's no way I'd abandon *Rhett* like that. Besides, you're not going to need a parachute, Ocean. It's far more likely the entire plane will plummet into the water."

"Scarlett." Oliver grimaced. "Did you really need to mention that last part?"

"Probably not. But it's worth it to see your expression." Scarlett grinned and shut the door with another grinding screech.

Shinji sat down on the uncomfortable seat, quickly clicking the seat belt into place. His heart was pounding so hard, it felt like drumbeats in his ears. Lucy wasn't looking much better, and even Roux, who had never flown with Scarlett, was already slightly green.

"All right, everyone buckled in?" Scarlett asked as she slipped into the pilot seat and flipped several levers. "I normally don't say this, but hold on to your hats, pants, lunch, or whatever you don't want to lose. It's going to be a bumpy ride."

"So completely normal," Oliver muttered, jamming his seat belt into place. Shinji curled his fingers tightly around the idol as the plane rumbled to life and began rolling down the runway. As much as Oliver joked about Scarlett's flying, he knew this particular flight was going to be much, much worse than usual.

As the plane left the ground and climbed shakily into the air, Shinji gazed out the window, and his stomach twisted so hard he felt sick.

A massive wall of black clouds hovered on the horizon, blocking out the sky. Lightning flickered in its depths, bluewhite strands crawling through the belly of the clouds. A sharp gust of wind tossed the plane, causing it to jerk up, and Shinji clenched his jaw.

"Yep, that is a hurricane," Scarlett observed. She didn't sound afraid. There was an undercurrent of excitement in her voice, as if she relished the challenge. "Looks like a nasty one, too. All right, *Rhett*. This is your moment. Don't let me down."

The plane seemed to surge forward in response, rising into the air toward the looming storm, and Scarlett chuckled. "All right, everyone! This is it. Into the heart of the storm we go!"

Fighting the gale that shrieked around them, they flew into the hurricane.

Curtains of water slashed at the windows while pellets of hail beat against the metal walls like tiny hammers. Lightning flashed, and thunder boomed all around them, rattling the glass and making the entire airplane shake. The winds were a constant, howling nightmare, ripping at *Rhett*'s wings and propellers, and the plane dipped, jerked, and bounced wildly as it fought against the storm.

Shinji's jaw hurt from clenching so hard, his knuckles white as they gripped the statue. Beside him, Lucy and Roux were tense, with Lucy trying not to gasp every time the plane fell from the sky. Oliver had both hands on the wall next to his seat, bracing himself, and even Phoebe looked a little green.

The plane rose sharply into the air, thrown by a gust of wind, and Shinji's stomach leaped to his throat.

"Woo-hoo!" Scarlett cheered, as if they were on a roller coaster at a theme park and not fighting a monstrous natural disaster. "Is that the best you got, you nasty thing? Come on, why are you holding back?"

"Scarlett, maybe we shouldn't taunt the angry, mythological hurricane god," Oliver said through a clenched jaw. "Call me crazy, but I don't think attracting the Storm Boar's attention is the best strategy. . . . Oh."

His voice trailed off, and Lucy let out a gasp. Shinji looked out the window, just as a section of clouds broke away from the rest, swirling into the form of an enormous boar. Not the Storm Boar itself, Shinji realized; this was a cloud shaped like a wild pig, not the massive, intimidating Storm Boar of legend. But it was still huge and powerful-looking, nearly as big as the plane, and clearly not happy.

With a thunderous roar that caused lightning to erupt around it, the cloud boar charged the plane.

Scarlett banked hard, barely dodging the boar as it thundered past, and Roux let out a yelp as the plane dropped from the sky. Oliver braced himself against the wall again, squeezing his eyes shut. "Right, I think my point has been made. If we live through this, remind me to tell you I told you so."

"Why is the stupid pig attacking us?" Roux wanted to know. "We're trying to give him back his statue. Stop trying to kill us, pig!"

"I think he's just too enraged to see reason," Phoebe said, grabbing her seat belt as the plane dodged the pig once more.

"He doesn't care who we are or what we're trying to do; he's just lashing out at everything in his anger."

The plane swerved away from the boar's next attack, but this time, it didn't move fast enough. A tusk clipped one of the wings, and a vicious blast of wind upended the plane, sending it spiraling away into the clouds. *Rhett* tumbled through the air, making Shinji feel like he was in the inside of a blender. Both Lucy and Roux screamed, and Shinji closed his eyes, gripping the idol and focusing on not throwing up.

Scarlett finally got the plane under control, stopping their free fall through empty space. "Okay!" she announced as they righted themselves. "That's not something they teach in flight school. How's everyone doing? Still hanging in there?"

"Great," Oliver wheezed. "Maybe when we're done here, we can go back for my stomach; I think it flew out the window and is floating around the ocean by now."

Shinji looked up. Overhead, the swirling clouds parted, revealing the wispy form of the pig glaring down at them. It pawed at invisible ground and tossed its head, squealing a challenge, as lightning flashed and thunder boomed around it.

"Well, that beastie is going to make it very hard to go any farther," Scarlett muttered, also watching the cloud boar with narrowed blue eyes. "Flying in a hurricane is tricky enough; another hit like that, and we might be swimming home."

Shinji set his jaw, feeling a tingling power stir within. Reaching down, he unbuckled his seat belt, causing the others to blink and frown at him.

"Shinji, what are you doing?" Oliver asked. "Sit down and buckle up. If we take another fall, your brains are going to be all over the seats."

"I know what to do," Shinji said quietly. The power swirled inside him, straining to be unleashed. "Scarlett, fly right at the Storm Boar," he said, pointing out the windshield. "No turning or swerving out of the way. Don't stop for anything."

"Oh," Scarlett said, glancing over her shoulder with a raised brow. "So, we're playing chicken with a giant mythological storm god, are we? Sounds like fun. Did you hear that, *Rhett*?" She patted the dashboard of the plane. "Time to show it what you can do. Let's go!"

The plane surged forward and up, rising through the clouds and driving rain, toward the cloud creature that was waiting for them. The pig roared a challenge, slashing the air with its tusks, then lowered its head and charged.

Shinji raised a hand, fingers spread wide, feeling the power of the storm whipping through the air. It churned inside him as well, as wild and unpredictable as the wind. This time, he didn't try to grab on to the magic or control it. He let it swirl around him, shaping it into what he wanted.

"Shinji!" Lucy cried, her voice seeming to come from far away. "The boar is going to hit us!"

No, it won't, Shinji thought, and let the magic go.

A long, serpentine form rose up from the roiling storm below the airplane. Its feathered body seemed made of clouds, though its eyes blazed emerald green as it soared into the air. On great, sweeping wings, the cloud Coatl flew like an arrow at the charging boar, who gave a snort of alarm and swerved aside at the last second. Wheeling around, the boar squealed in rage and came at them again. Shinji swept his hand out, and the Coatl flew between them, forcing the pig to change direction once more.

"It's working!" Roux cried, watching the battle rage between the two huge creatures in the sky. Abandoning its attempts to charge the airplane, the boar turned its fury on the Coatl. It darted and lunged through the clouds, slashing at the Coatl with its long tusks, but the winged serpent was quick and agile and dodged out of the way. Winds still buffeted the plane, tossing it like it was made of paper, but Scarlett kept the vessel under control as they continued through the storm.

"Hold on to your seats," she said. "I think we're just about there."

Almost as if it heard her, the boar spun around, blue eyes flashing dangerously. The Coatl lunged at it, but it leaped away and sprang into the clouds, vanishing from sight for a few seconds. For a moment, the winds died down, the lightning ceased, and the rain beating against the windows calmed.

"I don't like this," Oliver muttered, his gaze wary as he stared out the window. "It's too quiet. Usually that means something big is about to happen—"

The clouds parted, and the boar stepped directly in front of them. Eyes blazing, it raised its head with a squeal, and the sky overhead erupted with lightning. White-hot energy strands rained down, flashing like strobe lights.

"Hang on, everyone!" Scarlett cried as the plane swerved violently, throwing Shinji against the wall. His head struck the glass, and he slumped, dazed, to the floor, the world spinning around him. He tried getting up, but the plane was rocking wildly, pitching like a boat on the stormy sea. Shinji fell again, hitting his shoulder against the seat edge, and clenched his jaw around a gasp of pain.

Something grabbed his arm, pulling him upright. The plane swerved into the air and Shinji nearly fell again, but the grip on his shoulders tightened, keeping him on his feet.

"Come on, kiddo," Oliver muttered overhead. He braced himself against the wall, keeping them both upright. "Stay with us."

"It's charging again!" Roux cried.

Shinji looked up. The cloud boar was coming at them, plowing straight through the lightning storm.

And then something bright red flashed by the window. A crimson umbrella, spinning almost lazily on the wind. It soared past the plane, driven by the gale, and hit the cloud boar in the face, covering its eyes. The boar squealed and tossed its head, trying to throw it off, but the umbrella caught on its tusks, flapping wildly. Blinded, the boar veered to the side, barely missing the plane, and went charging past them into the storm. Shinji turned his head and saw the cloud Coatl lunge forward and wrap itself around the boar. Then lightning sizzled down, blinding him for a moment, and the two creatures were gone.

"Everyone, brace yourselves!" Scarlett cried, and banked hard to the left, causing the plane to nearly stand on a wing tip as it swerved to avoid the worst of the lightning strands. For a few seconds, the wind screamed in Shinji's ears, the rain pounded the windows, and everything was chaos and madness and noise.

Then, quite suddenly, the noises stopped. Sunlight poured through the windows, the plane stopped pitching and rattling, and the sound of the wind ceased. Breathing hard, still bracing himself against the wall, Shinji peeked out the window, and his heart leaped to his throat.

A ring of clouds surrounded them, still swirling and flickering with lightning, but in the center of it all, the sky was clear. They were in the eye of the hurricane, and something waited for them, there at the heart of the storm.

The Storm Boar loomed in front of them, a massive white creature with electric-blue eyes, a bristling mane, and curved tusks that were longer than Shinji's whole body. Not the pig-shaped cloud that had chased them through the storm; this was the real thing. The true form of the guardian at the heart of the hurricane. Strands of lightning snapped from its hide and flickered over the clouds, as if the guardian itself was the core that held the storm together.

Shinji's throat was dry, but he straightened and looked around the plane, heart pounding. "The idol," he gasped. "Where's the idol?"

"Here," Roux answered, holding it out to Shinji. "I grabbed it when you decided to stand up on a moving airplane in the middle of a hurricane," he explained. "Thought you probably didn't want it flying out a window."

Shinji took the statue, but the second he did, it pulsed in his hands. As they watched, the idol began to glow, becoming brighter and brighter by the second. The dead stone turned to rippling magma, not hot, but definitely warm, throbbing with a heartbeat that made it feel like it was alive.

"Oliver," Phoebe said, "open the door."

The ex-pirate gave her a dubious look but reached out and cranked the lever back, pulling the side door open with a grinding screech. Instantly, a blast of cold, damp wind rushed into the cabin, whipping at hair and clothes. Through the opening, Shinji saw the Storm Boar watching them, neon-blue eyes focused on the glowing statue in his hands.

Gripping the idol, he took a careful step toward the opening, deliberately not looking at the sheer plunge into the clouds below. Hoping Scarlett would keep the plane steady for once, he raised the idol in both hands and met the eyes of the Storm Boar through the opening.

"Guardian of the island," he called, "we return your statue to the heart of the storm. Take it and be at peace."

A gust of wind rushed into the cabin through the doorway, and Shinji released the idol. It floated in the air for a moment, still glowing brightly. Then the wind sucked it out the door and into empty space. It flew straight up, like a stray rocket into the storm, and disappeared into the clouds.

The great Storm Boar lowered his head, his blue eyes still fixed on Shinji. *Human with the spirit of a guardian within*, it rumbled. *You have risked much to return what was stolen from the island. I will not forgive, and I will not forget. But I will accept your offering. And I will spare your city the wrath of the storm. This will be my final deal with humankind. The pact with the Natia, broken when the heart of the island was stolen, will not be restored. No mortal will set foot on the island again, and the font will be hidden from human eyes forever.*

"Storm Boar," Shinji went on. He knew he might be risking the boar's wrath again, but the guardian seemed calm now with the return of his idol. "What happened to the Natia, the people who once lived on the island?"

They left, the Storm Boar said bluntly. *After they sealed me from the font, they departed the land and sailed away over the horizon. I do not know what became of them. I do not know if they perished, or if their ancestors live still, somewhere hidden and far away.* He tossed his shaggy head with a snort. *I am done with humankind, but if you wish to preserve the Natia, remember them. Their culture and their way of life. If they are remembered, they will never truly be gone.*

"We will," Shinji promised. "We won't forget."

Farewell, then, mortal. You, and the rest of mankind, will not see me again.

The Storm Boar tossed his head again. Bunching his muscles, he sprang into the air, threads of energy following him up into the clouds. Lightning flashed, turning everything white for a moment, and a boom of thunder rattled the plane. When the light cleared and the rumbles faded away, the Storm Boar was gone.

"Okay," Roux breathed. "I'm never going to sleep through a thunderstorm ever again. What do we now? Is it over?"

"Look," Lucy whispered as they all gazed around in confusion. "The hurricane is waning. The storm is breaking up."

Shinji peered out the window. Around them, the clouds were parting, dissolving on the wind. In a few minutes, the storm had disappeared, and a bright blue sky stretched before them over the ocean.

"We did it," he said. "It's over."

Oliver let out an explosive breath and collapsed onto the seats. "Well, this has certainly been an adventure," he said, grinning at them all. "Storm Boars, hidden islands, exploding volcanoes, and flying into a hurricane? Priya is never going to let me take you kids anywhere ever again."

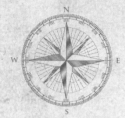

EPILOGUE

A bang on the door jolted Shinji out of bed.

Blearily, he peered at the clock on the nightstand, trying to remember where he was and how he'd gotten there. A snore sounded beside him, and he looked over to see Roux sprawled on a second bed, mouth hanging open, one arm and leg dangling over the sides. In the corner, Oliver slouched in the chair with his arms crossed and his chin on his chest.

That was when it all came rushing back to him. After the intense battle with the Storm Boar and releasing the idol into the heart of the storm, Scarlett had returned them to Los Angeles. After flying through a monster hurricane, she wanted to make sure *Rhett* was still flightworthy before she took them home. So they had gotten a hotel room while they waited for Scarlett to make repairs on *Rhett* and discussed what came next.

Unfortunately, with the exception of Phoebe, everyone was too exhausted to think of anything but sleep. There was still the question of Roux, and what was going to happen to him, but that seemed like a problem for the next day. Shinji had staggered into the hotel room with Roux and Oliver, collapsed on the bed, and was asleep almost before his head hit the pillow.

The knock came again, a sharp rapping against their door. Lucy and Phoebe were in the room across from theirs; Shinji wondered if one of them had gotten bored and decided to come over.

Rubbing his eyes, he slid out of bed, staggered across the room, and opened the door. It swung back, revealing the stern, unamused face of Priya Banerjee peering down at him.

"Hello, Shinji," Priya greeted as Shinji's stomach cartwheeled. Her voice was pleasant, but her eyes could freeze a lava pool. "I am very pleased to see you are all right. Where is Oliver?"

"Um," Shinji began, but Priya brushed past him into the room. Roux sat up quickly, glancing at Shinji in confusion, but Priya didn't stop. Striding over to Oliver's chair, she stood in front of it with her arms crossed, glaring down at him. Oliver didn't move, but after a few seconds, his brow furrowed, even though his eyes remained closed.

"I'd recognize that glare anywhere." He sighed, still without looking up. "Hello, Priya. I suppose you heard what happened in the South Pacific?"

"A bit" was the short reply. "Enough to give me heart palpitations and seriously reconsider my decision to send Shinji anywhere with you. Bad enough that you had to flee an island with an erupting volcano, but then I hear from Scarlett about flying Shinji and Lucy into a hurricane!" She took a breath, smiling, as Phoebe and Lucy poked their heads into the room, eyes wide as they spotted her. "So, I decided to come here and hear the story for myself. Perhaps I am missing something. Perhaps all these tales of fleeing an erupting volcano, nearly sinking your ship, breaking into Hightower private property, and flying into a hurricane have a perfectly reasonable explanation. I am willing to hear your side of the tale. We are adventurers after all. Even if some of us are too young to even drive a car, much less go flying into a hurricane." Priya shook her head and sighed. "So, we are going to sit down, make some tea, and then you all can tell me exactly what happened from the day Shinji and Lucy left with Oliver."

So, they did.

Starting with their arrival in Pula with Scarlett. They told her about Mano and the *Seas the Day*. They told her about meeting Roux, and though her eyes narrowed when they got to the part where he had stolen Tinker, she didn't say anything. Her lips thinned when they revealed that Hightower had beaten them to the shipwreck and had taken everything inside. When they got to the part about the island, the hidden village, the trapped guardian, and having to flee the volcano, she was looking rather nauseated. Finally they told her about sneaking into Hightower's warehouse, stealing the idol, and flying into the heart of the storm to return it to the Storm Boar.

"I see," Priya said when they were finished. Her voice, though it was as cool and unruffled as ever, was slightly breathless. It was nearly an hour later; there had been several interruptions as everyone added their own version to the story, with the tale getting longer and more exciting each time. Priya shook her head. "Absolutely incredible. If it wasn't for Shinji and his previous adventures with the Coatl and the font, I'm not sure I would believe any of this. I don't know whether to commend you, and Shinji especially, for appeasing the guardian and doing the right thing, or to lecture you all about your complete and utter recklessness."

"Come on, Priya," Oliver said, giving her a roguish grin. "We're the Society of Explorers and Adventurers after all. Death-defying escapes and leaping headfirst into danger is what we do."

She glowered at him with pursed lips. "You and I are going to have a conversation when we get back to headquarters,

Oliver," she warned, making him wince. "As for everything else, I wish we had gotten more information about the Natia people. It's a shame we weren't able to discover more about them."

"Not to worry, Ms. Banerjee," Phoebe announced loudly. "The expedition was not in vain. Before the volcano erupted, we were able to make some fascinating discoveries and find some extremely interesting artifacts that concerned the Natia and the island. Dr. Grant and I have already discussed teaming up on this project and sharing what we find. Maybe we will even discover where the Natia went! I will keep you informed as well, if you like."

"Please do." Priya nodded. "I would very much like that."

"Me too," Shinji said. "I want to know more, too."

They all stared at him in surprise. He shrugged. "There was an entire culture who lived next to a guardian and a font," he said. "I want to know more about them. The Storm Boar said if we remember them, they'll never truly fade away."

Priya, Oliver, and Phoebe all smiled. "No," Priya said softly. "They won't. We can make sure of that.

"Now," she continued, rising from her seat, "there is one more item of business we need to discuss, but not here. I have been asked to tell you that *Rhett*, according to Ms. Blaurhimmel, is, and I quote, 'too traumatized to fly anyone around right now.' So, after we stop by the harbor and I assure Captain Mano that he will be fully compensated for this fiasco, we will be traveling home. Via car." She glanced at Oliver, who was visibly slumping in relief, and chuckled. "Try not to be *too* disappointed."

The sun glimmered brightly off the water, and the ocean breeze was cool on Shinji's face as he leaned over the railing of the *Seas the Day*, watching the gulls wheel above him. Mano had greeted Priya and the others at the harbor and had nearly cracked Shinji's ribs in two with a very enthusiastic hug. They couldn't leave without saying good-bye to Mano and the *Seas the Day*; both had been a huge part of their adventure in the South Pacific. It seemed only right that they be there when it ended as well.

"Hey." Lucy joined Shinji at the railing, Tinker perched happily on her shoulder. The mouse squeaked a greeting, copper ears and whiskers glinting in the sunlight. Shinji's phone suddenly buzzed. He pulled it out, and the gif of a cartoon mouse waved cheerfully at him when he glanced at the screen.

"Roux is still talking with Priya, Oliver, and Phoebe," Lucy said, sounding slightly worried. "They've been in there for nearly an hour. What do you think is going to happen to him?"

"I don't know," Shinji muttered. "He hoped Roux wasn't in trouble. Sure, he had stolen Tinker when they first met, and had stowed away on the ship. Which was a fairly serious crime, according to Mano. But they wouldn't have gotten the idol, or stopped the hurricane, without his help. That had to count for something, right?

Lucy sighed, resting her chin in her hands as she stared over the water. "I think I'm going to need a vacation after this vacation," she muttered, earning a squeak of agreement from Tinker. "No more erupting volcanoes, angry guardians, and flying into hurricanes, thanks. I'm ready to go back to class, where the only thing I have to worry about is a pop quiz on spores and edible fungus."

"Professor Carrero will be very happy to hear it," Priya said.

Shinji turned. Roux was there, with Priya, Oliver, Mano, and Phoebe standing behind him. "We have come to a decision," Priya said, making Shinji's heart beat faster. "After talking to Roux, reviewing the events that led up to returning the idol, and speaking to some of the other board members, I have made the decision to offer Roux a trial internship in the Society of Explorers and Adventurers."

"Really?" Lucy gasped.

"Yes." Priya nodded gravely. "Which means I will be counting on you and Shinji even more," she went on. "Roux will be joining the pair of you in all your lessons and Society training. I expect you will show him what it means to be part of the Society of Explorers and Adventurers. If you are willing to accept him into the Society."

Shinji shared a glance with Lucy. She nodded. "Yeah," he replied, gazing back at Priya. "No problem."

Phoebe gave a squeal of excitement and clapped her hands. "Oh, this is excellent!" she exclaimed. "A new Society member, a font, and the discovery of a guardian and a hidden culture. I cannot wait to share this information with everyone back home in Tokyo. I haven't been this excited since we found that Bigfoot print in the mountains!" She beamed down at them, then gasped. "Oh, I should be writing all this down, shouldn't I? Journal! Where's my journal?"

She bounded off, teal coat flapping behind her. Oliver rolled his eyes. "Welcome to our little family, kid," he said as he turned away. "Never a dull moment around here. Oh, and don't forget to ask Shinji about Kali; I'm sure she's going to love you."

Shinji looked at Roux and grinned. "Congratulations. You're in the secret club now."

Roux broke into the biggest smile Shinji had ever seen on him. Not a smirk or a taunt or a sneer, but a real, genuine smile. "I know," he said. "Finally I get to leave that island and see what's out there. That's what you guys do, right? Travel around and dig up all the weird stuff no one knows about? Dragons and krakens and mermaids; all that stuff is real, and we get to find it."

"Sometimes," Lucy said. "It's not all sailing the world and finding mythical guardians. Sometimes it's memorizing lists of poisonous plants and figuring out which mushroom won't kill you if you eat it."

"Hey," Roux said, "if it means I get to be part of this, I'll learn everything there is to know about poisonous mushrooms."

Abruptly, Shinji's phone buzzed once more. Wondering if it was another text from Tinker, he pulled it out and flicked on the screen.

Hey, Shinji! It's Aunt Yui. I'm flying home from New Zealand tomorrow. Btw, how did your trip with Oliver go? Did anything interesting happen?

Shinji grinned. A few things, he texted back. I'll tell you everything when you get home.

ACKNOWLEDGMENTS

A huge and continuous thank-you to Mark, Frank, Kiran, Juleen, Charlie, Kelly, and everyone at Disney who made this experience completely unforgettable. Thank you to my agent Laurie for doing all the agent-y things. And finally, a ginormous and massive thank-you to my editor Kieran for bringing Shinji and co. to life. May your magic never fade.